A MANUAL OF PRACTICAL MAGICKAL QABALAH

Published by Avalonia

BM Avalonia
London
WC1N 3XX
England, UK

www.avaloniabooks.co.uk

First Edition 2005
Copyright © David Rankine

Design by Avalonia
Illustrations by Satori 2005

ISBN 1-905297-06-8

Climbing The Tree of Life

A MANUAL OF PRACTICAL MAGICKAL QABALAH

David Rankine

*"The Qabalah does not leave us creeping about on
the floor of the physical world, it draws us upward
into communion with God and the angels."*

De arte Cabalistica, Johannes Reuchlin (1507 CE)

Dedication

This book is dedicated to Stephen Skinner, whose work inspired me at a young age to start practicing magick, and who continues to inspire me today as a friend and colleague exemplifying all the best qualities of the magickal path.

Table of Contents

Foreword

The Qabalah has undergone a prodigious flowering during the last part of the 1990's. Not only has it become the object of attention by well known stars, but it has also been received by a new generation of Rabbinical scholars. Even the Zohar, the foundation text of the Qabalah is again being translated into English, this time by Daniel Matt in the Pritzker edition. His words are like a garland of roses compared with the rather stuffy Simon and Sperling translation. New aspects of the Qabalah are coming to light including new theories by Kieren Barry on important Greek links with the Hebrew Gematria and Notariqon.

The Qabalah is a difficult subject to write about, as it means so many very different things to different people. It is also a body of knowledge that has at different times been appropriated by Renaissance Hermeticists, orthodox Christians, twentieth century practitioners of magic, wonderworkers from Safed and Mediaeval Eastern European rabbis. When David showed me the manuscript of the present book, I was delighted to see that he had clearly made the distinction between these different approaches. I was also pleased to see that the book was not just another re-hash of the Christian Qabalah as filtered through the Golden Dawn, and that he had gone back to sources and made many new connections which I had not suspected before.

I particularly liked his survey of the differences between monotheism, polytheism and henotheism, which effectively slays a few pernicious misconceptions. It is good to see clear lines drawn between the Rabbinical practice of the Kabbalah, and its later incarnations as the Christianized Cabalah of the Renaissance, and finally in its incarnation as a repository and ground plan of the western magical tradition of the twentieth and twenty-first Century. Another strand which is brought to the forefront in this book is the sexual side of the Qabalah in the form of the Shekinah doctrines. The author also throws considerable light on the important issue of the Holy Guardian Angel, which he relates back to the original concept of the Maggid.

David is someone with a strict training in the Western magical tradition combined with a breadth of vision and scholarship which allows him to take in the wider perspectives of the Zohar, the Torah and Christianity, without shrinking from the religion of his forefathers or rebelling against it as did Crowley. For surely the Qabalah is part of the mystery tradition of Judaism and Christianity, as well as a universal system of classification which has been successfully used in theology, mysticism and magic.

The book is eminently readable and leads the reader logically through the Tree of Life, its Paths and the Four Worlds, making sure to quote the relevant passage from the Bible, Sepher Yetzirah or Zohar along the way, rather than just stating things as facts. In tying the Qabalah in with its roots, David is not leading off in a religious direction, but ensuring that the whole edifice of the Qabalah is firmly rooted in tradition, something that has not been of prime concern to many modern writers on the subject. Throughout the book numerical Gematria equivalents of key words are given, tying together words like 'unity' and 'love' and more interestingly 'serpent' and 'Messiah.'

Above all this book is designed for practical work, leading the student from simple visualisation exercises to major path and temple workings. The Sephiroth are compared to continents, and the reader encouraged to explore them. To aid the reader in doing this, a lot of symbolic and real correspondences are given in considerable detail. The list of gods and goddesses attributed to each Sephira is considerably more extensive than those listed in Aleister Crowley's 777, his tabular summation of Golden Dawn correspondences.

All in all one of the best books on the Qabalah to have been published, one that not only goes back to the roots, but also beyond the G.D, Crowley, Dion Fortune axis, whilst focusing on the use of the Qabalah in practical ritual, talisman making and pathworking.

Stephen Skinner
Singapore, 2005

Introduction

Qabalah is a dynamic system of esoteric philosophy that explores the nature of divinity, the universe, the human soul, creation, the function of life and a whole range of other philosophical and metaphysical subjects.

Many people actually mean the Tree of Life glyph when they say Qabalah. The Tree of Life is the pictorial representation of Qabalistic thought, a concentrated image containing all the philosophical and magickal concepts of Qabalah. However strictly speaking Qabalah is the whole tradition of thought as well, embodying a history of millennia of development and mystical experience, as well as the glyph.

Qabalah offers the student the opportunity to follow a well-defined and multi-layered map of consciousness expansion and self-integration and balance. For this reason it is no surprise that it is becoming increasingly popular today. Additionally it is extremely compatible with many other schools of thought, enabling existing beliefs and practices to often be fitted into Qabalistic ideas harmoniously.

The word Qabalah can be spelled in a variety of ways, the most common ways being Cabalah, Kabbalah and Qabalah. In common parlance the main differences between these different uses can be summarised very simply in different transliterations of the Hebrew root word QBL[1] – Cabalah refers to the Christianized branch of study, Kabbalah to the classical and original Jewish mystical study, and Qabalah to the Western Mystery Tradition branch of study. Although used to distinguish between different areas of study, it should be stressed that they are all acceptable translations of the same word.

The definition of Qabalah used within this book is thus in terms of the Western Mystery Tradition. The Western Mystery Tradition is the name given to a range of occult subjects and areas, which includes Ceremonial Magick (such as the Golden Dawn system and Thelema),

---

[1] *The Hebrew letter Qoph is most commonly translated as "Q" or "K", but also sometimes as "C".*

Alchemy, Christian Mysticism, Hermeticism, Rosicrucianism, Wicca, Druidry, and the Arthurian mythos. The mythologies of ancient Egypt, Greece, Rome and the Celts, and sometimes also ancient Babylon and Sumeria, are the most common ones to have been applied to the practical use of Qabalah in the Western Mystery Tradition in the last hundred and twenty years or so.

So within the specified context, Qabalah is a structure that lays the foundation for much of the theory and practice of many of these traditions. Of the aforementioned systems, only Druidry and the Arthurian mythos can claim not to have been heavily influenced by Qabalistic thought and practice. It should be stressed that Qabalah as practiced in the Western Mystery Tradition is very different to Jewish Kabbalah, having developed in different directions.

Qabalah offers a challenge to anyone who chooses to practice it, for it presents a path to the infinite, which unfolds conditioning and challenges views, whilst at the same time reinforcing all of the best qualities in the student. The success of Qabalah is demonstrated by the effectiveness of its practices, and the way that it has come to permeate so much of modern magickal practice. It provides a panoramic worldview and one can practice Qabalah with or without including ritual practice in your life. As with all other aspects of Qabalah, the choice of how you climb the Tree of Life is up to you.

David Rankine
London, 2005

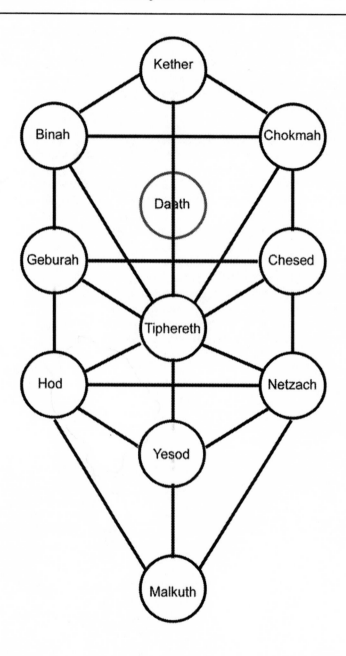

PART I

HISTORY & DEFINITIONS

1. A Brief History of Qabalah

As the English meaning of the word Qabalah being *"received teaching/wisdom"* implies, we know that it was originally an oral tradition. As such the Kabbalah may have existed for centuries before the first texts were recorded.

According to Jewish myth, the archangel Metatron or Raziel gave the knowledge of Kabbalah to Adam in the Garden of Eden. It passed down Adam's line to Noah, and to Abraham. In Egypt some of the knowledge was passed on to the Egyptians, supposedly influencing their development. Moses was said to be very learned in Kabbalah, and learned much more from the angels during the forty years in the wilderness. He subsequently taught seventy elders, so that the line of descent of knowledge would be secured.[2]

A largely ignored contributory factor in the early development of Kabbalah was the worship of Theos Hypsistos ("the highest God"). The cult of this highest god spread to various parts of the Hellenic Greek culture, as well as various Jewish communities. It was already established by the second century BCE, and provided a transitional state between pagan monotheism and the development of Jewish Kabbalah and Christian thought.[3] The inscription below clearly shows great similarity to later Kabbalistic thought.

"Born of itself, untaught, without a mother, unshakeable, not contained in a name, known by many names, dwelling in fire, this is god. We, his angels, are a small part of god. To you who ask this question about god, what his essential nature is, he has pronounced that Aether is god who sees all, on whom you should gaze and pray at dawn, looking towards the sunrise."[4]

We know that one of the earliest and greatest of Jewish Kabbalistic texts, the *Sepher Yetzirah* or *Book of Formation* was said to have been written by *Simeon ben Yochai* in about 70 CE. This book combines the earlier Merkavah Mysticism (which was practiced during the approximate period of 100 BCE – 1000 CE) and newer Kabbalistic thought, and lays the template for much of the subsequent Kabbalah (and Qabalah). The Kabbalah was often

---

[2] *Numbers 11:24-25.*
[3] *See particularly The Cult of Theos Hypsistos between Pagans, Jews, and Christians – Stephen Mitchell, in Pagan Monotheism in Late Anitquity edited by Polymnia Athanassiadi & Michael Frede, 1999, p81-148.*
[4] *Oracular inscription from Oenoanda in northern Lycia, translated by Stephen Mitchell.*

referred to as the *"workings of the Chariot"* (*Merkavah*), indicating its dynamic nature.

Merkavah Mysticism was highly significant and stems from Ezekiel 1:26-28, referring to the chariot of Ezekiel's vision. The Merkavah Mystic or Rider strove to enter into the throne world of God, using fasting and repetitious use of hymns and prayers, akin to mantra.[5] When in trance he would send his spirit upwards through the Seven Palaces, where he would encounter demons, and he needed to have prepared many magickal amulets and memorized long incantations to ensure successful passage.

This dynamism and use of direct practice to attempt to reach perfection is also characterized in the Renaissance appropriation of Kabbalah and its symbolism in the process of transformation into the modern practice of Qabalah. Hence we encounter references such as the *"Chariot of the Soul"* in magickal texts like *The Nine Keys*.[6]

A development of Merkavah mysticism was the German branch of Kabbalism, established by Aaron ben Samuel in 917 CE. This version concentrated more on prayer than the ascent to God's throne. The German branch also focused on the esoteric meanings of scripture, developing the techniques of Gematria, Notariqon and Temurah that have become a major part of modern Qabalah.

The other most influential Kabbalistic works, the *Bahir*[7] and the *Zohar*[8], were also said to have been written in the first century CE, but to have remained completely unknown outside of very small select circles until the twelfth and thirteenth centuries CE respectively. This view is one that is disputed by some, ascribing authorship of these works to much later historical figures. Gershom Scholem presents very lucid arguments ascribing these works to the thirteenth century in his classic work *Major Trends in Jewish Mysticism*. Nonetheless it could perhaps be said that these vital works represent the fruition of a train of thought which began in the first century CE.

The use of the word Kabbalah to describe the tradition, which had previously been known by phrases like *"the work of the Father"* or *"the hidden wisdom"*,

---

[5] *This theme is also found in some Gnostic texts, and may indicate cross-fertilisation of ideas between these two schools of mystical thought.*
[6] *"There are in Man the four Elements, with the most true proprieties of their natures, And also an Ethereal Body, Likewise the Chariot of the Soul in proportion Corresponding to the Heaven." See The Keys to the Gateway of Magic: Summoning the Solomonic Archangels & Demonic Princes by Stephen Skinner & David Rankine.*
[7] *The Bahir takes it name from Job 37:21 "And now they do not see light, it is brilliant (Bahir) in the skies."*
[8] *The full title of the work is Sepher Ha-Zohar, meaning "Book of Splendour".*

is attributed to the Jewish Rabbi Isaac the Blind (1160-1236 CE), in Provence, France, who was known as the "*Father of Kabbalah*". After Isaac the Blind a whole range of Rabbis across Europe spread the development of Kabbalah like wildfire.

The publication of the *Zohar* by Moses de Leon (1238-1305 CE) in 1290 CE in Spain, together with the use at this time of the first known images of the Tree of Life glyph created a surge of interest in this spreading emanation of Kabbalistic philosophy. It is significant that the *Zohar* places great emphasis on the Shekinah, bringing sexual polarity very much to the forefront of Kabbalah at this point.

These influential books introduced the Kabbalah to the developing branch of evocatory magick. Themes already familiar to philosophers and magickians from studying Hermeticism and Neoplatonism were found in Kabbalah, enabling a bridge to be made from Kabbalah back to the Christianity of the Old Testament.

Christian Cabalah, drawing on the mysteries of Jewish Kabbalah was now able to develop as a result of the availability of Kabbalistic material. Shortly after the publication of the *Zohar* one of the most important magickal grimoires appeared, which was to significantly influence the development of Western magick. This grimoire is *Liber Juratus* or *The Sworn Book of Honorius*.

This Grimoire used the Shemhamforash and other non-biblical angels, suggesting a strong influence from Merkavah mysticism. This book is also significant as it contains the first image of the *Sigillum dei Aemeth*, which was to play a major role in the development of Dr John Dee's system of Enochian magick.

Around the same time period that the *Zohar* was published and *Liber Juratus* was being produced, the magickian Ramon Lull was having a vision on Mount Randa (1274 CE) in Spain. Lull's vision included details of combinations of letters and speculations about the divine names, suggesting a Kabbalistic influence on his experience, possibly as the result of earlier study. Certainly Lull's writings were influential, as indicated by reference to them by later writers like Pico della Mirandola.

The Genovese magickian Pico della Mirandola (1463-1494 CE) then went further by publicly declaring the beauty, sanctity and efficacy of Qabalah as good magick in his writings, opening the door for the development of Western Qabalah. Significantly, he made seventy-two[9] of the nine hundred of his major religious work *Conclusions* about the Kabbalah. Although persecuted

---

[9] *The number of Shemhamphorash Angels, see the later chapter The Unpronounceable Name of God.*

by the Church, he managed to avoid imprisonment and the material was published before the church could suppress it. Pico della Mirandola can be seen as the key figure in the process of merging Kabbalah into Hermeticism and so creating the basis of what we today work as Qabalah.

Pico della Mirandola studied Neoplatonism, with its core of influence from the Hermetic texts of the *Corpus Hermetica*. Texts such as the *Orphic Hymns* and *Chaldean Oracles* also influenced him, and his friendship with Marsilio Ficino (1433-99 CE), translator of much of Plotinus and Plato is sure to have contributed to his opinions. All these strands came to influence the development of Qabalah as the great thinkers like Pico della Mirandola and his successors found areas of commonality in the various schools of thought.

From here the work of Johannes Reuchlin continued the development of both Cabalah and Qabalah. His writings on Cabalah referred back to Pico della Mirandola's work and furthered their development, concentrating more on areas like the angels and manipulation of numbers, and expanding Pico della Mirandola's associations with Pythagorean Numbers and mathematics. Particularly influential was his work *De arte Cabalistica*, published in 1517 CE.

The work of Heinrich Cornelius Agrippa von Nettesheim (1486-1535 CE), friend of Johannes Reuchlin and student of the extremely influential and significant scholar-magician and cabalist Abbot Johannes Trithemius, continued this development of the integration of Kabbalistic thought into acceptable Western magickal doctrine. His classic work *De Occulta Philosophy*[10] marked the full acceptance of Qabalah as part of the corpus of European magick, to be embraced by those who would follow.

By the late sixteenth century to early seventeenth century Kabbalah was well and truly integrated into the developing Western Mystery Tradition branches of Hermeticism, Alchemy and the newly developing Rosicrucianism. This is best illustrated by a book called *The Nine Keys*, which deals with evocation of the Archangels and orders of angels attributed to the Sephiroth.[11] This period marks the *"coming of age"* of the transition from Jewish Kabbalah to magickal Qabalah, with the emphasis being on practical angelic magick rather than devotional mysticism as was largely the case with Kabbalah.

Another important work from this period is *The Thirty-Two Paths of Wisdom* by Joannes Stephanus Rittangelius (1606-52 CE), published in 1642 CE. This book gives descriptions of the qualities of the Sephiroth and paths, and is

---

[10] *Published in 1531 CE, and available today as Three Books of Occult Philosophy.*
[11] *See The Keys to the Gateway of Magic: Summoning the Solomonic Archangels & Demonic Princes by Stephen Skinner & David Rankine.*

often erroneously referred to as part of the *Sepher Yetzirah*, due to its inclusion in Wynn Westcott's edition of that latter work.

In the mid nineteenth century the French occultist Eliphas Levi added a further major development to the evolution of Qabalah. In his book, *Sanctum Regnum*, Levi attributed the twenty-two trumps of the Tarot onto the twenty-two Hebrew letters and thus the paths of the Tree of Life. This action was to lay the groundwork for much of the modern perception of Qabalah, including the whole art of pathworking the Tree of Life using the Tarot cards as astral doorways.

The last great refinement of Qabalah can be said to have occurred with the Hermetic Order of the Golden Dawn, founded in 1887 CE.[12] Certain of the major figures within the Golden Dawn, notably Samuel Liddell MacGregor Mathers, Wynn Westcott and Allan Bennett synthesized much of the corpus of material we now use. Examples of this are the Colour Scales, the Lesser Banishing Pentagram Ritual, the Middle Pillar, Telesmatic Imagery and many of the correspondences.[13]

---

[12] *For more on the foundation, role and members of the Golden Dawn, there are many good works available, such as The Magicians of the Golden Dawn by Ellic Howe, and Golden Dawn: Twilight of the Magicians by R.A. Gilbert.*
[13] *Although Aleister Crowley published these correspondences in 777 claiming them as his own, much of the work he "borrowed" though some is his original work.*

2. Otz Chiim - The Tree of Life

"All the divine powers form a succession of layers and are like a tree."[14]

The Tree of Life is on one level a symbolic glyph which embodies the prime magickal axiom of *"As above, so below"*, representing as it does both the universe (macrocosm) and the body of man (microcosm), each reflecting the other, but on a different scale. On another level it is a map of the psyche, enabling the practitioners to explore their own mental and emotional landscapes with a well-used and effective map that is designed to facilitate growth and realisation of the self through integration of the parts of the psyche to create a unified consciousness and soul.

The Tree of Life is a geometric glyph comprising ten circles, the *Sephiroth*[15], meaning *"Emanations"*, arranged in three vertical columns and connected by twenty-two diagonal, horizontal and vertical paths. Each of the Sephira within the Tree of Life has unique qualities as an expression of the different aspects of the divine manifesting on different levels.

The first recorded images of the Tree of Life occur in thirteenth century CE Spain, and this underwent some changes as different models were postulated. The version we are familiar with in modern Qabalah dates back to around sixteenth century CE Europe.

The twenty-two paths express the subjective experiences of the self and the world necessary for the development and realisation of inner potential. To each of the paths is attributed a letter of the Hebrew alphabet, and a whole host of symbols.

The Tree of Life may be divided into parts by a variety of classifications, each of which give insight into the nature of Qabalah. These divisions include the Three Pillars, the Four Worlds, the Triads and the Seven Palaces.

---

[14] *Bahir, from Gershom Scholem's translation.*
[15] *Sephiroth is the plural term, and Sephira or Sephirah the singular.*

3. Terms used in Practicing Qabalah

Modern Qabalah is usually categorised into four areas. These are *Practical Qabalah*, *Literal Qabalah*, *Unwritten Qabalah* and *Dogmatic Qabalah*. Of these the first two are those that are the main concern of this present work.

Practical Qabalah is the area concerned with the magick of Qabalah, including such subjects as divination, meditation and the creation and use of amulets and talismans. This branch of Qabalah is largely derived from Merkavah mysticism.

The Literal Qabalah is the area concerned with the manipulation of the Hebrew alphabet and its associated numbers, i.e. Gematria, Notariqon and Temurah. As with Practical Qabalah this branch also grows from roots found in Merkavah Mysticism.

The Unwritten Qabalah is the material that has always remained oral or has never been circulated. The bulk of the Kabbalistic texts (in their thousands) have never been translated from the Hebrew or been available to a wide audience.

Finally the Dogmatic Qabalah is the study of classic Qabalistic texts, such as the *Sepher Yetzirah*, *Sepher ha-Zohar*, *Sepher Bahir* and of course the *Torah* (*Old Testament*). Reference to these texts will be made through the book to illustrate concepts and their origin and development. Both Kabbalah and Cabalah as previously defined focus mainly on this branch of Qabalah.

PART II

DIVIDING THE TREE OF LIFE

4. The Four Worlds

The Tree of Life may be represented through the Four Worlds. These are Olahm ha-Atziluth *(Archetypal World)*, Olahm ha-Briah *(Creative World)*, Olahm ha-Yetzirah *(Formative World)* and Olahm ha-Assiah *(Making or Active World)*

The World of Atziluth

Atziluth is also known as the World of Emanations, where God manifests as the archetypes expressed through the Sephiroth. For this reason it is also sometimes called the World of the Sephiroth (Olahm ha-Sephiroth) as this is where they first exist in potential. These archetypes of the Sephiroth are the templates of creation; the ideal representations of what will be when evolution to the highest has occurred. They may also be seen as the pantheistic deities of the pagan religions whose natures embody facets or faces of the ultimate unknowable divine.

Atziluth is hence the hidden form of God's creation, the laying out of the perfect model of how things will be when complete harmony is reached. Atziluth can also be seen as the world of pure will, before it is manifested into action. In Atziluth the Ultimate acts without intermediaries, expressing itself through emanation of concepts.

Atziluth is also said by some to be the World where God unites with the Shekinah to produce the lower three Worlds. Atziluth takes its name from the Hebrew in Numbers 11:17 *"And I will take [Atziluth] of the spirit which is upon these, and will put it upon them."*

The numerical significance of Atziluth adding to 537 can be seen through all the letters attributed to the vertical paths on the three Pillars adding to the same (i.e. 537), demonstrating that the beginning of the three Pillars is contained within the Supernal Triad of the Sephiroth of Atziluth.

The World of Briah

Briah is the world of creation, where the Archangels are formed from the emanations as they become more manifest. The ultimate force is taking form into patterns of order that enable the further manifestation of energy towards matter. The pure will of Atziluth becomes formed into ideas in Briah.

Briah is the universe of the Throne (Khorsia), the foundation upon which creation is formed. Many analogies to that of Ezekiel (the sapphire throne of 1:26 and 10:1) of the throne of creation may be found in world myths, such as the quartz throne of the creator god Daramulun in Aboriginal myth, and also Isis as the throne[16] of Osiris in Egyptian myth.

The Archangels are created in Briah as expressions of the energy of spirit in its purest form. Briah takes its name from the Hebrew in Isaiah 43:7 *"I have created [Briah] him for my glory, I have formed him; yea, I have made him."*

Briah adds to 218 (BRIAH), which is the same as *ether* (AVIRA), *multitude* (RBVA) and *the benignity of time* (ChSD AaVLM). Looking at these words we can see that Briah is the place where the Archangels *(the multitude)* are formed from spirit *(ether)* to act in the universe as directors of the divine will *(the benignity of time)*.

The World of Yetzirah

Yetzirah is the world of formation, where the Angels come into being and act as distributors of the patterns of order created by the Archangels who rule them. Hence it is also sometimes referred to as the Universe of Angels. Rising to the level of Yetzirah is known as *"ascending to the orchard"*. The orchard is another name for Eden, so it indicates a return to the perfection without evil (negativity). To appreciate this further we need to consider the glyph known as Jacob's ladder, which will be considered subsequently in this section.

Yetzirah is often seen as containing the six Sephiroth from Chesed to Yesod, which are also collectively called the Sephiroth of Construction (Sephiroth ha-Benyin[17]) in this context, and correspond to the six days of the creation in Genesis.[18] Yetzirah takes its name from the same verse as Briah, i.e. Isaiah 43:7 *"I have created him for my glory, I have formed [Yetzirah] him; yea, I have made him."*

Yetzirah adds to 305 (ITzRH), the same as *dazzling white light* (AVR TzCh) and *appointed time* (QTz HIMIN). So in Yetzirah occurs the formation of the choirs of angels (embodying the dazzling white light) who perform the tasks assigned to them by their governing Archangels (their appointed time). Appointed time also refers to the six days during which the creation of the world took place.

---

[16] *Isis means "throne" and the throne is also her primary symbol.*
[17] *Zohar.*
[18] *Though it is also sometimes seen as containing the Astral Triad of Netzach, Hod and Yesod. See the following chapter.*

The World of Assiah

Assiah is the world of making, where matter is formed. Here man resides, and strives to rise back up through the Worlds to the divine. Assiah is the universe of forms. It is also sometimes referred to as the *"Vale of Tears"*.

Assiah also takes its name from the same verse as the previous two worlds, Isaiah 43:7 *"I have created him for my glory, I have formed him; yea, I have made [Assiah] him."*

Assiah adds to 410 (HTzShIH), the same as *liberty* (DRVR), *holy* (QVDSh) and the *Tabernacle* (MShKN). So in Assiah the world was formed (Tabernacle) as a holy place that man might achieve his liberty.

World	Atziluth	Briah	Yetzirah	Assiah
Action	Emanating	Creating	Forming	Making
Process	Intent	Concept	Realisation	Manifestation
Divinity	Divine Name	Archangel	Angels	Heaven
Colour	King Scale	Queen Scale	Emperor Scale	Empress Scale
Tetragrammaton	Yod	Heh	Vav	Heh
Element	Fire	Water	Air	Earth

Meditation – The Coin

A simple meditation performed on a coin can illustrate the action of the Four Worlds very well. Hold a coin in your hand and contemplate it. First see it as a man-made disk, used in commerce; this is the level of Assiah, the manifestation of the coin. Next see it as a metal alloy, blended together and stamped to form it, this is the level of Yetzirah, the formation of the coin.

Now see the coin as a structure of bonded atoms of different elements, such as copper or silver and nickel, this is the level of Briah the creation of the alloy that makes the coin. Now see the atoms of the coin as part of the manifest universe, like everything else around you, this is the level of Atziluth, the emanation, where the coin is seen as part of the whole that is also you.

Meditation – The Grain of Sand

This principle can also be used very well to demonstrate the veracity of William Blake's classic line *"to see a world in a grain of sand"*.[19] Hold a grain of sand in your hand and meditate on it through the levels of the four Worlds.

---

[19] *From Auguries of Innocence by William Blake.*

At Assiah it can be seen as a grain of sand, weathered over millennia to its current shape.

At Yetzirah it may be seen as silicon dioxide, a combination of silicon and oxygen in solid shape. At Briah it is perceived as a structure of bonded atoms, two oxygen to each silicon, forming the grain. At Atziluth it can be realized as the visible form of millions upon millions of atoms, a microcosm or universe in miniature. Truly it can be seen as a world in itself, and we, though far vaster, are but as grains of sand in the universe.

5. The Sephiroth in the Worlds

There are four models used to do this, so I will consider them in turn.

Western Magickal Model

This model is based on the triads of the Tree, and also is the most used for working magickal Qabalah, as the divisions are also indicated by the presence of the three veils on the Tree. For the purpose of the soul divisions however this model is not so valid and the classical models have a number of advantages (see the later chapter *The Human Soul on the Tree*).

World	Contains	Part of Soul
Atziluth	Kether Chokmah Binah	Yechidah Chayah Neshamah
Briah	Chesed Geburah Tiphereth	Ruach
Yetzirah	Netzach Hod Yesod	Nephesh
Assiah	Malkuth	

Yechidah *(unique one, immortality)* and Chayah *(vitality)* are both higher aspects of the Neshamah *(upper soul, breath* or *pneuma)* respectively. The Ruach is the middle soul or spirit, and the Nephesh is the lower soul or animal soul.[20]

Classical model

This is much more the mystical perception of the Qabalah, tying in with the soul, the dimensions and the hidden meanings of the Divine Names. Here Kether is beyond the Four Worlds and corresponds to the Yechidah, and the upper two Worlds contain Chokmah and Binah respectively, which correspond to the Chayah and Neshamah, Yetzirah contains the six Sephiroth from Chesed to Yesod *(the Lesser Countenance)* corresponding to the Ruach, and Assiah contains Malkuth and the Nephesh.

---

[20] *See the chapter The Human Soul on the Tree for more details.*

World	Contains	Part of Soul
Atziluth	Chokmah	Chayah
Briah	Binah	Neshamah
Yetzirah	Chesed Geburah Tiphereth Netzach Hod Yesod	Ruach
Assiah	Malkuth	Nephesh

Alternative Classical model

This is a variant of the more mystical perception of the Qabalah, also tying in with the soul, the dimensions and the hidden meanings of the Divine Names. Here Kether is the highest of the Four Worlds, corresponding to the Chayah and the second World contains Chokmah and Binah, corresponding to the Neshamah, Yetzirah contains the six Sephiroth of the Lesser Countenance corresponding to the Ruach, and Assiah contains Malkuth and corresponds to the Nephesh.

World	Contains	Part of Soul
Atziluth	Kether	Chayah
Briah	Chokmah Binah	Neshamah
Yetzirah	Chesed Geburah Tiphereth Netzach Hod Yesod	Ruach
Assiah	Malkuth	Nephesh

Jacob's Ladder

In this model each of the Four Worlds has its own complete Tree of Life, with the Malkuth of the first being the Kether of the second, and so on, down the Tree. This is known as Jacob's Ladder, and refers to Jacob's vision in Genesis 28:12, *"And he dreamed, and behold a ladder set up on the earth, and the top of it reached to heaven; and behold the angels of God ascending and descending on it."*

It is also referred to in *The Book of Razial* (part 4): *"The great ladder is placed in heaven. The top reaches to the firmament."* A variant of this has the Kether of the lowest Tree of Life being the Tiphereth of the second, and so on, making a more compact version of Jacob's Ladder.

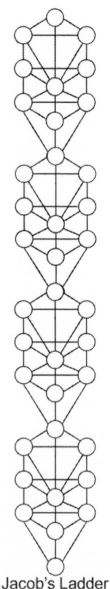

Jacob's Ladder

6. The Three Pillars on the Tree

The Sephiroth of the Tree of Life all lie vertically within three columns, known as Pillars. These three pillars represent many concepts and symbols, most of which revolve around the idea of a harmony between two opposing forces. The three pillars are sometimes referred to as the *zahzahoth* (hidden splendours), a term used to denote the underlying balance of opposing forces of primordial mercy and primordial justice by primordial will.

The Black Pillar

The Black Pillar is also known as the Pillar of Severity or Judgement, the Pillar of Fire, Primordial Justice, or the Feminine Pillar. The Black Pillar is considered to be negative, in the sense of negative charge as opposed to bad. The Black Pillar also represents night. As we look at the Tree of Life the Black Pillar is on the left facing us, as it corresponds to the right side of the body. This Pillar equates with *Boaz* (BAaZ), one of the pillars in the Temple of Solomon.

The Black Pillar contains the Sephiroth of Binah, Geburah and Hod. Adding together the numbers corresponding to the letters joining these Sephiroth on the Black Pillar we have the total of 48 (Cheth: 8 + Mem: 40). 48 is the total for *black* (ChM) recalling the name of the pillar, and also *star/planet*, the heaven of Hod (KVKB) at its base. Hence the nature of this pillar, which represents form, is clearly indicated by the letters totalling the same number as its colour and the heaven of its base.

This point is further developed if we consider the Divine Names of the Sephiroth on the Black Pillar. All three of these Divine Names contain the plural Elohim (Gods) – Yahveh Elohim (Binah), Elohim Gibor (Geburah) and Elohim Sabaoth (Hod). This demonstrates the association with form, for form does not occur in singularity, but rather in relationships that define the form.

The White Pillar

The White Pillar is also known as the Pillar of Mercy or Love, the Pillar of Water, Primordial Mercy, or the Masculine Pillar. The White Pillar is considered to be positive in the sense of charge. The White Pillar also represents day. As we look at the Tree of Life the White Pillar is on the right facing us, as it corresponds to the left side of the body. This Pillar equates with *Jachin* (IAChIN), the other pillar in the Temple of Solomon. It is no coincidence that both the names Boaz and Jachin add to the same total of 79.

The White Pillar contains the Sephiroth of Chokmah, Chesed and Hod. Adding together the numbers corresponding to the letters joining these Sephiroth on the White Pillar we have the total of 26 (Vav: 6 + Kaph: 20). 26 is also the total for *Tetragrammaton* (IHVH), so we can see this pillar expressing the divine force, as Chokmah at its top corresponds to force.

The Middle or Grey Pillar

The Grey Pillar is also known as the Pillar of Equilibrium or Harmony, or Pillar of Balance, or Pillar of Consciousness, or the Primordial Will. The Grey Pillar is considered to be neutral, the equilibrium and union of the two opposing pillars. The Grey Pillar represents the times in-between day and night, i.e. dawn and dusk. Hence we see that the word *conjunction* or *union* (AaDH) also adds to 79, showing the linking of the black and white pillars on either side of it.

If we add together the numbers corresponding to the paths on the Middle Pillar, we get 463 (Tav: 400 + Samekh: 60 + Gimel: 3). Now *"a rod of almond"* (MTH HShQD) also adds to 463, which is why the Middle Pillar is also known as the almond rod or wand. The word *"crowns"* also adds to 463 (ThGIN), illustrating the crowning glory of Kether manifesting itself down the Middle Pillar in the Royal Child (Tiphereth) and the Royal Bride (Malkuth). The Middle Pillar is also sometimes called the Shekinah, possibly also to indicate this descent of divine wisdom from the highest through to manifestation (see later chapter *The Shekinah*).

By combining the totals for the letters on all three pillars we get the total of 537 (463+48+26). Significantly 537 is also the total for *Atziluth* (ATzILVTh), the Archetypal World of the Supernal Triad. So the three pillars represent the expression of the Archetypal World, each descending from one of the three Sephiroth of the Supernal Triad – Black Pillar from Binah, Middle Pillar from Kether, and White Pillar from Chokmah.

Although the Black Pillar is referred to as negative and the White Pillar as positive, there is another consideration when looking at the Sephiroth individually. This is that each Sephira is considered positive to the one below it, and negative to the one above it. E.g. Chokmah is negative to Kether, but positive to Binah. This may also be why the three Veils of Negativity are so called, for they are negative to each other in sequence, but positive to Kether, which expresses the veils in its manifestation.

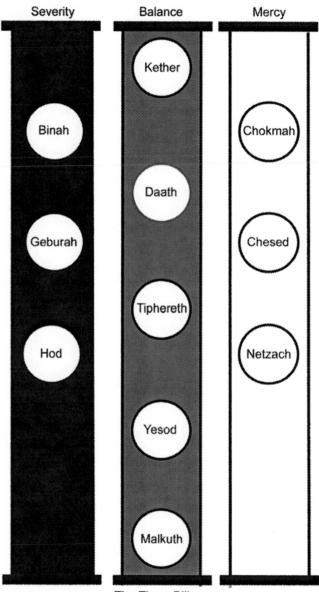

Severity   Balance   Mercy

The Three Pillars

Pillar of Severity	Pillar of Harmony	Pillar of Mercy
Black	Grey	White
Negative	Neutral	Positive
Passive	Stillness	Active
Feminine	Androgyne	Masculine
Form	Transition	Force
Matter	Spirit	Energy
Fire	White Light or Fire	Water
Restraint or Constriction	Equilibrium	Expansion
Right side of Body	Centre Line	Left side of Body

Practical Work

To further develop your appreciation of the pillars, especially the Middle Pillar, you should start practicing the Middle Pillar exercise as a daily practice.

7. The Triads on the Tree

The Sephiroth of the Tree of Life may be divided into three triads of three, with Malkuth being the only Sephira not included in a triad. These triads can be seen as a repeating pattern that occurs down the Tree, of force and form balancing into action or intent.

The Supernal Triad

The first triad on the Tree is that made by the first three Sephiroth of Kether, Chokmah and Binah, contained within the Archetypal World of Atziluth. It is the only triad that forms a triangle with its apex upwards, indicating the divine nature of the forces contained in this triad. It also shows the initial separation of the divine essence into separate components. The Sephiroth of the Supernal Triad are sometimes referred to as the *Superior Crowns*.

The Supernal Triad is referred to in some texts and by some modern writers as the Intellectual World (Olahm Mevshekal). Obviously this is only appropriate if using the model of the Tree with each triad as one of the Worlds with Malkuth as the fourth World.

The Supernal Triad establishes the pattern repeated in the rest of the Tree – of the pure force (Kether) which is the balance and union of the opposing forces, in this case Masculine (Chokmah) and Feminine (Binah), which can also be seen as force and form respectively.

This triad is referred to in Job 28:11-12 *"He bindeth the floods from overflowing; and the thing that is hid bringeth he forth to light (i.e. Kether). But where shall wisdom (Chokmah) be found? And where is the place of understanding (Binah)?"*

Subsequent verses in Job 28:21 also illustrate a further point that many magickians have ignored in their desire to prove they are the supreme magus, despite having supposedly overcome their egos and made them a vessel rather than a master. For the Supernal Triad is not accessible in human form, only when one transcends this and is a being of pure energy, such as the seven Archangels who stand in the presence of God.

---

[21] *Job 28:20-21 "Whence then cometh wisdom? And where is the place of understanding? Seeing it is hid from the eyes of all living".*

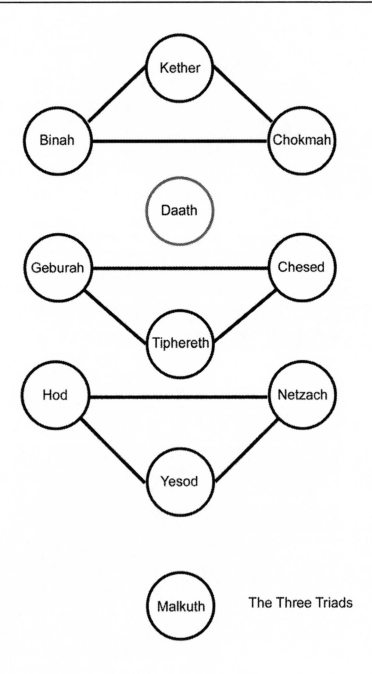

The Three Triads

This point is illustrated both in classical Kabbalah, and also in more modern Qabalah as practiced by the Golden Dawn. For the skullcap (*kippah*) worn during worship protects from the influence of the Supernal Triad, which man cannot survive, and the nemys or headdress worn in Golden Dawn rituals also served this function, as well as ensuring the magickian was not possessed by the deities that were called to.

The Ethical Triad

The second triad on the Tree is made by the fourth, fifth and sixth Sephiroth of Chesed, Geburah and Tiphereth. It is also known as *"the Children"*, referring to the position below the Father (Chokmah) and Mother (Binah) in the Supernal Triad. Other names include the Moral World (Olahm Morgash) or Sensuous Triad and it could also be called the Triad of the Adept.

Many people claim to be exalted grades that correspond to these Sephiroth of the Tree, but this is ego delusion. To master Tiphereth one should know and be practicing the true will, a rare occurrence amongst spiritual seekers. To master Geburah that individual should be ceaselessly radiating the magickal current they are following, and to master Chesed they should be manifesting spiritual truths through a mystery school selflessly teaching that magickal current and aiding others to ascend the Tree of Life. Many may make such lofty claims, but they rarely stand up to scrutiny.

The Astral Triad

The third triad, also known as the Vegetative Triad, comprises the seventh, eighth and ninth Sephiroth of Netzach, Hod and Yesod. It is also known as *"the Grandchildren"*, referring to its position as the third triad, under *"the Children"* of the Ethical Triad.

Other names include the Natural Triad or Material World (*Olahm Ha-Mevetbau*). Strictly speaking these terms might be more appropriate for the final Sephira of Malkuth, though they do express the faculties of man which need to be developed – to master the unconscious, the intellect and the emotions that the seeker may then burst through the rainbow of Paroketh to the realisation of true will that is Tiphereth.

The Knowledge Triad

A triad may also be made downwards from Chokmah and Binah, with its apex in Daath. This triad is also known as the Triad of Truth, for Truth is said to be made of Wisdom, Understanding and Knowledge. From this triad comes the saying *"Knowledge is the child of Wisdom and Understanding"*.

Significantly, the total for *Kether* is 620 (KThR), which is also the same as the total for these three Sephiroth added together – *Chokmah, Binah and Daath* (ChKMH BINH VDAaTh). This equation demonstrates the expression of the ultimate divine that is Kether through the Sephiroth that lead directly to it. Thus we see that *"the Doors"* (ShAaRIM) to the divine also adds to this total of 620.

The Knowledge Triad is especially referred to in the book of Proverbs. Hence we see it in Proverbs 2:6[22], *"For the Lord giveth wisdom [Chokmah]: out of his mouth cometh knowledge [Daath] and understanding [Binah]."*

It is found again in Proverbs 3:19-20 in connection with the dew which represents the divine light, *"The Lord by wisdom [Chokmah] hath founded the earth: by understanding [Binah] hath he established the heavens. By his knowledge [Daath] the depths are broken up, and the clouds drop down the dew."*

Dew was a term often used to denote the gaining of heavenly knowledge (of Kether), for it is found in the morning as the sun rises, having descended from the heavens to settle on the grass (earth).

---

[22] *And also Proverbs 2:2-3, "So that thou incline thine ear unto wisdom, and apply thine heart to understanding; Yea, if thou criest after knowledge, and liftest up thy voice for understanding.*

8. The Seven Palaces

The Seven Palaces is a model that was used in the early Merkavah branch of Kabbalah. Within this the palaces are also referred to as halls or chambers (*hekhalot*). Texts referring to the practice of the Merkavah branch of Kabbalah are known as *Hekhalot texts*.

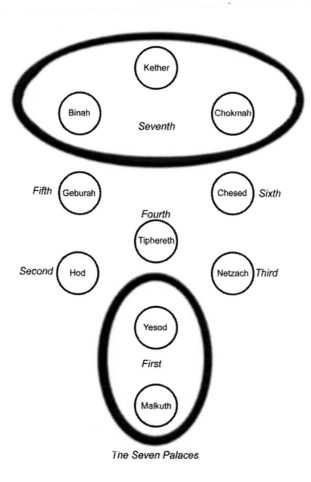

The Seven Palaces

The first palace contains the Supernal Triad of Kether, Chokmah and Binah. This could be considered the palace of the ultimate and incomprehensible God, residing above the Abyss. Physically this represents the unknowable beyond the outer boundaries, for Saturn is the Heaven of Binah, the outermost of the classical planets and beyond which man perceived the vastness of infinity, i.e. God.

This palace is also the world of Atziluth or Atziluth and Briah, depending on which model you use. This palace was the ultimate goal of the mystic, or chariot rider, as they were known, to enter into the seventh palace, which represented the Throne room of God, as described in the vision of Ezekiel.

The next five palaces contain a Sephira each, i.e. Chesed, Geburah, Tiphereth, Netzach and Hod. It can be seen that essentially the palaces are a planetary model, representing the seven classical planets, and adding in the Sephiroth at the top and bottom of the Tree to keep to the number seven.

The last palace contains Malkuth and Yesod. This pairing is very important as it emphasises the close relationship between the lowest two Sephiroth, which are the most relevant to humanity in general as containing the direct experience of life shared by all – the physicality of Malkuth, and the unconscious and dream worlds of Yesod. Also of course the Moon is the Earth's satellite.

As a planetary model, the seven palaces obviously then correspond to the days of the week, though not in a strictly consecutive order, as the days are not. The important thing to note here is that within the context of the seven palaces, the first palace, containing the supernal triad, corresponds to Saturday, the Sabbath or holy day.

By the same consideration, in modern terms it is interesting to note that the last palace, which is the palace we exist in, corresponds in planetary terms to the Moon and Monday, the beginning of the working week for the bulk of the population.

PART III

THE VEILS OF THE TREE

9. The Veils of Negativity

By their very nature the three Veils of Negativity are abstract concepts, symbols of the infinite and unknowable. Whereas Kether is the unknown divine that we strive to know and ultimately achieve, the veils are beyond Kether, which is their manifestation.

The Veils of Negativity are the absolute ultimate and remain forever beyond our grasp, defining the limits and then removing them. As such they are very difficult to write about, but hopefully the ideas set out below will give the reader some thoughts to begin their own realisations.

The abstraction of the infinite perceived through the absence of everything, of nothing or no-thing, has been seen in many religions. This is why the ancient shrines or *"Holy of Holies"* were empty rooms, and why religions like Islam do not allow representations of the divine. This is referred to in Deuteronomy 27:15, *"Cursed is the man who makes any image ... and puts it in a hidden place."* The hidden place is the veils beyond Kether, which are unrepresenteable.

Even though Kether is brilliant and unbearable light, it is as darkness next to the Veils of Negativity, cast into shadow by the limitless light of the Ain Soph Aur.

Ain - Negativity

Ain is nothingness. It is incomprehensible, the void of potentiality, before creation. In this respect it can be seen as the primal divine essence, without form or restriction, without expression, outside of time and before extending itself into being and creating anything or anywhere.

Ain is also referred to as negative existence, as can be seen in the Sepher Yetzirah, which says *"He formed substance out of chaos and made non-existence into existence."*[23] This is interesting for as well as bringing existence (Ain Soph – limitlessness) from non-existence (Ain); it also indicates the divine will as the ultimate principle of order. For without the divine will

---

[23] *Sepher Yetzirah 2:6.*

there is chaos (*tohu*), and by the divine will is order imposed on the chaos of creation.[24]

The Zohar says of the Ain: *"It is so named because we do not know, and also it cannot be known, what was in this principle as this, to our understanding, yea, even by our wisdom is unattainable."* We may note that the supernal Sephiroth of Chokmah (Wisdom) and Binah (Understanding) are implied by this sentence, as is the transitional non-Sephira of Daath (Knowledge). Therefore the Ain may only be understood from the viewpoint of Kether, which is the expression of the ultimate divine, and not the other supernal Sephiroth or the Abyss.

This view is made clear by another quote from the Zohar which used one of the titles of Kether (Holy Ancient) in connection with the Ain: *"The most secret of mysteries is that which is called Nothing, the most Holy Ancient, from whom the light flows forth."*

It is interesting to note that by rearranging the letters of Ain (Aleph, Yod, Nun) we also make the words *Daughter* (NIA) and *I* (ANI). From this we can see that Kether, which we may consider to be the Ani, the identity of the Creator God that is expressed by the first Sephira, is an expression of the fullness of emptiness that God exists as before choosing to manifest.

The lesson we can learn from this is that even the unmanifest finds ways of expression when it is named, and given representative letters and numbers. Ain and its permutations add to 61, and we may note that so does Kali, the great black goddess of creation and destruction of the Hindu pantheon. You may wish to meditate on this and see what results you get.

Meditation - Ain

Meditate on the void, the complete absence of anything – no images, no sounds, no smells, no feelings, and absolutely no sensory input at all. See how this makes you feel. You may find your internal dialogue becomes annoying, and should try to silence it. When you can shut off the internal dialogue at will and enjoy the stillness of nothing you will have achieved a major step in your spiritual growth.

---

[24] *This perspective is also the underlying philosophy of ancient Egyptian religion, where the preservation of Maat (truth and cosmic harmony) was the most important consideration, to prevent isfet (disorder and chaos), and this view may have influenced early Qabalistic thought.*

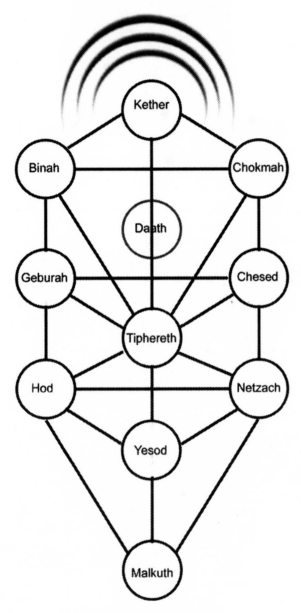

The Three Veils of Negativity

Ain Soph – Without End

Ain Soph is the divine as Infinite Being, immanent in everything. Because Ain Soph is eternal (without end) it is the eternal moment of transition, expressed as the creation of form, the beginning of the universe. From Ain Soph is Kether born, containing within it the plan of all the other Sephiroth to be unfolded. Kether is but a drop compared to an ocean when held next to the Ain Soph. Ain Soph is the unity beyond unity.

As well as being translated as *"without end"*, Ain Soph could also be described as limitlessness. Limits are a constraint of not only form, but also force, as they imply activity. An appropriate phrase for the Ain Soph is *"beyond the limits there are no limits"*.

To attempt to describe the incomprehensible, the best illustration I can suggest is the ancient Chinese book *The Tao Teh Ching*. This comes closer than any other work to expressing the concepts found in the Veils of Negativity. Verse fourteen is a particularly fine example:

> *"Look, it cannot be seen – it is beyond form.*
> *Listen, it cannot be heard – it is beyond sound.*
> *Grasp, it cannot be held – it is intangible.*
> *These three and indefinable;*
> *Therefore they are joined in one.*
>
> *From above it is not bright;*
> *From below it is not dark:*
> *An unbroken thread beyond description.*
> *It returns to nothingness.*
> *The form of the formless,*
> *The image of the imageless,*
> *It is called indefinable and beyond imagination.*
> *Stand before it and there is no beginning.*
> *Follow it and there is no end.*
> *Stay with the ancient Tao.*
> *Move with the present.*
>
> *Know the ancient beginning is the essence of Tao."*[25]

Meditation – Ain Soph

In modern terms you may find it useful to meditate on the Ain Soph as dark light and dark matter – invisible and unseeable, yet present everywhere, and by its existence, enabling the light to be known.

---

[25] *Translation by Gia-Fu Feng & Jane English, 1972*

Then expand this meditation to include all the energy we perceive as light and matter, realising that it is part of a much greater whole, that is completely unknowable, and beyond human comprehension. Visualise the whole cosmos, and keep drawing back, until the immensity of the universe overwhelms your mind.

Ain Soph Aur – Infinite Light

> *"You are eternal light, eye of mind longs and is startled at you, seeing only the edges, never all."* [26]

The Ain Soph Aur is the expression of the divine through the process of creation. The utterance of the words *"Let there be light"* [27], can be seen as the expression of the divine essence into its first point of manifestation. It is from the Ain Soph and Ain Soph Aur that Kether comes into existence. With infinite light comes infinite sound, for infinite light is really expressing infinite energy.

> *"Then, when all was yet undistinguished and unwrought, there was shed forth holy light."* [28]

The Ain Soph Aur can be likened to the divine light described by mystics in their attempts to express states of oneness with all of life and creation. The Indian Saint Allama Prabhu describes Shiva in a manner that can be used to demonstrate a glimpse of the concept expressed in Ain Soph Aur:

> *"It was like the sudden dawn of a million million suns, a ganglion of lightnings for my wonder. O Lord (of Caves) if you are light, there can be no metaphor."* [29]

It should be further mentioned that the divine light (Aur), which is also expressed by the term Lux or LVX (as in Fiat Lux – *"Let there be Light"*), is also represented by the term crystalline dew, and that references to dew in Kabbalistic texts may refer to this light, [30] or in some instances to Kether, which is said to be filled with the light. [31]

---

[26] *Kether Malkhuth, The Crown of the Kingdom, 8, Solomon the Sephardi, 11th century.*
[27] *See Genesis 1:3*
[28] *Libellus III, Corpus Hermetica. The similarity of Hermetic thought and Qabalistic thought is demonstrated repeatedly, and this is an obvious example.*
[29] *From Speaking of Siva, Translated by A.K. Ramanujan, 1973*
[30] *Isaiah 26:19, "The dew of the lights is Thy dew."*
[31] *"The head which is incomprehensible is secret in secret [Kether]. But it hath been formed and prepared in the likeness of a cranium, and is filled with the crystalline dew." The Book of Concealed Mystery 1:9-10 (Zohar)*

We may also note that the dew is referred to as being two colours – white and red[32], which are classically associated with male and female (e.g. in alchemy). Thus the dew can be seen as a union of both the male and female energies.

Meditation – Ain Soph Aur

Try meditating on the image of a desert, full of grains of white sand, reflecting the light of the fierce midday sun. Then imagine yourself as one of the grains of sand, within that desert, and consider yourself in relation to the desert. Expand this to the world, and then to the cosmos, and your mind may open more to the concept of Ain Soph Aur.

Alternatively, meditate on a drop of dew hanging off a blade of grass in a field as the sun rises, reflecting the light through itself in a prismatic spread of rainbow colours. Imagine yourself as the tiniest particle of water within that drop, which becomes your universe. Then expand your perceptions to the field you are in, then the whole landmass, then the world, and ultimately the cosmos.

---

[32] *"And that dew, which distilleth … in colour white and red." The Greater Holy Assembly 553 (Zohar).*

10. The Veils dividing the Tree

There are three main veils within the Tree of Life, which divide the Sephiroth horizontally into the three triads and Malkuth. These are the Veil of the Abyss, the Veil of Paroketh and the Veil of Malkuth.

The Veil of the Abyss

This veil lies beneath the Supernal Triad, and runs through Daath, the non-Sephira, dividing Kether, Chokmah and Binah from Chesed, Geburah and Tiphereth. The Abyss is the barrier dividing force (the Supernal Triad) from form (the lower Sephiroth). Above the Abyss is the time before time and after time, and below the Abyss the seven Sephiroth which refer to the seven days of the week (though the Seven Palaces model works slightly differently, attributing one day to the combination of Yesod and Malkuth, and one to the Supernal Triad).

This is mentioned in 1 Chronicles 29:11 *"Yours O God are the Greatness (Chesed), the Strength (Geburah), the Beauty (Tiphereth), the Victory (Netzach) and the Splendour (Hod), All (Yesod) that is in heaven and earth, Yours O God is the Kingdom (Malkuth)."*

The Veil of Paroketh

This veil is also known as the Veil of the Temple. The word Paroketh means *"veil"*, so it is usually simply referred to as Paroketh, otherwise you are saying the *"veil of veil"*! This veil lies beneath the second triad, dividing Chesed, Geburah and Tiphereth from Netzach, Hod and Yesod.

Paroketh is usually described as being like a rainbow, and is the barrier separating the aspirant from the adept. When a seeker has mastered the Astral Triad, and has emotions, intellect and unconscious working in harmony, then they are ready to move to the realisation of the true will expressed by Tiphereth, and gain understanding as to their true purpose in life.

The 25th path, connecting Yesod to Tiphereth, passing through Paroketh, is attributed to the Hebrew letter Samekh and the Tarot Trump Art, which is associated with Sagittarius, the archer. This path is sometimes referred to as the arrow on the bow of the Veil of Malkuth.

The Veil of Malkuth

Also referred to as the Veil of the Profane, this veil lies beneath the Astral Triad, dividing Netzach, Hod and Yesod from Malkuth. This veil passes through the 31st, 32nd and 29th paths on the Tree, to which are attributed the letters Shin, Tav and Qoph. Combining these letters we make the word QShTH, meaning bow (or rainbow).

The Veil of Malkuth is the barrier separating the spiritual seeker (aspirant) from those whose focus is purely on the material. This is also indicated in the *Zohar*, where it says that until the Nephesh (animal soul) is purified, man cannot aspire to the Ruach (middle soul), which corresponds to the Sephiroth between the Veil of Malkuth and the Veil of the Abyss. This is illustrated in Genesis 9:13-17 when the Covenant between God and man is established. The first of these verses implies the Veil of Malkuth and the ascent to the Ruach: *"I have set My bow in the cloud, and it shall be for a token of a covenant between Me and the earth."*

The Veil of the Presence of the Most High

Sometimes a veil is also drawn on the Tree below Kether, separating it from the other two Sephiroth of the Supernal Triad. This is the final barrier for the perfected soul to pass across to achieve union with Godhead.

11. Other Important Relationships

As well as the variety of ways of dividing the Tree of Life, there are also a number of important relationships that should be mentioned to expand the awareness of the student.

Divine Triad

Although not a standard Qabalistic triad, the relationship of Chokmah, Binah and Tiphereth should also be mentioned. This is the template of many world pantheons, and indeed of humanity and the animal kingdom generally. The father (Chokmah) and the mother (Binah) unite to produce the child (Tiphereth).

Kether-Tiphereth

Tiphereth is the manifestation of the divine energy of Kether. It is the reflected mirror (a title of Tiphereth) in the Veil of the Abyss, giving form to the divine energy in physical form. This is why rulership and sacrificial gods are associated with Tiphereth, as representations of the ultimate divine ruler of Kether.

The Yesod-Daath Mirror

This is a relationship that is sometimes mentioned but rarely explored. Daath is a curious enigma, as it is considered to be and yet not be a Sephira at the same time. In some respects Daath is the gateway between the Supernal Triad and the rest of the Tree of Life below the Abyss.

However if we look at the principle of reflection that occurs repeatedly in Qabalah, Yesod is considered to mirror Daath, with Tiphereth being the axis of that mirror. This is reflected in the attributions to the human body, for Daath corresponds to the throat and Yesod to the genitals. Both of these areas are the centres of creativity – the voice and the sexual energy.

The Eclipse Line

If we start at the bottom of the Tree of Life and move up the Middle Pillar, we have the Earth, Moon and Sun all aligned. In nature the effect of this is a total solar eclipse. On the Tree of Life this alignment indicates the aspects of the consciousness in man.

Malkuth represents the conscious world, Yesod the unconscious world and Tiphereth being the super-conscious. So the alignment in the spiritual seeker of these energies results in the opening of the mind to develop greater *"cosmic"* consciousness, where the individual realises his or her place in the universe.

This is why the 25th path, joining Yesod to Tiphereth, is known as the path of the honest or righteous man, for it requires the balance and purity associated with the alignment of the different worlds for the perfection of the moment.

The Expansion of Chokmah

Chokmah is the second Sephira, and we see its energy manifesting lower down the Tree in different aspects. It may be seen in Chesed and Hod, demonstrating the expansion of the dyad, from two (Chokmah) to four (Chesed) to eight (Hod). The flow from Chokmah to Chesed is mentioned in Proverbs 3:35, *"The wise (Chokmah) shall inherit glory (Gedulah): but shame shall be the promotion of fools."*

The Expansion of Binah

Binah has a strong relationship to both Netzach and Malkuth. This can be seen as the form of Binah being expressed as the emotions (Netzach) and the final physicality of matter (Malkuth). Also of course Malkuth is the lower reflection of the Shekinah, expressed from the higher aspect of Binah. Binah is the Mother and Wife, and Malkuth the Daughter and Bride.

And if we recall the statements in the *Zohar* that all women embody the Shekinah, then Netzach as the ultimate expression of the Venusian energies may also be seen as the Shekinah in the individual. Also Binah and Venus are the two earthiest planets, a fact which is relevant to their association with the elemental plane of Malkuth.

PART IV

IMPORTANT CONCEPTS

12. The Lightning Flash

"Ten Sephiroth of Nothingness, Their vision is like the 'appearance of lightning'". [33]

The Lightning Flash is the name given to the path of creation through the Sephiroth of the Tree of Life. It is the quickest route, taken by the energy as the emanation of energy in each Sephira overflowed and rushed into the next Sephira below. The Lightning Flash does not follow all the paths of the Tree of Life, as it is taking the quickest route from each Sephira to the next one.

If we consider lightning, we know now that it actually strikes initially from the ground to the heavens, and then back to the earth. This illustrates the point that the quickest way to achieve enlightenment is the path of the Lightning Flash. However lightning is pure energy travelling at the speed of light, and can be immensely destructive. For us as humans, the Path of the Serpent is a much more balanced path, which is far less prone to the potential "crash and burn" effects we may experience if we try to always take the quickest route.

The Lightning Flash is also known as the Flaming Sword, a phrase that occurs in connection with the Tree of Life in Genesis. In Genesis 3:24 it says *"So He drove out the man; and He placed at the east of the garden of Eden the Kerubim, and the flaming sword which turned every way, to keep the way to the tree of life."*

That the angels are Kerubim must also be considered significant. The Kerubim *("the strong")* have the heads of the four elemental creatures, i.e. the eagle, the lion, the bull and man. So the elemental energies that are repeated throughout the Tree as the building blocks for higher energies are emphasised here. Also the Kerubim are the angels of Yesod, the Foundation, implying that the Garden is not totally lost, as it is in the realm of the imagination, waiting to be manifested again by man, if he can take responsibility and regain the former harmony he had with the universe around him.

As spiritual seekers it is essential to realise the difference between the energy itself, and the symbols and vessels through which that energy is understood and manipulated.

---

[33] *Sepher Yetzirah 1:6.*

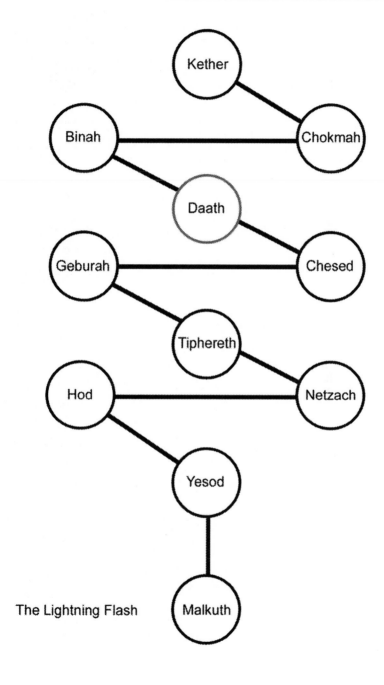

The Lightning Flash

It is through developing your awareness and giving it every opportunity to expand and develop that you move along your path. As the Indian Saint Basavanna said:

> *"Bowl and mirror are one metal. Giving back light one becomes a mirror. Aware, one is the Lord's; unaware, a mere human."*

Practical Work

Start performing the Lightning Flash affirmation and familiarise yourself with the energies you will be working with through the Tree of Life.

Next time there is a storm, take the time to sit in the dark and watch it, feeling the energy change occur whenever there is a flash of lightning.

13. The Serpent

The Path of the Serpent is the name given to the meandering path up the Tree of Life from bottom to top, which takes in each path in reverse numerical order. The image of the Serpent on the Tree of Life is initially a negative one in Biblical terms when considering its most superficial level, when the serpent tempts Eve in Genesis 3:1-4. However as with many other phrases in Qabalah, when we look at the Gematria a completely different meaning is revealed.

Nechesh (NchSh), the serpent on the Tree, adds to 358. The word for *shame* also adds to 358 (GShNH), which confirms the obvious interpretation, as Eve and Adam knew shame after eating the fruit and wore clothes to cover their bodies (Genesis 3:7). However 358 is also the total for *Messiah* (MshICh). The serpent is the root cause of the Messiah, for without the serpent there would be no original sin, and no need for the Messiah to sacrifice himself and redeem mankind. Hence the Serpent and the Messiah are equivalent in this context.

This is confirmed by the location of the crucifixion. The crucifixion occurred at Golgotha (place of the skull), where Adam was buried. The blood of Christ dropped onto the ground there, redeeming the original sin of Adam. Looking at the word for *Skull* (GLGLTh), this adds to 466, the same as "*The World of Formation*" (AaVLM HITzIRH). So the skull is the link between Assiah, the World of the physical, and the purity of Yetzirah, the World of the Angels, and through it the redemption was able to occur.

The Path of the Serpent is the path of completion. By following the Path of the Serpent up the Tree of Life, every experience is achieved, so that the seeker does not fall on their path. The Path of the Serpent will be considered in more detail in the second volume of this work, which will concentrate more on the paths on the Tree of Life.

Meditation

Meditate on the movement of a serpent. The following piece by John Ruskin from "*A Serpent in Motion*" provides an excellent focus for meditation.

> "*That rivulet of smooth silver – how does it flow, think you? It literally rows on the earth, with every scale for an oar; it bites the dust with the ridges of its body. Watch it when it moves slowly; a wave, but, without wind! A current, but with no fall! All the body moving at the*

same instant, yet some of it to one side, some to another, and some forward, and the rest of the coil backwards; but all with the same calm will and equal way – no contraction, no extension; one soundless, causeless march of sequent rings, a spectral procession of spotted dust, with dissolution in its fangs, dislocation in its coils. Startle it: the winding stream will become a twisted arrow; the wave of poisoned life will lash through the grass like a cast lance.[34]

---

[34] *From Treasury of Snake Lore – B Aymar (ed), 1956, p83.*

14. Tzim-Tzum

Tzim-Tzum, or Zim-Zum (pronounced *tzeem-tzum* and meaning *"contraction"* or *"constriction"*), is a term that refers to the concept of a contraction of the Ain Soph to form a *"space"* into which all of creation could and would manifest (i.e. the Sephiroth of the Tree of Life). The presence of God still permeates the space, but withdraws his dynamic essence, like a beautiful fragrance lingering in a room.

The *Zohar* refers to this process:
> *"In the beginning of the King's authority*
> *The Lamp of Darkness*
> *Engraved a hollow in the Supernal Luminescence*
> *And there emerged out of the Hidden of Hidden*
> *The Mystery of the Infinite*
> *An unformed line, imbedded in a ring*
> *Measured with a thread."*[35]

The best description of Tzim-Tzum can be found in the writings of one of the great Jewish Kabbalists, Rabbi Isaac Luria (1534-72 CE), better known as the Ari:
> *"Before all things were created ... the Supernal Light was simple, and it filled all existence. There was no empty space ... When His simple Will decided to create all universes ... He constricted the Light to the sides ... leaving a vacated space ... This space was perfectly round ... After this constriction [Tzim-Tzum] took place ... there was a place in which all things could be created ... He then drew a single straight thread from the Infinite Light ... and brought it into that vacated Space ... It was through that line that the Infinite Light was brought down below."*[36]

This could be thought of like a sand grain in an oyster, which accretes layers and forms a beautiful pearl. The sand grain is the space within the Ain Soph. This creation of space is the preparation for creation, and is the first instance of separation, where God moves from immanence to transcendence in the prepared space.

However separation then allows for a disharmony through lack of unity. The light of God entered the empty vessels of the Sephiroth, of which all but the

---
[35] *Zohar 1:15a.*
[36] *Etz Chaiim.*

upper three broke, unable to hold the divine emanations. This *"breaking of the vessels"* (shevirah) as it is known, resulted in the shards falling into the prepared space and taking sparks of the divine light with them. Most of the divine light returned to the Ain Soph, apart from these sparks.

This is then viewed from two different perspectives, which can be considered the optimistic and pessimistic. The optimistic view is that this was the birth of the universe, with all the pain and difficulties we as humans have come to expect from birth, but on a universal scale. The pessimistic view is that the universes slipped, and Assiah (the world we live in) is now in the World of Shells, and to restore it we have to free all the sparks of light trapped in this realm. This doctrine is sometimes known as *"restoration"* (tikkun), and can be seen as restoring the divine spark within everything to the primal divine.

15. The Unpronounceable Name of God

"Of the sublime name of the unity of the Lord, the name of four letters is most glorious. According to the image of Yod Heh [IH], the power and the glory. According to Vav Heh [VH], the secret of the name of every name."[37]

Tetragrammaton (IHVH) is the most significant word in Qabalah, as it contains many mysteries within it. It is known as the unpronounceable or unspeakable name of God. It has been given the vocalization of *"Adonai"* when pronounced by Kabbalists, though in Qabalah it is usually pronounced in one of four ways. It is either taken letter by letter as *"Yod Heh Vav Heh"*, or it is pronounced *"Jahveh"*, *"Yahweh"* or *"Jehovah"*.

The word Adonai (ADNI: Lord) was substituted when texts were spoken out loud, and eventually the correct pronunciation was said to have been lost. Prior to this the High Priest spoke it once a year in the holy of holies in the temple, and teachers could pass it on once every seven years to students. To allow the Tetragrammaton to be written down, it would be written as IHVH, with the vowel points from the word ADNI written underneath it, rendering it unpronounceable.[38] Even today "God" is often written as G-d in many Hebrew writings and online as a mark of respect for the divine.

The four letters correspond not only to the Four Worlds, but also to the Sephiroth (apart from Kether), and our place in the universe. Some texts also give Kether as the point of the Yod, thus including the whole of the Tree of Life within the word.

IHVH	Sephiroth	World	Time/Space
Point of Yod	Kether	Adam Kadmon	Timelessness
Yod	Chokmah	Atziluth	Past
Heh	Binah	Briah	Future
Vav	Chesed - Yesod	Yetzirah	Space
Heh	Malkuth	Assiah	Now

---

[37] *The Holy Names, Book 3, part 4, The Book of Razial.*
[38] *Hence the line in The Book of Concealed Mystery (Zohar) 5:29, "Four kings slay four kings", referring to the two Divine Names and the use of the vowel points.*

The letters are also attributed to the four elements and to the Tarot suits, thus:

(Point of Yod	Spirit	Trumps)
Yod	Fire	Wands
Heh	Water	Cups
Vav	Air	Swords
Heh	Earth	Disks

It has also been observed that the three tenses of the verb *"to be"* can be made from the letters of Tetragrammaton, further reinforcing the associations of time with this word. Thus *"He was"* (HIH), *"He Is"* (HVH) and *"He shall be"* (IHIH)[39].

The letters comprising IHVH (shown above) add up to 26 (10+5+6+5). All sorts of ideas spring to mind when we look at the sequence made by adding the letters – 10 (I) is $\Sigma(1-4)$[40], 15 (IH) is $\Sigma(1-5)$ and 21 (IHV) is $\Sigma(1-6)$. The final total is not $\Sigma(1-7)$ (28), but rather 26, which immediately brings to mind 2x13. As both *love* (AHBH) and *unity* (AChD) add to 13, it can be seen as saying by Gematria that Tetragrammaton is the unity of divine love.

This is particularly emphasised by the famous medieval Jewish Kabbalist Rabbi Abulafia, who said:

> *"The name of God is composed of two parts since there are two parts of love (2x13) [divided between] two lovers, and [parts of] love turn one [entity] when love became actuated. The divine intellectual love and the human intellectual love are conjuncted being one. This is the great power of man: he can link the lower part with the higher [one] and the lower [part] will ascend and cleave to the higher and the higher [part] will descend and kiss the entity ascending towards it, like a bridegroom actually kisses his bride out of his great and real*

---

[39] *Though this does require repetition of the yod. There is a distinct similarity to the ancient Egyptian description of the God of Writing and Magick Thoth as yesterday, today and the brother of tomorrow; and the Goddess Isis as "She who is, was and ever shall be".*

[40] *I.e. the sum of the numbers 1-4: 1+2+3+4 = 10.*

desire, characteristic to the delight of both, from the power of the name [of God].[41]

This number is also significant as it is the sum of the numbers of the Sephiroth on the Middle Pillar (1+6+9+10). We can thus describe the Middle Pillar of Balance as a manifestation of the unpronounceable name, demonstrating its inherent harmony.

Tetragrammaton is the most prevalent divine name through the medieval grimoires, as the ultimate power of God. This concept had already found its way into other streams of religious thought long before this, such as the Gnostics.

This is well illustrated in *Pistis Sophia*:

> *"And if that Name is said to the judges of the wicked, and to their lords and all their powers . . . . As soon as that Name is uttered in those regions they will fall one upon the other, so that being destroyed they perish and exclaim: 'Light of all the Lights, who art in the infinite lights, have mercy upon us and purify us.'"*

If IHVH is placed in a Pythagorean triangle the total of the letters is seventy-two, the number of letters in the Shemhamforash. The expansion of the name from the initial Yod (I) to the full Tetragrammaton (IHVH) can be seen as the Tree of Life manifesting through the Four Worlds. For there are ten letters corresponding to the ten Sephiroth, and the apex is Yod, which is sometimes used as shorthand for Kether.

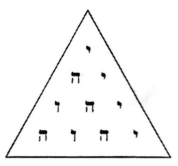

The Shemhamforash can be perceived as an expansion of the Tetragrammaton into an expression that can be used to ascend the Tree of Life through the four Worlds. The word Shemhamforash, or Shem ham M'forahs is a Hebraicized Aramaic term, usually translated as the *"ineffable Name"* or *"explicit name"*.

The Shemhamforash is derived from Exodus 14:19-21. Each of the verses contains seventy-two letters in the original Hebrew, which are translated into the English language thus:

---

[41] *'Or HaSekhel, MS Vatican 233, fol 115a Abulaifa*

> *19: And the angel of Elohim, who went before the camp of Israel,*
> *removed and went behind them; and the pillar of cloud removed from*
> *before them, and stood behind them;*
> *20: And it came between the camp of Egypt and the camp of Israel;*
> *and there was the cloud and the darkness here, yet gave it light by*
> *night there; and the one came not near the other all the night.*
> *21: And Moses stretched out his hand over the sea; and Adonai*
> *caused the sea to go back by a strong east wind all the night, and*
> *made the sea dry land, and the waters were divided.*

Not only is this the case, but verse 19 contains the words *"The angel of the Gods (Elohim)"*. The letters of verse 19 are written down, with the letters of verse 20 written down underneath them in reverse, and the letters of verse 21 in normal order underneath them. Reading downwards seventy-two three-letter names are obtained.

To these are added the suffix AL or IH to make the names of the seventy-two angels of Jacob's Ladder.[42] The angels whose names end in –al are taken as being angels of mercy attributed to the Pillar of Mercy, and those whose names end in –iah (as –ih is often written) are taken as being angels of severity attributed to the Pillar of Severity.

An early Merkavah text refers to the Shemhamforash specifically, demonstrating its importance and relevance: *"On His forehead the crown of the explicit name,[43] composed of fire and hail, and on His head a crown of glory."[44]*

Now as there are seventy-two names, made from three letters each, the total number of letters is two hundred and sixteen. This is significant as it demonstrates the flow of energy being expressed in these names. For 72 = *Chesed* (ChSD) and 216 = *Geburah* (GBVRH), so these names are indicative of the flow of energy between the highest two Sephiroth of the Tree of Life below the Abyss.

This is further emphasised in The Greater Holy Assembly (volume 2 of the Zohar), for the figure of seventy-two as the product of eighteen and four is referred to in verse 499:

> *"And between one column and another column[45] are contained*
> *eighteen bases of columns: and they shine forth with brilliancy in the*
> *openings carved out in that veil, and so on all four sides."*

---

[42] *Also implied in Exodus 14:19 by the "pillar of cloud".*

[43] *In the Hebrew this is Kether Shem ha-meforash.*

[44] *Hekhalot Zutarti (The Lesser Hekhalot).*

[45] *I.e. the White and Black Pillars.*

As is discussed later in the section entitled *A Note on Visualisation* within the chapter on *Pathworking*, the term *carved* is used to describe visualisation, especially of magickal words, and so this can be seen as referring to the seventy-two names (4x18) of the Shemhamforash. The number 18 here is significant as it refers to the numeration of the word for *life* (ChI), which is then expressed through the Four Worlds.

So the Shemhamforash is literally the life that shines through the veil expressed through the worlds, i.e. the divine creative power. Hence we see the line in The Book of Razial: *"Of the unity of one, the secret of the seventy-two most glorious. Proclaim the Shem Hamphorash."*[46]

It is also interesting to note that the Egyptians chasing the Jews in Exodus remove their chariot wheels and are drowned by the deluge of the waters. This recalls the whole idea of Merkavah (chariot) mysticism and the quest for the presence of God.

Meditation on Tetragrammaton

In your mind's eye see a clear cloudless blue sky. See yourself rising up into the sky, passing through it into the heavens. Keep rising into space and see the stars all around you. Keep rising until the blackness of space is all around you, and the stars have all disappeared. Now rise again, and see the infinite blackness that surrounds you become infinite whiteness. You are surrounded by a huge white curtain that seems to go on forever.

Now visualise the letters of Tetragrammaton in black, huge in front of you. See the colour of the letters and of the curtain intensify, so that it seems the letters are burning black fire, and the background is burning white fire. The letters become bigger and bigger as you move towards them, until your whole mind is swallowed by the Divine Name.

To further develop this meditation you can use the letters as astral doorways, and pass through each letter in turn, exploring the different experiences you have when passing through each of the letters.

---

[46] *The Holy Names, Book 3 Part 1.*

16. The Shekinah

The Shekinah is described in a number of different ways through the different branches of Kabbalah, and this has greatly affected the modern perception. The word Shekinah is from the root *Shakhan* meaning *"to dwell"*.

The German branch of Kabbalah described the Shekinah as the flame encircling God, causing the throne, angels and human souls to come into being.[47] This fits with the idea of the Shekinah being the divine bride, who unites with God in Atziluth, causing the other three Worlds to come into being. The Worlds of Briah, Yetzirah and Assiah are thus implied by the throne, angels and human souls respectively.[48]

When the Shekinah descends into Briah, the highest of the Archangels gather around her, that they may help her light become formed into her body, indicating the nature of Binah both as the residence of the Greater (or unmanifest) Shekinah and as the place where force is at the moment of transition to form.

Having descended through Yetzirah and taken on form, the Shekinah is then manifest in two main ways in Assiah. As the Lesser or Exiled Shekinah she is perceived as being the world soul, somewhat akin to the concept of Gaia as postulated by James Lovelock. However as the source of souls, Shekinah is also present in every person, as the spark that seeks to reunite with the Greater Shekinah and thus to God.

Thus when the Bible likens man to a tree, saying *"Man is a tree of the field"*[49], it refers to the presence of both the Tree of Life and the Shekinah within every one of us, for the Shekinah is also known as the *"Field of Holy Apples"*[50].

The Shekinah can also represent the Middle Pillar, uniting the Exiled Shekinah with the Creator, Malkuth and Kether. The Shekinah as Binah is also known as the Superior Supernal Mother, and the Exiled Shekinah as Malkuth is known as the Inferior or Infernal Mother. These titles and attributions are part of the idea of the Shekinah as the two Heh's of Tetragrammaton.

---

[47] *Kabbalah – Charles Ponce, 1974. p62.*
[48] *For which consider the Book of Ezekiel.*
[49] *Deuteronomy 20:19.*
[50] *Zohar 2:60b.*

"Her ways are of pleasantness, and her paths are peace.
She is a tree of life to them that lay hold upon her; and happy is
every one that retaineth her."[51]

That Shekinah is seen as wisdom, and Chokmah (Wisdom) is seen as a masculine Sephira may be seen by its relative position on the Tree of Life. For as each Sephira is negative to the one above it and positive to the one below, so is it also the case that each Sephira is feminine to the one above it and masculine to the one below[52]. This is why we find quotes such as *"Of understanding, receive wisdom."[53]*

Hence although Chokmah is known by titles such as the Father (Aba), this is in respect of its relationship with Binah as the Mother (Ama), not in its relationship to Kether, where it is perceived as feminine. Hence quotes such as the following one from The Zohar: *"And that Spirit (Shekinah) issued forth from the concealed brain (Kether). She is called the Spirit of Life and through Her do all men understand Chokmah, Wisdom."*

Some modern practitioners see the Shekinah as being the Holy Spirit (Holy Ghost), and others as a feminine aspect of the Holy Spirit. However this view is somewhat denigrating and does not really place sufficient emphasis on the importance of the Shekinah. The Shekinah is literally the "indwelling" presence of God, the divine spark within every human being.

The Shekinah is clearly described in all of Proverbs 8, but especially verses 1-11:

"1. It is wisdom (Chokmah) calling, understanding (Binah) raising her voice.
2. She takes her stand at the topmost heights, by the wayside, at the crossroads,
3. Near the gates at the city entrance; At the entrance she shouts,
4. O men, I call to you; My cry is to all humankind.
5. Simple ones, learn shrewdness; O dullards, instruct your minds.
6. Listen, for I speak noble things; Uprightness comes from my lips;
7. My mouth utters truth; Wickedness is abhorrent to my lips.
8. All my words are just, None of them perverse or crooked;
9. All are straightforward to the intelligent one, And right to those who have attained knowledge.

---

[51] Proverbs 3:17-18.
[52] *Hence Kether being seen as the only purely masculine Sephira and Malkuth as the only feminine Sephira. This in itself is a balance of the two extremes in the Tree of Life.*
[53] *Book of the Vestment (Sepher Hamelbosh), part 1 of The Book of Raziel.*

10. Accept my discipline rather than silver, Knowledge (Daath) rather than choice gold.
11. For Wisdom (Chokmah) is better than rubies; No goods can equal her."

This amazing chapter goes on to describe how the Shekinah existed before creation (7:22-31), being the first act of the divine impulse. Proverbs 7 is an incredible piece of literature regarding the divine feminine and it is astonishing that it has been ignored for so long.[54] The next but one chapter, Proverbs 9, begins with a verse which alludes to the doctrine of the Seven Palaces, referring to seven pillars, indicating how all-permeating the Shekinah is when we start to look for her.

Wisdom hath built her house, she hath hewn out her seven pillars ..."[55]

To really appreciate the Shekinah and her influence, try re-reading *The Song of Solomon* in the Bible. However read it as an expression of the love between Shekinah and God, and see how the context of what is written there changes. The great beauty of this piece then gains a very different perspective.

Meditation on the Shekinah

Prepare your space by burning pure frankincense and myrrh on your censer. Drink from a cup of milk and honey, so the taste fills your mouth. Sing the phrase *"I am the rose of Sharon, and the lily of the valleys"* as a mantra, whilst visualising yourself surrounded by a circle of flames. Stimulated by these sensations, allow your mind to focus on the concept of the Shekinah.

Flame Meditation on the Shekinah

This meditation can be done with a beeswax candle, but ideally should be done with a small oil lamp, with olive oil and a linen wick. Olive oil burns with a flame that is particularly clean. The lamp (or candle) should be placed at least a metre (just over three foot) from the wall, and there should be no other light source in the room, curtains should be drawn.

Contemplate the flame, and see the white, yellow and red. Then become aware of the surrounding blackness around the flame. After a while you may

---

[54] *The exception being the superb Mirror of His Beauty by Peter Schäfer, 2002.*
[55] *Proverbs 9:1.*

perceive a sky blue colour in the blackness around the flame.[56] This blueness is representative of the Shekinah. Gaze into the blueness and allow it to transport your consciousness into awareness of the Shekinah.

---

[56] *According to the Zohar there are said to be five colours seen when contemplating a flame – white, yellow, red, black and sky-blue.*

17. Adam Kadmon

To understand the concept of Adam Kadmon (or Qadmon) it is important to realise that the Adam who is expelled from Eden with Eve is actually the fourth of the Adams. The first Adam was Adam Kadmon, the primordial man. Adam Kadmon was traditionally viewed as the fifth World, above Atziluth, containing the potential of the other four Worlds within him (expressed as IHVH representing the body as shown below). This fifth World is sometimes referred to as being the Ain Soph, and as being the dwelling place of Tetragrammaton, the unpronounceable name. It is sometimes equated with the dot on the Yod of Tetragrammaton, as the first impulse of the ultimate.

Adam Kadmon was formed by a single beam of light sent forth from the Ain Soph, which burst forth from his eyes, ears, nose and mouth as the lights of the Sephiroth. The light from the eyes filled the vessels of light that were the Supernal Triad of Kether, Chokmah and Binah. However when the light filled the vessels of the lower Sephiroth it was so intense that the vessels broke. This is the act known as the *Breaking of the Vessels* (*Shevirah*), and described elsewhere in the text.

The Sephiroth correspond to different parts of the body of Adam Kadmon, which are sometimes given inaccurately in modern Qabalistic works. It will be seen that Adam Kadmon is viewed from behind, with the right side of the body aligned with the right side of the observer, unlike many modern authors claim.

Note this is not the same as the attributions of the Tree of Life onto the human body, which is an important attribution for personal work with Qabalistic practice, although many works make this mistake and call those attributions Adam Kadmon.

Adam Kadmon

Sephira	Part of Body
Kether	Head
Chokmah	Brain
Binah	Heart
Chesed	Right Arm
Geburah	Left Arm
Tiphereth	Chest
Netzach	Right Leg
Hod	Left Leg
Yesod	Genitals
Malkuth	The Completion and Harmony

The Five Adams

Some sources consider Adam Kadmon to have been the first template of divine manifestation, the *"first Adam"*, reflected through the Four Worlds in different manifestations. This is part of a doctrine known as the *"Five Adams"*.

The second Adam is the one referred to in Genesis 1:27, *"And God created man in His own image, in the image of God created He him; male and female created He them."* This hermaphroditic Adam contained both male and female, undivided, and is known as the Atziluthic Adam, or *"Adam of light"*.

The third Adam is referred to in Genesis 2:7, *"And the Lord God formed man of the dust of the ground, and breathed into his nostrils the breath of life; and man became a living soul."* This Adam is known as the Briatic Adam, or the *"Adam of dust"*. This is the Adam who gives names to all the creatures (Genesis 2:19-20).

The fourth Adam is the Adam from whom Eve is created in Genesis 2:21-23[57], formed by the separation of the third Adam. There is dispute about the idea of

---

[57] *And the Lord God caused a deep sleep to fall upon the man, and he slept; and He took one of his ribs, and closed up the place with flesh instead thereof. And the rib, which the Lord God had taken from the man, made He a woman, and brought her unto the man.*
And the man said: "This is now bone of my bones, and flesh of my flesh; she shall be called Woman, because she was taken out of Man."

the rib being what is taken, and it is written in the *Zohar*[58] that in fact the term was *"side"*, implying that the third Adam was still a hermaphrodite. The expression *"closed up the flesh"* and *"bone of my bones, and flesh of my flesh"* also lends credence to this argument. This Adam is known as the Yetziric Adam, and was said to be the source of all human souls.

The fifth Adam is Adam after expulsion from the Garden of Eden (Genesis 3:23-24). This Adam is known as the Assiatic Adam. Mankind, as children of the fifth Adam, are striving to return to the state of the fourth Adam, dwelling in the perfection and paradise of Eden. This is why ascending to the World of Yetzirah on the Tree of Life is also known as *"ascending to the orchard"*, as the orchard is another name for Eden.

Meditation on Adam Kadmon

Use this classic image as a gateway image, closing your eyes and seeing it in brilliant white on a black background. See it get larger and larger, until it is big enough for you to step into, like a curtain or screen over a doorway. When you have sent your consciousness through to the other side, explore what you find there. After a period of 5-10 minutes, concentrate on seeing yourself again, and bring your awareness back to your body.

---

[58] *"And when He wisheth to separate them He causeth an ecstasy to fall upon Microposopus, and separateth the Woman from His back."* Greater Holy Assembly 13:1028.

18. The Qliphoth

The word Qliphoth means *"shells"* or *"husks"* (singular Qliphah). It is also sometimes written as Klippot or Kellipot. There is much confusion about the nature of the Qliphoth. Many modern writers will describe the Qliphoth as being evil and negative entities, but this viewpoint is extremely limited and entirely misses the point.

This is recognised in the inner order writings of the Golden Dawn, where they and their role are referred to very concisely:

> *"To bring perfect order into the Six Sephiroth of his Ruach, then will the Qliphoth who may be called the Wild Beasts of the Nation, be forced to retire, they only having been permitted to remain through Disorder .... Their synthesis will become as a strong yet trained animal, whereupon the man rideth, this bringing added material strength unto the man."*[59]

Consider the Four Worlds – there is Atziluth, Briah, Yetzirah and Assiah. To each of these Worlds corresponds different qualities, which may be seen operating in each of the Sephiroth. Hence the Divine Name corresponds to Atziluth, the Archangel to Briah, the Choir of Angels to Yetzirah, and the Heaven and Qliphoth to Assiah.

The Divine Name corresponds to the essence of a Sephira, its inherent divinity, this is its presence in Atziluth. The Archangel is the lens, focusing that divine essence and directing it according to the will of that essence, this is its presence in Briah. The Choir of Angels fulfils the will of the Archangel, ensuring that all runs according to the divine plan, this is its presence in Yetzirah. The Heaven is the manifestation of the Sephira in the physical, this is its presence in Assiah. However this leaves a residue of undirected energy, which does not necessarily follow the divine will – this is the Qliphoth.

The concept of the Shevirah or *"Breaking of the Vessels"* describes how the Qliphoth came into being. There is a teaching that the lower Sephiroth (below the Abyss) of the primeval and original ten Sephiroth could only receive the divine emanations, but could not interact or give.[60] As a result they were overwhelmed and shattered. This is known as the *"Breaking of the Vessels"*,

---

[59] *Know Thyself, Flying Roll 21, by Mina Mathers*
[60] *See the section on Tzim-Tzum.*

and is what is referred to symbolically in Genesis 36:31-43 describing the Kings of Edom.

The broken pieces of these vessels fell to Assiah, and the ten Sephiroth were then created anew in the form where they could interact, giving the Tree of Life. The broken pieces are also considered to be the Qliphoth, which can challenge but cannot give, so they need to be overcome to gain an understanding of the true nature of each of the Sephiroth.

The name of the Qliphoth indicates their nature to anyone who looks at it and thinks for a moment. They are the shells or husks. When you eat a nut, say a hazelnut, you first remove the shell. The inner fruit within is guarded by the outer shell without. Thus are the Qliphoth also. Without a shell or husk, how can the essence within have form? Once the nut is eaten the shell may seem useless, but that does not mean it did not fulfill a necessary function, and indeed will continue to do so as it breaks down and is transmuted into other forms as it rots in the earth.

Another way to look at the Qliphoth would be to imagine a cross-section of a tree. There are many concentric rings indicating the growth of the tree, all interconnected. Imagine all those inner rings as being the energy of the Sephira, and the Qliphoth would then be the rough dead bark enclosing and protecting all the living wood within.

Our daily waking world is sometimes referred to as the *"World of Shells"*, and if you think about this for a moment you will soon see why. Modern buildings are like concrete shells, cars are mobile shells, the rubbish from all the processes of modern life can be seen as shells, the list goes on and on.

> *"Shape without form, shade without colour,*
> *Paralysed force, gesture without motion;*
> *Those who have crossed*
> *With direct eyes, to death's other Kingdom*
> *Remember us - if at all - not as lost*
> *Violent souls, but only*
> *As the hollow men*
> *The stuffed men."*[61]

T.S. Eliot's wonderful poem is one of the most vivid descriptions of the idea of the Qliphoth, and also the World of Shells that life can become if we do not keep the fire of our spirits alive and strive ever forwards towards beauty and truth.

---

[61] *From The Hollow Men by T.S. Eliot.*

So although the Qliphoth are the shells that give necessary form, we must not allow ourselves to become comfortable in the mundane. We must recognise the nature of the Qliphoth, and also that we must break through them to reach the fruit of wisdom beyond.

Likewise when you meditate, banish all thoughts. In this context, those thoughts can be seen as the Qliphoth, for they are unwanted shells distracting you. This is why my discussion of the Qliphoth within the chapters on the *Sephiroth* will not present them as evil but rather as challenges, as shells to be cracked to reach the kernel of truth within.

This is a point made in Psalm 7, where David prays against the malice of his enemies, e.g. 7:14, *"Behold, he travaileth with iniquity, and hath conceived mischief, and brought forth falsehood"*, and 7:16,*"He made a pit, and digged it, and is fallen into the ditch which he made."* The emphasis of this whole Psalm is on behaving properly, to enable one to overcome the challenges presented by the Qliphoth.

The Tree of Evil

A modern perception of the Tree of Life has been the idea of an averse Tree, or Tree of Evil. This is said to be the Tree of the Qliphoth, and derives from medieval hierarchies of demon kings and princes, whilst failing to consider the true nature of the Qliphoth. Such a perception is derived from the idea of an imbalance in the Tree on the Pillar of Severity, resulting in the creation of this Qliphotic Tree. Such a distorted perception holds little value for the Qabalist beyond a cautionary note to avoid obsession with such ideas.

Meditation

Allow your mind to contemplate the physical shell of your body – your nails, skin and hair. All of these are dead, yet they enclose and protect all the living tissue within. Meditate on your shell, and keep your attention focused entirely on it.

PART V

MAN AND THE QABALAH

19. The Human Soul on the Tree

The different models of the Tree of Life also incorporate a fundamental aspect of Qabalah, that of the aspects or parts of the human soul. Exploring this helps demonstrate the depths of Qabalah, and helps show that each Sephira and level are like onions, with more layers always ready to be unpeeled to gain deeper understanding as you approach the core essence of the Sephira or level of the Tree of Life.

The human soul may be divided into several major aspects, which are considered as each existing in a different world simultaneously, demonstrating once more the interconnectedness of man, the universe and the Tree of Life as all being manifestations of the same creative divine impulse.

One of the key Qabalistic teachings about the soul is that originally all souls were one (as the original hermaphroditic Adam Kadmon), and they became separated into male and female as they began the descent into matter. This means that on earth all souls are separate from their other half. To reach completion a person must find their other half (their "soul-mate"), which may only be done by walking in truth. An old Qabalistic saying is that when two such souls meet, *"their union was pre-ordained by virtue of the fact that they were originally one"*.

The Glassblower Model

The classic Kabbalistic analogy of the soul was described by Rabbi Moshe Chayim Luzatto as of a glassblower performing his craft. The glassblower is the divine, and the glass vessel is the person. The process of blowing the glass begins with the glassblower breathing (Neshamah) into the tube that connects his mouth to the vessel he is blowing.

The breath then travels through the tube as a wind (Ruach) until it reaches the vessel. Finally the breath enters the vessel and shapes it according to the glassblower's plan, and it comes to rest (Nephesh).

The Nephesh

This is the animal soul or lower soul, which corresponds to Malkuth in the classical model and the Astral Triad in the modern model. The animal soul is of the nature of the world of Assiah, of physical existence, and it remains in this world even after the death of the body and transmigration of other parts of the soul. The Nephesh has the lowest aspects of the soul – the instincts and cravings. The Nephesh is the raw energy necessary for making the body function.

Until the Nephesh is refined the seeker cannot move on to purification of the Ruach. This is referred to in The Book of Razial, which says *"Conceal the Nephesh in the Foundation"*,[62] referring to Yesod (Foundation) as the lowest part of the Ruach. When the Nephesh is purified, it then becomes a throne for the Ruach to reside in, enabling the seeker to strive towards the Neshamah. By purification the control of the bodily desires is indicated, such as the overcoming of addictions.

This overall attribution is easy to appreciate when we consider that the Nephesh was thought to reside in the blood during life, and to pass into the earth after death (and Nephesh means *"resting soul"*). These beliefs are illustrated in Genesis 4:10 after Cain has slain Abel, *"And He [God] said: 'What hast thou done? The voice of thy brother's blood crieth unto Me from the ground."*

It is also demonstrated in Deuteronomy 12:23-24, *"Only be sure that thou eat not the blood: for the blood is the life; and thou mayest not eat the life with the flesh. Thou shalt not eat it; thou shalt pour it upon the earth as water."*

This line of *"the blood is the life"* has been the inspiration for a whole genre of authors writing books on the theme of vampires, and is probably one of the most-quoted lines of the Old Testament in fictional works.

In I Samuel 28 this concept of the Nephesh going into the Earth after death is clearly described, when Saul goes to the witch and persuades her to raise the shade of Samuel (i.e. his Nephesh). The witch sees the shade *"ascending out of the earth."*[63]

Earlier in Genesis 9:3-4 we read, *"Every moving thing that liveth shall be for food for you; as the green herb have I given you all. Only flesh with the life thereof, which is the blood thereof, shall ye not eat."*

Strictly speaking the Nephesh is perceived as residing in the liver, or that the liver (*kaved*) is the main dwelling place of the Nephesh. The liver as the largest organ in the body is responsible for breakdown and synthesis of complex sugars and proteins transported in the blood. So all the blood gets pumped through the liver, the dwelling place of the Nephesh.

---

[62] *Book of the Vestment, Part 2.*
[63] *I Samuel 28:13.*

The Ruach

The Ruach is the middle soul or spirit, sometimes known as the Intellectual Spirit. It is the seat of the moral qualities of the individual, and represents the purity of the self when it is fully realised. The Ruach may be divided into five sub-parts, corresponding to the faculties of Memory, Will, Imagination, Desire and Reason.

The Ruach is said to dwell in the heart (*lev*) of man, corresponding to Tiphereth as the centre of man. The Ruach is connected with spiritual experience, being associated with inspiration and prophecy, which is easy to see when we consider that Ruach literally means either *"wind"* or *"spirit"*.

By gaining control of the faculties of the Ruach, you have placed yourself on the path of your true will, aligning yourself to the purpose of the divine and traveling through the experiences of life that bring fulfillment of the self in striving for perfection.

The Neshamah

The Neshamah is the upper soul, breath or pneuma. It is first referred to in Genesis 2:7 - *"Then the Lord God formed man of the dust of the ground, and breathed into his nostrils the breath of life; and man became a living soul [Neshamah]."*

The Neshamah is also referred to as the Shekinah, and is always depicted as being female. Only a person who has discovered their true will and aligned himself with the flow of the divine can experience their Neshamah. The Neshamah resides in the brain (*moach*) of each person. It is also said that all people see the Neshamah at the moment of death.

> *"Quintessence of the universe, Distilled at last from God's own heart, In me concentred now abides, Of all that is the subtlest part."*[64]

All women are said to be in the shelter of the Shekinah, and so it is said to be easier for a woman to reach the Neshamah than a man. The higher aspects of the Neshamah remain unknown and unknowable to a person until they have become aware of their Neshamah.

For a person to progress spiritually they must have refined their Nephesh and Ruach and harmonised these with their Neshamah. Now the main dwelling places of these three parts of the soul in the body are the liver, heart and brain. Thus if we take the Notariqon of the names of these three organs we get M(oach) L(ev) K(ayed), making the word MLK, *Melekh*, meaning King. So

---

[64] *Minot Judson Savage (1841-1918), from "My Birth".*

a person who has developed themselves to the extent of refining their internal spiritual aspects is known as a king. For anyone interested in Thelema, this has considerable bearing on certain lines of *The Book of the Law*, especially chapter 2:57-8.

Chayah

Chayah (or Chiyah or Chiah, meaning *"life force"* or *"living essence"*) is a higher aspect of the Neshamah that is the vitality, the creative impulse. This is often equated to the true will. There is a dichotomy here, as the true will is often equated with Tiphereth. It would perhaps be more appropriate to say that Tiphereth corresponds to the realisation of the true will or Chayah, but to actualise and fully realise the true will is an ongoing process that continues as you keep travelling up the Tree.

The Chayah and the Yechidah are known as *envelopments* (makifim), that is to say they are not perceived as being internalised within the human body. These more subtle aspects of the soul are believed to be present in our auras around us, literally enveloping us.

Yechidah

The Yechidah (*"unique essence"* or *"unity"*) is the highest aspect of the Neshamah, and can be seen as corresponding to the divine and immortal spark of the soul that is eternal. It is the most ephemeral and transcendental part of the soul, where the highest essence of man becomes the divine.

The parts of the soul correspond to the force of creation moving through the Four Worlds. Hence any creative impulse within us moves from nothingness to thought, and then to speech and action. To assist in the ascent of the Tree, we must strive to purify and unite the parts of our soul, each in turn, bringing them into harmony so that we can gain the majesty of the king (or queen) that comes from pure pursuit of the true will, and then we can be open to the force of the Chayah and ultimately the Yechidah.

Part of Soul	World	Impulse
Chayah	Atziluth	Nothingness
Neshamah	Briah	Thought
Ruach	Yetzirah	Speech
Nephesh	Assiah	Action

Part of Soul	World	Classical Model	Modern Model
Yechidah		Kether	Kether
Chayah	Atziluth	Chokmah	Chokmah
Neshamah	Briah	Binah	Binah
Ruach	Yetzirah	Chesed – Yesod	Chesed – Tiphereth
Nephesh	Assiah	Malkuth	Yesod – Netzach
Guph (body)	(exists in Assiah)		Malkuth

20. Reincarnation and Qabalah

The idea of reincarnation, or transmigration of souls, known as *"gilgul"* (meaning revolving or swirling) was one that became integrated into Kabbalistic belief, being first published in the *Bahir* in the late thirteenth century CE. On death the parts of the soul all go to their appointed places. The Nephesh sinks into the earth, to go to Gehinnom (hell) if the person has been bad, the Ruach stays with the body, and the Neshamah ascends to the Throne of God, where the Throne sustains it until it is ready to descend back into physical form.

This doctrine is hinted at by the name of the heaven of Kether, i.e. *Rashith ha-Gilgalim* (the first swirlings), coming from the same root as the word gilgul. The soul aspires to its highest aspect, the Yechidah, seeking to elevate the lower aspects so they may be united with the highest and then re-merge with the ultimate divine.

There are a number of variants of this belief, such as where the souls go depending on conduct. A soul that has fulfilled its spiritual destiny does not need to continue reincarnating, and is said to be stored in holiness by God until the end of time, when it is rejoined with its body, its Ruach and its Nephesh. God will then cause dew (which is the divine light) to exude from His head that will flow through the Sephiroth until it reaches the earth. The dew is said to be that which would have caused Adam and Eve to have become immortal, and will enable the resurrected soul to be remerged with the primal Adam.

When all the souls have remerged with Adam, he can be restored to his state of grace from before the Fall and exile. In this way every person is part of the process of restoration, *"tikkun"*.

A soul that has knowingly perpetrated evil will return to a lesser form, such as an animal, plant or even stone. This doctrine is analogous to the Hindu concept of karmic reincarnation, and is thought to have its roots in Platonic and Neo-Platonic philosophies.

A later version of this doctrine changed the concept of rebirth until perfection is reached with a cycle of only four incarnations. If by the end of the fourth life the soul had not reached a basic level of development it would roam the earth as a spirit (called a *dybbuk*) that sought to possess other people to control their bodies and be returned to the flesh. If the soul did reach a level of attainment it would find sanctuary until the day of restitution.

21. The Guardian Angel

> *"There are as many orders of human souls as the stars and legions of dæmons numbered together, and that souls are allotted the nature, function, and name of their respective dæmons and stars. Now they call these dæmons spirits, the innate guides of our being, each assigned to an individual soul by the law of fate."*[65]

Modern Qabalah includes the concept of the Holy Guardian Angel, made popular particularly by the works of the Golden Dawn and Aleister Crowley, but often not very clearly explained or considered. However this idea also has its roots in ancient Kabbalah and other schools of religious philosophy, such as Zoroastrianism.

In Kabbalah a type of angel called a *Maggid* (pl. Maggidim) is discussed. These angels are said to be created when a person performs good actions, and if a person is consistently good and disciplined, then the Maggid will reveal itself to him. Interestingly if the person kept a commandment but not according to the law it was said the Maggid would be made up of both good and evil, combining truth and lies.

The way to recognise a true Maggid was to test that it always told the truth, motivated one to do good deeds, and always gave accurate predictions of the future. Magickians will recognise this is akin to the concept of the Holy Guardian Angel. This is verified by the following description of a Maggid: *"It is a voice sent from on high to speak to a prophet … such a voice cannot enter the prophet's ear until it clothes itself in a physical voice. The physical voice in which it clothes itself is the voice of the prophet himself."*

However this idea also found its way into the Renaissance Grimoires, and hence we see them filled with such quotes as:

> *"And as there is given to Every man, a good spirit, so there is given to him an Evil spirit; & each of them seeketh an union with his spirit, & endeavours to attract it to itself, and to be mixed with it."*[66]

---

[65] *How each person has a guardian angel, letter by Marsilio Ficino to Filippo Callimachus, 1484*
[66] *Sloane 3825: for the full text of this Grimoire see The Keys to the Gateway of Magic: Summoning the Solomonic Archangels & Demonic Princes by Stephen Skinner & David Rankine.*

> *"Now when a good spirit hath influence upon a holy soul, it doth exalt it to the Light of Wisdom, & all things that conduceth to an Intellectual Benignity"*[67]

Indeed some versions of the Goetia even contain a prayer for conjuration of the Holy Guardian Angel, reproduced here in full.

The Conjuration of the Holy Guardian Angel[68]

> *"O thou great and blessed [Name] my angel guardian vouchsafe to descend from thy holy mansion which is Celestial, with thy holy Influence and presence, into this crystal stone, so that I may behold thy glory; and enjoy thy society, aid and assistance, both now and for ever hereafter. O thou who art higher that the fourth heaven, and knoweth the secrets of Elanel. Thou that rideth upon the wings of the winds and art mighty and potent in thy Celestial and superlunary motion, do thou descend and be present I pray thee; and I humbly desire and entreat thee. That if ever I have merited Thy society or if any of my actions and Intentions be real and pure & sanctified before thee bring thy external presence hither, and converse with me one of thy submissive pupils, By and in the name of the great god Jehovah, whereunto the whole choir of heaven Singeth continually: O Mappa la man Hallelujah. Amen."*

When you have said this over several times you will at last see strange sights and passages in the stone and at last you will see your genius: Then give him a kind entertainment as you were before directed declaring him to your mind and what you would have him do, &c.

To achieve the state of balance and harmony required to maintain your existence in Tiphereth or above is a lifelong task. However you can experience visions of your guardian angel in meditations and dreams, and it may even communicate with you in these instances. As has been previously mentioned, any contact with the guardian angel will be characterised by truth and accuracy, which are your guidelines for determining the validity of such perceived encounters.

---

[67] *Ibid.*

[68] *Sloane MSS 2731: reproduced also in The Lesser Key of Solomon, edited by Joseph H. Peterson.*

PART VI

EXPANDING PERCEPTIONS

22. Working with the Tree of Life

At first glance the Tree of Life can be a perplexing glyph. The complexity of all the attributions and forms of division into different categories can seem overwhelming, numbing the mind and can often be daunting to the newcomer. However all these categories and attributions are much easier to come to grips with than you may think.

The correspondences are there to help explore the symbolism inherent in Qabalah, and open the mind up to the wisdom it contains. By considering one aspect at a time and not rushing at it like a bull in a china shop, Qabalah can be appreciated as ultimately simple, with layers upon layers to be unravelled and marvelled at, like a cosmic onion.

To appreciate the way in which Qabalah can cover so many different areas, we need to look at the role of gods, Archangels and the planets.

23. Qabalah and the Gods

Many people have dismissed Qabalah by giving it a cursory glance and declaring *"I'm not interested in that Judeo-Christian monotheistic worldview"*. However such a dismissive attitude displays a woeful ignorance, both of the versatility and depth of Qabalah, and of the history of their own beliefs.

Monotheism is not merely the belief in a single deity – it is the belief in an ultimate deity. Other divine and immortal beings may also be perceived as existing, and fulfilling roles and functions subservient to the will of the ultimate. This is known as Henotheism, and is still essentially a monotheistic view, with the inexplicable forces and occurrences of the natural world being qualified through association with divine entities.

At the end of the day, the perceptions man has placed on gods – seeing them as human, animal or a combination of the two, are an attempt to create a workable interface between him and the otherwise unknowable forces of the universe. Images of the gods are gateways for human interaction with divine force.

Whilst Polytheism undoubtedly did occur in ancient times, and has its place as part of the development of religion, nonetheless it is not as widespread as it may first appear.[69] Consider some of the most influential ancient civilizations that are held up as models of the virtues of polytheism.

Ancient Egypt, whilst celebrating a multitude of gods, was essentially henotheistic. To clarify this statement – there is a creator deity (*Atum/Re*), who then subsequently sires a race of gods who fulfill different functions. What is the difference between this and an ultimate deity who is served by Archangels and angels fulfilling different functions?

Likewise if we consider ancient Greece, and study the writings of most of the philosophers, it quickly becomes clear that they are expressing the same henotheistic principle, i.e. there is an ultimate god, who expresses itself through the gods as they are worshipped and celebrated in the myths.

Let me conclude this point with a modern example of religious development. Wicca is seen as being polytheistic, yet it contains a goddess who contains all goddesses, and a god who contains all gods, and the two are part of a greater

---

[69] *See Pagan Monotheism in Late Antiquity – Polymnia Athanassiadi & Michael Frede (editors), 1999.*

whole. This is a henotheistic worldview. Celebrating the ultimate through different names that represent different manifestations of that energy is ultimately monotheistic, not polytheistic. Ultimately, almost all religions have a deity who is the original source, and of whom any other deities can be seen as developments, so in a way they can all be seen as monotheism being expressed through different faces.

From this position the uniquely effective role of the Qabalah as an expression of the creative divine emanations through different manifestations becomes clear. Qabalah works, and the Tree of Life as a symbol holds true whether you apply it to Christian, Hebrew, Egyptian, Greek, Celtic or any other pantheon. This is part of the beauty of Qabalah, that it does not deny the beliefs of the practitioner, but is all-encompassing to a degree that it can accommodate such a wide range of perceptions, as any true spiritual path should be.

Study of the Torah (*Old Testament*), which is full of Qabalistic symbolism, can greatly enhance the appreciation of Christianity for any adherents of that religion, giving insights of beauty and wisdom that enrich the religious experience. Likewise although this is a book on Qabalah from the viewpoint of the Western Mystery Tradition, to illustrate many of my points it will be necessary to quote from the Torah, to show the origins of terms and the concepts they were used to illustrate.

24. The Archangels

Within the Western Mystery Tradition, to work with the Qabalah as a spiritual system of seeking the divine, one must come to grips with the Archangels. Any hang-overs regarding Archangels and angels from previous religious conditioning must first be overcome. The reason for this is that the Archangels are the lenses through which the pure and unknowable energy of the divine is comprehended. The Archangels are the distributors of that divine energy, and partake of it in their essence. Therefore to know the divine, it is imperative that one becomes familiar with the Archangels, and develops a good relationship with them.

The Magickian William Gray came out with a very good description which I will include here to illustrate the point:

> "We must get out of the bad habit of seeing Angels and Archangels as fairy-like winged creatures created entirely for the good of mankind. They are units of specialized energy with an inherent awareness which enables them to accomplish or at least attempt the Original Intent behind them. Angels are more like guided missiles than bodiless babies with wings!"[70]

A critical reference is found in the book of Genesis, referring to the Fall and hinting at the path back up the Tree that man needs to walk. Genesis 3:24 says: "So He drove out the man; and He placed at the east of the garden of Eden the cherubim, and the flaming sword which turned every way, to keep the way to the tree of life." I.e. to walk the way of the Tree of Life you must establish a positive relationship with the entities that guard its mysteries – the angels and Archangels.

Many people operate under the misconception that the angels are a Christian concept. In fact the word angel comes from the Greek *angelos* meaning messenger. Further study shows that angels as they are generally perceived today, i.e. as winged guardian entities, come from ancient Sumeria, over five thousand years ago. Winged human and animal-headed human guardian spirits were a common occurrence within the ancient Sumerian culture, which also gave us writing.

---

[70] *Ladder of Lights* – William G. Gray, 1975, p18.

The Archangels are specialized functionaries, each fulfilling their function within the scheme of the universe. Do not underestimate their importance or ability to create change and direct energy towards a particular end. Working with the Archangels will help keep you very focused on your path, and ensure you do not stray into too many bad habits.

25. The Planets

The attributions of the planets to the Sephiroth of the Tree of Life are one of the keys to its understanding. An alternative set of attributions for the highest Sephiroth has come about in the last 150 years or so, in line with scientific discoveries of the outer planets. Both these sets of attributions have their own mysteries, and both also maintain an integral spiritual truth.

Number	Sephira	Classical	Modern
1	Kether	First Swirlings	Pluto
2	Chokmah	Zodiac	Neptune
3	Binah	Saturn	Saturn
4	Chesed	Jupiter	Jupiter
5	Geburah	Mars	Mars
6	Tiphereth	Sun	Sun
7	Netzach	Venus	Venus
8	Hod	Mercury	Mercury
9	Yesod	Moon	Moon
10	Malkuth	Earth	Earth
11	Daath	-	Uranus

If we look at the initial attribution of Malkuth to the Earth, this is eminently obvious and sensible; it is the realm of the physical where we exist. If we then add to this the next four Sephiroth, we add the Moon, Mercury, Venus and the Sun. This is a journey inwards, to the Sun, which is the centre of the universe, as all these planets are between the Earth and the Sun, which is the centre of the Tree of Life as it is the centre of our universe.

The lower half of the Tree shows us that we have to perfect ourselves first on our spiritual journey, directing our energies inwards to create the inner harmony that allows spiritual growth to thrive. We balance the first Triad of the unconscious/imagination (Yesod), the intellect (Hod) and the emotions (Netzach) to reach the true will (Tiphereth), and are at the centre of our universe, our path and purpose clear.

The upper half of the Tree shows us that when we have balanced ourselves, we then need to radiate our energies outwards to improve our environment, and make the world a better place. In both the classic and modern sets of attributions this is clearly shown by the fact that the planets are those whose orbits are outside that of the Earth.

In the past, man saw the universe as comprising the seven classical planets, i.e. Sun, Moon, Mercury, Venus, Mars, Jupiter and Saturn, plus the Earth, and the stars. The attribution of the Zodiac, or fixed stars, and the first swirlings, which represent the creative urge of Divinity, complete the classical attributions for the Tree of Life. Beyond Saturn are the stars, and beyond the stars the ultimate unknowable force that is deity.

With scientific advances came the discovery of the trans-Saturnian planets. By adding Uranus as Daath, i.e. Knowledge, the central role that the scientific approach has played in shaping modern civilization is represented. However Daath is also the gateway, where man can either soar to the divine power within the supernal triad, or fall into the Abyss and an eternal damnation. This also reflects the power of science, to be used to help the evolution of man, or to drag his soul into servitude.

Uranus also symbolizes revolution. This implies change to the current order, which is definitely true between the lower Tree and the Supernal Triad. To reach the pure divine energy above the Abyss, you must path through Daath and undergo the transformation and revolution this brings. The word revolution also hints at the process of reincarnation, as the concept of *gilgul* ("revolving"). So Daath also hints at the potential for divinity when one has passed through all the incarnations needed to attain perfection.

The attributions of Neptune and Pluto to Chokmah and Kether fit with the model of reaching to the outer limits, with Pluto being the outer guardian of the solar system, and at the same time the underworld. So in this sense Kether is not only the zenith of the Tree, but has come full circle to be beneath the Earth that is Malkuth. This paradox is resolved within the axiom of *"As above, so below"*[71], i.e. ultimately everything is connected, it is for us to discover the connections and marvel at the wonder of life.

---

[71] *This axiom is found in Alchemy and Hermetics. See the Emerald Tablet of Hermes Trimegestus.*

PART VII

COLOURS & NUMBERS

26. The Colour Scales

"Life, like a dome of many coloured glass,
Stains the white radiance of Eternity."[72]

As with many other aspects of the Qabalah, the Colour Scales correspond to the Four Worlds, which by association means they also correspond to the four letters of the Unpronounceable Name and the four elements. The founders of the Golden Dawn introduced the Colour Scales, so they can be traced back to the late nineteenth century. The Colour Scales are strictly a part of the Western Mystery Tradition, and differ greatly from the much older Hebrew attributions of colours to the Sephiroth.

The Colour Scales represent expressions of the essences of the Sephiroth and Paths. The colours both illuminate the natures of the energies and also draw attention to other forces that influence those energies.

When drawing the Tree of Life for reference, it is better to make separate representations, rather than mix the Colour Scales on the same image. These images make excellent meditation tools for gaining inspiration and understanding of relationships and subtleties contained within the Qabalah. At the end of the day Qabalah is ultimately a practical system, and needs to be worked to be appreciated and to gain its benefits.

The Colour Scales are used for visualisation of divine names, Archangels, angels etc, as well as for the Sephiroth during exercises like the Middle Pillar and Lightning Flash. They are also to be used for the construction of talismans. By using the appropriate Colour Scale you are focusing on the energy appropriate to that world.

The King Scale

In IHVH:	Yod
Element:	Fire
World:	Atziluth
Tarot:	Wands

---

[72] *From Adonais, Percy Blythe Shelley.*

The King Scale is used when drawing or visualising the Divine Names of the Sephiroth, and associated deity forms. It is the primary illumination of the force of the Sephira or path.

The Queen Scale

In IHVH:	Heh
Element:	Water
World:	Briah
Tarot:	Cups

The Queen Scale is used when drawing or visualising Archangelic names and forms. It is also used for demi-gods and the Elemental Rulers as the highest aspects of the elements.

The Emperor Scale

In IHVH:	Vav
Element:	Air
World:	Yetzirah
Tarot:	Swords

The Emperor Scale is used when drawing or visualising Angelic names and forms. It is also used for the Planetary Spirits and Planetary Intelligences, and the Olympic Spirits.

The Empress Scale

In IHVH:	Heh (final)
Element:	Earth
World:	Assiah
Tarot:	Disks

The Empress Scale is used for drawing and visualising all other names and forms. This includes Elemental and Qliphotic spirits, humans, and the spirits of the animal, vegetable and mineral kingdoms. This Scale is that of the manifest, physical plane on which we exist.

The Hebrew Kabbalistic Colour Attributions

You may wish to experiment with the earlier set of colour attributions, which is a single scale rather than four different ones. You will see that most of the attributions are very different to those of the four Colour Scales. This was also used for the making of talismans, and for robe colours for appropriate magickal working or meditation.

Sephira	Colour
Kether	Blinding Invisible White
Chokmah	A Colour that includes all Colours
Binah	Yellow and Green
Chesed	White and Silver
Geburah	Red and Gold
Tiphereth	Yellow and Purple
Netzach	Light Pink[73]
Hod	Dark Pink[74]
Yesod	Orange
Malkuth	Blue

---

[73] *Described as the colour of the upper eyelid.*
[74] *Described as the colour of the lower eyelid.*

27. The Magick of Numbers

Gematria

Gematria is the comparison of words whose constituent letters create the same total. So for example, *Unity* (AchAD) and *Love* (AHBH) both add to 13, and we can say from this that the *nature of unity is love*, or *love promotes unity*. Because of the magickal nature of the Hebrew alphabet and the Tree of Life, this is a technique that is used a great deal in Qabalah, and you will come across many examples of Gematria in this present work.

Gematria encourages you to develop your intuition by looking at possible links between words with the same numerical total. Some magickians use this to develop very tenuous links that do not stand up to examination. Personally I would suggest that if you do not spot a link within about fifteen seconds, do not try and spend hours on it. If you wish to meditate on the different words and see if you produce interesting links from your unconscious that is fair enough.

Notariqon

Notariqon takes its name from the Latin *"notarius"* meaning *"shorthand writer"*. Notariqon is the creation of a word by taking the first letters of a sentence and forming them together, essentially an acronym. E.g. AGLA is Notariqon of *Ateh Gibor Le-olahm Adonai* ("To Thee O Lord the Glory"), and the prayer ending of Amen which is used throughout Christianity is Notariqon of *Al Mlk Natz* ("The Lord and faithful King).

This technique is also sometimes applied by taking the first and last letter of each word to form the new words. So if we took the phrase *Chokmah Nistorah* (Secret Wisdom, a name ascribed to Qabalah), the first letters give us *chen* (ChN) meaning *grace* and the last letters give us *Heh* spelt in full (HH), meaning *window*. So from this we could say that secret wisdom is the window to grace.

Notariqon can also be applied as an expansive principle rather than a contractive one. In this instance a word is expanded out, so that each letter in the word becomes the first letter of a word in a sentence. So e.g. *Berashith*, meaning *"In the beginning"*, is the first word of Genesis. In Hebrew it is written BRAShITh, which could be expanded to *"Berashith Rahi Elohim Sheyequelo Israel Torah"*, meaning: *"In the Beginning the Gods saw that Israel would accept the law."*

Temurah

Temurah is the transposition of the letters of the Hebrew alphabet, so that each letter is consistently replaced by another one, given by the particular cipher used. By this means different words are created. Temurah was used largely in the making of talismans. There are many different forms of Temurah, so I will give the best known and easiest to work.

The Atbash Cipher, is where the letters are reversed (so Aleph is replaced by Tav, Beth by Shin ... Shin by Beth, Tav by Aleph).

The Avgad Cipher, where each letter is replaced by the one following it (Aleph replaced with Beth, Beth with Gimel, etc).

Boustrophedon, is where alternate lines are written right to left and then left to right (i.e. reversed). Reading downwards then gives new words. This technique was used to form the seventy-two names in the Shemhamforash.

Thashrag, is where the word is written backwards, e.g. AIN becomes NIA, AL becomes LA, etc.

David Rankine

PART VIII

THE SEPHIROTH

28. The Sephiroth

"The most Ancient One is at the same time the most Hidden of the hidden . . . He made ten lights spring forth from his midst, lights which shine with the form which they have borrowed from Him."[75]

"The ineffable Sephiroth give forth the Ten numbers . . . Behold! From the Ten ineffable Sephiroth do proceed – the One Spirit of the Gods of the living."[76]

The Sephiroth[77] represent states of being and knowing, parts of the body, spiritual truths, astrological bodies, and many other things. As your understanding of Qabalah grows, what each Sephira means to you will also change and grow.

The Sephiroth can be seen like road maps of the continents. To travel the whole world you have to go to every continent, and you might visit a continent more than once so you can explore different parts of it.

To help you in this process a lot of information about the symbols of each Sephira is given in the next section, together with explanations of where the symbolism derives from, and also connections made through using Qabalistic techniques like Gematria. Additionally correspondences for a whole range of areas are given, and pathworkings for you to explore the Sephiroth firsthand for yourself.

For each of the Sephira the following information is given:

i.   Description from *The Thirty-two Paths of Wisdom*. Reference is made in the discussion of the nature of the Sephira to this text, which can often help illuminate more of the nature of the Sephira.

ii.   Discussion of the nature of the Sephira. The nature of the Sephira expresses the way the energy of the Sephira works from the point of view of human understanding.

---

[75] *From the Zohar.*
[76] *From Sepher Yetzirah.*
[77] *Some older texts call the Sephiroth "Ma'amaroth", meaning "Utterances", referring to the idea of their formation through the Word of God.*

iii.   Analysis and discussion of the Divine Name, the manifestation of the divine energy in the World of Atziluth. The Divine Name is the formula encapsulating the mode of manifestation of the ultimate divine energy as it is expressed in the Sephira.

iv.   They are extremely powerful words, which can be used in different ways to tap into the essence of the Sephira. The Divine Names can be repeated as a mantra, included in prayers or meditated on to help gain a greater understanding and insights into the nature of the different Sephiroth, and also how those forces are present and function within you. These words have been used for thousands of years, so be aware that they can create powerful changes in you and your circumstances when used regularly.

v.   Analysis and discussion of the Archangel, including a description for the purpose of visualisation. The archangel is the manifestation of the divine energy in the World of Briah. In the same way that the Divine Names are said to be aspects of the supreme divine power, so all Archangels are said to be manifestations of Metatron, as the voice of God.

vi.   The Archangel of each Sephira is like the overseer, directing the energies of that Sephira so they flow correctly. The Archangel acts as a lens for the Divine Essence, enabling us to interact with it and comprehend our role within the universe. Archangels are extremely powerful beings, as they are directing the energies associated with a whole Sephira of the Tree of Life. Developing a good relationship with the Archangels that will stand you in good stead as you interact with them on your journey up the Tree of Life.

vii.   Analysis and discussion of the Order (or Choir) of Angels, the manifestation of the Divine energy in the World of Yetzirah. As the archangel focuses the will of the divine, so the angels effects the work directed by the archangel.

viii.   The Angelic Hosts are easy to contact, and may be petitioned through the appropriate Archangel to assist you in your journey and to help you open up your heart to the divine influence and increase your understanding and wisdom as you travel up the Tree of Life. Remember Angel means "messenger", and do not hesitate to ask for their help with resolving issues, as they are happy to help those who are willing to work and help themselves.

ix.   Analysis and discussion of the Heaven, the manifestation of the Divine energy in the World of Assiah, also equating to the planets. The

Heaven is referred to in some works as the Mundane Chakra, a rather confusing and inappropriate term that does little to express the nature of the Heaven. A more appropriate term would be cosmic correspondence, indicating the physical planetary or stellar correspondence.

x.   The Heaven of each Sephira is its physical manifestation. So Malkuth corresponds to the Earth, Yesod to the Moon, etc. As you work with the energies of each Sephira, its corresponding energies and qualities in your life will come to prominence in your life. So when you start in Malkuth, issues like your physical situation (home, job) will be emphasised, and in Yesod lunar issues like your dreams, and dealing with hidden issues from the past. Each level needs to be worked through systematically, so you have good foundations in yourself to build upon, to fulfill your potentials to be the best you can be.

xi.   Analysis and discussion of the Qliphoth, the surplus energy in Assiah, representing challenges to be overcome. Although considered by many to be evil, it is more appropriate to view the Qliphoth as necessary tests to the development of the seeker. To use an analogy, in a video game the Qliphoth would be the "end of level baddie" who needs to be defeated before moving on to the next level.

xii. Analysis of the Titles of the Sephira, giving further insight into the nature of the Sephira. Some of these titles are also used as alternative names for Sephira, specifically Gedulah (Glory) for Chesed, and Pachad (Fear) for Geburah. The titles are usually found in Kabbalistic texts, and have found their way into modern Qabalah.

xiii. Discussion of the Experience of the Sephira, the benchmark of full integration of the energies of the Sephira. This is also sometimes known as the Magickal Power of the Sephira, though Spiritual Experience is a more appropriate term, as it demonstrates the expansion of perception and consciousness that develops as the energy and experience of the Sephira are integrated into the being of the seeker.

xiv. Discussion of the Virtues of the Sephira that should be cultivated. The Virtues act as a reference point for the seeker, indicating personality traits that if not already developed should become so before the energies of the Sephira can be fully integrated.

xv.   Discussion of the Vices of the Sephira that should be overcome. Again these traits, if not already dealt with in the self, should be fully overcome or eradicated before the energies of the Sephira can be considered to be fully integrated.

xvi. Some vices can never be fully eradicated, and the seeker must always remain vigilant against such vices, for their recurrence in life usually indicates an imbalance in the energy of the appropriate Sephira, which can indicate the energies are not as integrated as you might have thought, or an imbalance caused by events within the mundane or magickal life.

xvii. Discussion of the Colours of the Sephira in the four Colour Scales, and the symbolism of these. The Colour Scales indicate the energy aspects for working with the different Sephiroth in the different Worlds.

xviii. Analysis of the Magickal Formula associated with the Sephira. The formula can be seen like a key, to help you unlock the energies of the Sephira, and focus your thoughts on the concepts associated with the Sephira.

xix. Analysis and discussion of the Magickal Image of the Sephira and its relevance. The Magickal Image acts as a gateway for accessing the energy of the Sephira, giving a simple image that can be meditated upon, and worked with to help develop the positive qualities of the Sephira.

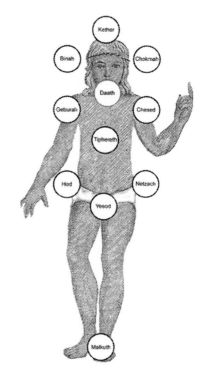

xx. Discussion of the corresponding parts of the human body to the Sephira.

xxi. Analysis of Numbers associated with the Sephira. These numbers can help your mind to have insights and realisations regarding the nature of the Sephira.

xxii. Consideration of the associated Tarot cards.

xxiii. Discussion of the Symbolism of

associated Animals. The relevance of the animals to the energy of the Sephira.

xxiv. Discussion of the Symbolism of associated Minerals. The relevance of the minerals to the energy of the Sephira.

xxv. Discussion of the Symbolism of associated Vegetables. The relevance of the vegetables to the energy of the Sephira.

xxvi. Discussion of the Scents associated with the Sephira. The scents are attributed by their qualities and the effects on the psyche that they create. Not for nothing is scent known as the "evoker of memory".

xxvii. Analysis of the Magickal Tools and Symbols associated with the Sephira. These tools and symbols are often used to represent or to direct the energies of the Sephira. By working with the tools and symbols more understanding of the nature of the Sephira may be gained. Some of the items under this category are symbols that may be meditated on to gain greater understanding of the Sephira.

xxviii. Symbolism of Deities associated with the Sephira from various pantheons, including the Celtic, Egyptian, Greek, Roman and Sumerian pantheons. Some deities may be attributed to more than one Sephira, as deities usually have a number of aspects. Where this is the case the appropriate aspect of the deity will be indicated.

xxix. Meditation on the planetary glyph of the Sephira. For the planetary sigil see what images and insights come to you. Consider how all of the planetary symbols are made of a combination from the circle, the crescent and the equal-armed cross. How is their position in the symbol relevant, what do the component parts represent?

xxx. A pathworking to the temple of the Sephira is then given for the Sephiroth below the Abyss. Before you perform any of these pathworkings, read the section in part IX Ritual Techniques on Qabalistic pathworking to avoid any confusion. That section explains the techniques used to begin and end pathworkings, and also how to travel between the temples as you move up and down the Tree of Life. The archangelic encounter described need not be repeated every time you go to the temples, but the appearance of the temple is constant, and the Archangels usually appear in the same form.

29. MALKUTH (MLKVTh) – The Kingdom

"The Tenth Path is called the Resplendent Intelligence because it is exalted above every head and sits upon the Throne of Binah. It illuminates the splendour of all the Lights, and causes an influence to emanate from the Prince of Countenances, the Angel of Kether."[78]

Malkuth (pronounced *Mal-koot*) is the Sephira of the Elements. This refers to the four elements specifically; spirit is not included in this. This is why the image of Malkuth is usually the circle divided into four by an X, separating it into equal quarters for the four elements. This division is also symbolic of the magick circle, with the quarters indicated by the fourfold division.

In terms of our existence some say it is the physical plane that we operate upon. However as a concept it would perhaps be more accurate to liken Malkuth to Eden, the perfected Kingdom of Nature. Malkuth is the way we would like to see the physical plane. We live in the lowest part of Malkuth – if you imagine every Sephira having a complete Tree of Life in it, we are in the Malkuth of Malkuth.

When we visit the Malkuth temple we are strengthening the process of manifestation of the ideal to the actual. For although we all live our lives as part of the elements around us, most "civilized" people function in their own little bubble, rather than in a dynamic harmony with their environment.

Malkuth is made up of the principles of the four elements. It is the point of stability and solidity, the objective reality that comprises our existence. As such the process of balance is vital, for when we start on our spiritual journey, we are in the middle of that circle standing at the centre of the crossroads. What path we take is up to us, though the spirit of growth encourages us to have firm roots in the physical but to strive upwards for the light – to become the Tree of Life in miniature, balanced and spreading our branches to realise the potential within.

Malkuth is the only Sephira that is not part of a triad, though it is linked to the three Sephiroth of the Astral Triad (Yesod, Hod and Netzach). Malkuth is said to receive the energies of all the other emanations of the Tree. This is why so many of the titles of Malkuth describe it as a Gate, for it is the Gate to the rest

---

[78] *The Thirty-Two Paths of Wisdom - Joannes Rittangelius*

of the Tree of Life, i.e. both the actualisation of the self as the inner Tree, and to other realms as symbolised by the Sephiroth and worlds.

The relationship between Malkuth as the physical realm of the elements, with Binah, the beginnings of form, cannot be overemphasised. When Malkuth is described as *"sitting on the Throne of Binah"*, the relationship is being highlighted. The Throne is a title of Binah, and demonstrates the power of Saturn as the highest aspect of the element of Earth to give solidity and form.

The Shekinah must also be considered within any analysis of Malkuth. Within the Tetragrammaton we see the feminine influence of the Shekinah (Divine Presence), who is expressed as first as the mother who is the Understanding of Binah (the first Heh) and then through manifestation as the daughter of Malkuth (the final Heh).

The energy of Creation that is the initial manifestation of the Greater Shekinah, i.e. the World of Briah containing Binah (Understanding), is manifested in Malkuth through the daughter as the World of Assiah, or Making, also known as the Lesser or Exiled Shekinah. Malkuth represents the making of the creative ideas, the reification of the generative principle in nature, hence nature, the Earth and indeed the Garden of Eden are all referred to as feminine in Qabalah.

There is a Qabalistic saying, *"Kether is in Malkuth, and Malkuth is in Kether, but after a different fashion".*[79] This is a cumbersome way of expressing the first axiom of magick, *"As above, so below"*.

Malkuth is the ultimate reflection of Kether, the manifestation of pure spirit as physical form. Indeed the perception of light as a wave-particle is perfectly described by this relationship. Kether is the light wave, and Malkuth is the manifestation of this energy as the light particle.

Divine Name (1): Adonai Melekh (ADNI MLK)

Usually translated as *"My Lord the King"*. Adonai is also the Divine Name which most ties in with man, implying the inherent divinity in each person, as it is the way the unpronounceable name was spoken. When used in the personal sense it implies the Holy Guardian Angel (referred to as the HGA) or higher self, as a King (Melekh) is one who has refined himself and balanced the aspects of his soul (see the earlier chapter entitled *The Human Soul on the Tree*) enabling realisation of the HGA.

---

[79] *This is also recorded in Sepher Yetzirah 1:6 – "Ten Sephiroth of Nothingness. Their end is imbedded in their beginning and their beginning in their end." I.e. Kether (the beginning) contains Malkuth (the end), and vice versa.*

The king is also he who wears the crown, i.e. Kether, and so this divine name also implies the *"As above, so below"* formula inherent in the relationship between Kether and Malkuth. This divine name suggests the idea of divine kingship, and the association of such a figure with the land.

Another consideration for this name is that it totals 155, which is also by Gematria the sum of the letters corresponding to the four kerubic signs of the elements (i.e. Tzaddi (90) – Aquarius, Teth (9) – Leo, Nun (50) – Scorpio and Vav (6) – Taurus). So this Divine Name also contains the balance of the four elements that is Malkuth itself.

The Hebrew word for *seed* (QNH) also totals 155, bringing the concept of Malkuth as nature, and the magickal image of the veiled and crowned young woman as the potential of nature to mind.

Divine Name (2): Adonai ha-Aretz (ADNI HARTz)

This Divine Name means *"Lord of the Earth"*. It emphasises the divinity inherent in each person as a physical manifestation of spirit, and it is worth noting that by Gematria, 361 also adds to *Men* (ANShI). Whereas Adonai Melekh implies the formula of divine kingship, Adonai ha-Aretz implies the ability of every person to be a king or queen. Once again we see the principle of *"As above, so below"* in operation.

Considering 361 as the square of 19, we see that *Eve* (ChVH) adds to 19, so 361 also implies the power of woman magnified, the generative principle of nature.

Archangel: Sandalphon (SNDLPhVN)

Sandalphon is thought to be derived from the Greek *synadelphos* meaning *"brother"* or *"brotherly one"*. In this context he is the brother to Metatron, for Sandalphon transmits the prayers of man to the heavens, and also stands behind the divine throne making garlands or crowns for the head of the most high. These crowns are made from the prayers of the faithful, which Sandalphon has received.

In his full glory he is said to be more than five hundred years taller than his brother. Sandalphon is also known as Hadraniel, Haviviel and Yagidiel. In appearance he is usually visualised a beautiful, androgynous (though slightly feminine) figure standing about 3m tall, wearing a citrine, olive, russet and black tunic and sandals.

Modern writers often say that Sandalphon means *"the sound of sandals"*. The reason given for this spurious attribution this is that sandals are worn on the feet, connecting us to the ground we walk on, i.e. Malkuth.

The Gematria of his name indicate some of the nature of this archangel, who is one of the most mysterious of those you will encounter. Sandalphon adds to 280 (final nun not counted), which is the number of tiles in the Vault of the Adepti in the Rosicrucian Mysteries (7 x 40).

The mysteries of the earth and the influence of the planetary energies on the earth, as described by the VITRIOL formula, are thus contained within the name of this archangel. He is the master of alchemy, the inner alchemy of the soul and the outer process of transformation in nature. Sandalphon is said to differentiate the sex of the embryo in the womb. Sandalphon was also identified with Elijah, who was said to become assumed into Sandalphon on his translation to heaven.

As you can see Sandalphon is an archangel you should cultivate your relationship with, he is an agent of balance of the elemental energies, unlike the elemental Archangels of the next four Sephiroth who embody the qualities of their particular element.

Order of Angels: Ashim (AShIM)

The angels of Malkuth are the Ashim meaning *"Flames"*. They appear as small dancing blue flames. The Ashim are also called the Issim, and referred to as the Order of Blessed Souls in medieval texts.

As with Sandalphon, a mystery is concealed in their name. For the three primal forces of creation, the three mother letters, are all in their name, representing air, fire and water (Aleph, Shin & Mem), along with Yod, which corresponds to Virgo, an earthy letter. So all four elements are represented in their name, which is totally appropriate for the angels of Malkuth, Sephira of the Elements. Not only that, but Virgo is the Virgin, and one of the titles for Malkuth is The Virgin.

Heaven: Cholim Yesodoth (ChLM ISVDVTh)

Cholim Yesodoth translates as either *"Dream Foundations"* or *"Mundane Foundations"* and adds to 564. Both of these are appropriate, as Malkuth is the Sephira of the Mundane elements, and is also connected with dreams (Yesod) by the doctrine of the Seven Palaces. 564 is also the total for the sentence *"And the Adam was formed into a living Nephesh"*. The Nephesh is the animal soul, the feeling part of the divine spark in man that corresponds to Malkuth in the human body. The soul seeks to return to the divine, and the first step on the way is to move from Malkuth to Yesod – from Kingdom to Foundation. Dreams are attributed to Yesod, and provide part of the interaction between the conscious mind experiencing Malkuth and the unconscious mind (Yesod).

Qliphoth: Lilith (LILITh)

As a classic attribution this is a negative view of Lilith, that a Goddess is a Qliphoth. However if we look deeper, the concept of sovereignty of the land being bestowed on the king can be seen as a formula of this attribution of Lilith as the Qliphoth. For she is the night-hag who is also the beautiful maiden, the formula of transformation which is that of the trial undergone by the aspirant to kingship, who must display discrimination and compassion to achieve kingship by kissing the hag.

Lilith could not be harmed by the angels, and had the power of the name of God, so in another sense she can be seen as the mirror image of the transcendent absolute in the immanence of nature, the reflection of the divine name of this Sephira.

Titles of Malkuth

Atarah (Diadem)
A diadem implies a queen, symbolising Malkuth as the Queen (*Malkah*) and also recalling the magickal image.

The Exiled Shekinah
As has been discussed elsewhere, the manifestation of the divine feminine (Shekinah) as nature is attributed to Malkuth.

The Gate
Malkuth is the starting place, the physical world we live in, so to progress we must choose to pass through the Gate to which we ourselves hold the key. That gate is discrimination and the key is action, which opens the lock of inertia. The Gate can also be seen as the uterus, the Gate to the womb, through which we all pass at birth.

The Gate of the Daughter of the Mighty Ones
This is symbolic of the first stage of womanhood, the daughter, and also the first stage on the path of wisdom, entering the first of the four quarters of Malkuth to begin the balancing process of the material world before attempting to ascend spiritually with firm foundations. The Daughter is the child of the Mighty Ones, because she represents the divine power within in its nascent stages of realisation.

The Gate of Death
Death is the natural conclusion of life. So as all life in nature (Malkuth) experiences birth, so too must it pass through the Gate of Death at the end of its days. Life returns to the earth through decomposition after death, from Malkuth to Malkuth, the shortest and longest journey.

The Gate of the Garden of Eden
This title recalls the full title of the Tree of Life, as the Tree of Knowledge of Good and Evil, as described in Genesis chapter 2 as the cause of man's fall from grace.

The Gate of the Shadow of Death
The shadow of death is always with us, and as a Gate it can be perceived as the transition between states, where the body returns to its constituent elements and the soul continues on its journey.

The Gate of Justice
Justice is the balancing effect of law to ensure that all are treated equally irrespective of status. So again this title indicates a prerequisite for spiritual growth – you must be prepared to treat all fairly and not pay undue attention to material trappings, for in passing through the Gate of Justice you are declaring your intent to purify your spirit.

The Gate of Prayer
The classic posture for prayer is kneeling, which places more of the body in contact with the earth beneath. This title demonstrates the nature of man, combining the earthy and animal side with the aspirational and spiritual side. Prayer is a medium for the spirit to rise, and the Gate of Prayer indicates that we should always keep our feet on the ground even when we seek to rise to the heavens.

The Gate of Tears
This title recalls the link between Malkuth and Binah, for tears are associated with Binah as the result of the Vision of Sorrow, which is the experience of Binah. The world of Assiah, which contains Malkuth, is also called the Vale of Tears, so this title refers to this as well. Also tears can be seen as a purification of the eyes, giving clearer vision to begin the quest – to pass through the gate you must be able to not only look but also to see.

The Inferior Mother
This title emphasises the link between Binah, the Great Mother, and Malkuth. It is a representation of the relationship between the Saturnian energies of Binah as the beginnings of form, where force gains the capacity to manifest, with the end result of physical manifestation as the earthly energies of Malkuth. Hence the line in *The Thirty-Two Paths of Wisdom*, which says *"The*

Tenth Path is called the Resplendent Intelligence because it is exalted above every head and sits upon the Throne of Binah."

The Mother is also the fourth quarter of Malkuth, having expressed potential through birth, creating life and showing her representation of the generative power of nature. The Inferior Mother is also a title used for the Shekinah, indicating the presence of the divine feminine within each of us (as the Neshamah) and within nature.

Kallah – The Bride
This title emphasises the relationship between the Earth as Mother (Malkuth) with the idea of the Sky Father (Kether), once again recalling *"As above, so below"*. The Bride is the second quarter of Malkuth, where the potential of the virgin daughter is about to be realised through union (marriage).

Malkah – The Queen
This title indicates the cyclicity of nature through the cyclic nature of womanhood. Having passed from virgin daughter to bride, the third stage is queen, having been through the union of marriage.

Mother of All Living Things
This title reminds us of the position of Malkuth as the sphere of life that we reside in, i.e. the world, and nature as the mother of life.

Shabat (the Lower Crown)
This title reminds us of the link between Kether and Malkuth, that Malkuth is the lower reflection of Kether (the Crown) and is hence the Lower Crown.

The Unreflecting Mirror
As the final physical manifestation, Malkuth does not reflect its light down the Tree like the Reflecting Mirror (Tiphereth).

The Virgin
This title reminds us of the magickal image of Malkuth, and also the astrological image of Virgo, which is mutable earth. The virgin depicts unexpressed potential, and can be seen as the first of the four quarters of Malkuth.

The World of Shells
This title refers to the presence of the Qliphoth in the physical world, as the essential residues giving form.

The Experience of Malkuth

Vision of the Holy Guardian Angel

The experience of Malkuth is the vision of the Holy Guardian Angel, i.e. the initial impetus that stirs the fires of spirituality and desire to evolve in the individual. The vision does not aid us beyond giving a goal to aim for, the Knowledge and Conversation of the Holy Guardian Angel that comes from having worked through the Sephiroth up to Tiphereth and balanced all the qualities and polarities in ourselves.

Virtues of Malkuth

Discrimination

This is a vital quality, yet one that seems so hard for people to cultivate. Discrimination enables us to see through the illusions that people (including ourselves!) create about us. It also teaches us when to speak and to act, and to gauge the effects of our actions. The result of this is taking personal responsibility for your actions, a core lesson to learn for any spiritual seeker.

Vices of Malkuth

Inertia

The negative side of the physical is a tendency to remain static. The easiest and laziest route is to do nothing. This vice is one that is ever-present and must always be combated. When inertia or stasis sets in, spiritual growth stops. By overcoming inertia we push ourselves to grow, and cultivate the desire to strive for the best we can achieve. Of course this means hard work, but the rewards are always worth the effort.

Avarice

The other vice of Malkuth is avarice, a desire to possess without earning. This is another aspect of inertia but more negative, for not only do you not want to do anything, but you want to be rewarded for it. Once you start on your path and develop momentum, avarice is more easily banished as you develop discrimination and can question your motives more honestly.

Colours:

King Scale: Yellow

Although yellow is often perceived as the colour of Air in the Qabalah, it is also sometimes attributed to Earth as its highest aspect. This is reflected in the Indian Tattvas, where the element of Earth is represented by a yellow square.

Queen Scale: Citrine, Olive, Russet & Black

The four elements are all represented here, as sub-elements of Earth. Citrine, russet and olive are all combinations of the three primary colours of red, yellow and blue representing fire, air and water. So citrine is blue, red and yellow with a predominance of yellow, representing Air of Earth; russet is red, yellow and blue with a predominance of red representing Fire of Earth; and olive is red, yellow and blue with a predominance of blue, representing Water of Earth. Black, as is shown below, represents earth of earth.

Emperor Scale: Citrine, Olive, Russet & Black, flecked with Gold

The four sub-elements of Earth are again depicted, but flecked with gold to show the marriage of the symbolisms of the King and Queen scales that the Emperor Scale usually contains.

Empress Scale: Black rayed with yellow

Black represents the element of Earth in Western Occultism. To see why we have only to consider the fertilising black Nile mud that flooded the lands around the Nile and ensured the growth of the crops in ancient Egypt. So Malkuth in the Empress Scale is Earth of Earth, the ultimate fertilising principle, which is further emphasised by the rays of yellow representing the fertilising influence of the sun helping promote growth.

Magickal Formula of Malkuth

V.I.T.R.I.O.L.

VITRIOL is the formula associated with this Sephira. This formula, found in alchemy, is an acronym for the Latin phrase, *"Visita Interiora Terrae Rectificando Invenies Occultum Lapidem"*. The combination of the energies of the seven classical planets may be found in this formula, each letter corresponding to one of the planets.

With its entreaty to *"visit the interior of the earth and there by rectification find the hidden stone"*, VITRIOL teaches us the lesson of Malkuth. For to move forward we must look within. Without balance of the self, progress will be erratic and ultimately result in devolution not evolution.

The *"hidden stone"* emphasises the nature of Malkuth, the physicality of matter and the presence of spirit within matter for all to see when they open their eyes and their minds. As with all things Qabalistic there is more than one interpretation to this formula. For the hidden stone is the Philosopher's stone, representing the perfection of the self. It is also the Emerald Tablet, containing the laws of magick, which are Nature's laws.

Magickal Image

A young woman crowned and veiled

This woman is none other than Nature Herself. For although Malkuth is the base of the Pillar of equilibrium, yet still it must be seen as being more feminine in nature, for the generative principle in all species is the female. She is the Virgin who becomes the Bride and Queen through Her union with the divine male principle.

The presence of the crown is significant, for it is Kether (the crown), showing Her divinity and that She is the manifestation of the pure divine energy of Kether, beyond form or gender. She is the Queen of Nature and the Earth.

The veil first gives us the idea of the veil of the mysteries, the preconceptions we must draw aside to begin our spiritual journey. We draw the veil of inertia aside and learn the virtue of discrimination, the ability to appreciate the value of perceptions and experience.

The veil can be perceived in sexual terms as the virgin's hymen. For the virgin to become the bride she experiences the union of opposites through sexual union that comprises the nature of growth. The hymen that is broken also can be seen as an underlying theme of the loss of innocence and sexual awareness of Eve and Adam in Genesis.

We must remember though that the Virgin is here representing Malkuth, i.e. nature. So her virginity can also be seen as the unmanifest potential, the seeds in the earth and the ungathered harvest. This image shows us the potential waiting to be expressed, needing action by the union of opposites to create expression.

The veil is also worn by a mourning woman, and in this form represents the mortality of life. The woman is young, showing the generative power of nature, but she also wears the veil of death, for all life must die, as expressed through some of the titles of Malkuth.

Human Body

The feet

The feet link us to the earth; they are our connection to the ground beneath us. The feet contain ten toes, the ten of Malkuth. The early footwear of man, still used greatly for comfort, were sandals, recalling the modern perception of Sandalphon, the archangel of Malkuth.

The anus

Our anus is the other body part that tends to link us to the earth, when we sit on it! The anus excretes the solid waste products (faeces) from the body, and the faeces has fertilising qualities for the plants in nature. In alchemy to produce the Philosopher's Stone the alchemist must first begin with the base matter, the waste product. The important lesson contained within this image is that of transformation. Nothing needs to be wasted. The Malkuthian symbolism is self-evident.

Numbers

Malkuth is the tenth Sephira on the Tree, and accordingly has the number ten associated with it. Ten is the number of solidity, for not only is it the basis of our numerical system (denary - base 10), but is also the sum of the first four numbers $\Sigma(1-4)$, showing the union of the four elements in this Sephira.

The mystical number of Malkuth is 55, i.e. $\Sigma(1-10)$. Significantly, one of the main titles of Malkuth, Bride (KLH), also adds to 55. 55 is 5 x 11, the number of the elements multiplied by the number of magick, emphasising the nature of the magick of Malkuth as that of the manifestation of the elements including spirit (the divine spark within all life) in the physical plane. And of course 55 reduces to 10 (5 + 5).

Malkuth itself adds to 496 (MLKVTh), which is the sum of the numbers 1-31 $[\Sigma(1-31)]$. This shows us how all the previous thirty-one emanations of the Tree come to fruition in Malkuth at the very base of the Tree as the final physicality of form (i.e. it "receives all the other emanations"). We may also note that 496 reduces to 10, the number of Malkuth (4 + 9 + 6 = 19, 1 + 9 = 10). This ultimately reduces to 1 (1 + 0), again recalling the polarity of Kether (1) and Malkuth (10).

Tarot

Unsurprisingly the four Tens are attributed to Malkuth, as are the four Princesses, due to the link with the titles of Malkuth.

Animals associated with Malkuth

The Bull & Cow
The Bull is the animal classically associated with Earth, and represents the Element of Earth, and the cow is the feminine counterpart to the bull.

The Sphinx
The sphinx combines the four elements in its form, and is the poser of the riddle. The magickal virtue of discrimination enables the mental clarity to solve the riddle and move on without being torn to pieces by the sphinx.

Minerals associated with Malkuth

Aventurine
Aventurine is green and was believed to be formed where lightning struck the ground, giving it perfect Malkuthian symbolism.

Coal
Coal is attributed to Malkuth, and reflects the axiom of *"As above, so below"*, for diamond, the pure product of coal that has been subject to hue quantities of heat and pressure (which can be seen as the trials and tribulations of the spiritual journey), is attributed to Kether.

Chrysocolla
Chrysocolla when carved is a combination of blue and green, recalling the images of Earth from space. It is also used for working with earthy energies, and so is appropriate for Malkuth.

Marble
Marble is a very earthy stone, used to adorn and make temples, giving physical form to the place of worship. Also marble may be veined with red, yellow, blue or black, recalling the colour scale combinations of the Queen and Emperor Colour Scales.

Onyx
Onyx is a very earthy stone, and the legend of its formation indicates why it should be attributed here. The myth recounts that Cupid was paring the Goddess Venus' nails one day and threw the parings into the Indus River, where they became onyx. The combination of throwing away waste body parts, and that they should be nails, the physically hardest part of the nail that is continually growing, are perfect Malkuthian symbols.

Salt
Salt as representing the element of Earth. Salt is an essential for human life and is also a purifier, representing the highest aspect of Malkuth. Also we may consider the link between salt and ley lines as salt tracks.[80]

Staurolite
Staurolite is also known as Cross Stone due to the "X" mark frequently found on it, making it highly Malkuthian. It is also used in witchcraft for working with nature spirits.

---

[80] *See The Old Straight track by Alfred Watkins.*

Plants associated with Malkuth

Corn
Corn is one of the staple crops that gives man bread, which helps sustain life, and has a long history of sacramental use and also for grounding after ritual. So bread also contains the polarity of Kether-Malkuth, as the sacramental symbol of spirit and also as the grounding principle that helps us keep our feet on the ground, i.e. balanced.

Ivy
Ivy as a plant that may grow on the ground, but that also climbs up trees!
Rice
Rice as a staple plant, which grows in the mud, and is nourished by the waters (Yesod) to produce one of the world's major crops.

Scents associated with Malkuth

Dittany of Crete
Dittany of Crete, due to its use in evocation by producing the large amounts of smoke which help in manifestation.

Patchouli
Patchouli has a very earthy scent, and is used heavily in wealth magick, both very appropriately Malkuthian.

Pine
Pine, being a scent associated with growth and fertility, and deities of the forest like Pan.

Vetivert
Vetivert, for the same reasons as patchouli, i.e. it has a very earthy scent and also its use for wealth magick.

Symbols & Tools associated with Malkuth

The Magick Circle of Art
The magick circle is the magickian's representation of the universe. It represents the symbolic creation of the universe, and is the place of action, the union of the elements that is Malkuth.

The Triangle of Evocation
The triangle of evocation is the place of manifestation, where non-physical spirits are given form through the use of earthy herbs that generate the smoke to give them a medium to manifest in. As such the triangle of evocation represents the physicality of Malkuth. The triangular shape also reminds us of

the connection between Malkuth and Binah, where form begins, and of which the triangle is a symbol.

The Double Cube Altar
The altar is the central focus of the circle, the physical form that supports the tools representing the elements and forces. Consider, when two cubes are placed one on top of the other, ten faces are exposed, ten being the number of Malkuth. Now the four sides will all be equal size, which is twice that of the top and bottom. So the four sides can be seen as the four elements in balance, with the bottom being the linking of the elements to the ground below (or physical plane). The top is the place where the tools of the art are placed, and also is exposed to the heavens above. So the top and bottom again reflect the axiom of *"As above, so below"*. This altar also represents the axis mundi, the central pole connecting the worlds, and could be seen as symbolic of the Middle Pillar as a whole.

The Equal-armed Cross
Again the balance of the four physical elements is implicit in the equal-armed cross. Physically of course it also depicts the crossroads. The crossroads is the meeting place of four ways, and has traditionally been seen as a place of magick.

Deities associated with Malkuth

Celtic
— *Abellio* as God of apple trees.
— *Amaethon* as God of Agriculture.
— *Boann* as a Fertility Goddess, with the white cow as her symbol.
— *Ceridwen* as an Earth Goddess, with her cauldron and herb craft.
— *Cernunnos* as the Horned God and Lord of the Beasts and the Forests.
— *The Daghda* as the Earth God, and through his cauldron of rebirth and consumption of vast quantities of porridge (oats).
— *Epona* as a Fertility Goddess and Goddess of Horses.
— *Sucellus* as God of Forests and Agriculture.

Egyptian
— *Geb* as the Earth God, his body being the Earth.

Greek
— *Demeter* as the Goddess of the fertility of the Earth and growth of vegetation.
— *Gaia* as the Earth Goddess, representing the whole of the Earth.
— *Hestia* as Virgin Goddess of the Hearth.
— *Pan* as God of the Woodland and the fertilising principle.

— *Persephone* as the Maiden and Bride.

Roman
— *Ceres* as an Earth Goddess linked with corn and the harvest, both Malkuthian symbols.
— *Fauna and Faunus* a pair of deities associated with woodlands and fertility and growth.
— *Ops* as Goddess of the Wealth of the Earth.
— *Pomona* as Goddess of Apples and Orchards.
— *Proserpine* as an Earth Goddess and also as the Maiden and Bride.
— *Terra Mater*, literally the Earth Mother.
— *Vesta* as Virgin Goddess of the Hearth.

Sumerian
— *Abu* as a minor Vegetation God
— *Ashnan* as Grain Goddess.
— *Ki (Urash)* as the primal Earth Goddess.

Meditations & Exercises

Heaven

Meditate on the symbol for planet Earth, a circle quartered by an equal-armed cross, and see what thoughts and images come to mind.

Magickal Formula

Spend a few minutes reciting the formula of VITRIOL as a mantra and record the impressions you get.

Magickal Image

Meditate on the Magickal Image of a young woman crowned and veiled, sitting in a garden, with fields of wheat behind her. Try varying the background through each of the seasons, visualising the flowers and wheat accordingly for the season.

Tarot

Lay out the four Tens in an equal-armed cross. Put the 10 of Disks at the top and the 10 of Wands at the bottom, the 10 of Cups on the left and the 10 of Swords at the right. Contemplate the images and see what inspiration arises.

Elemental Awareness – the Body as Elemental Temple

Contemplate in turn the effect of the elements and their presence within your body. Start with air, and concentrate on the breath entering and leaving your body. Focus on how oxygen is transported in your blood all around your body, how carbon dioxide is transported to your lungs to be exhaled, and the spaces in your body occupied by air, such as in your mouth, ears, lungs, etc

Next concentrate on the element of fire within yourself. Feel the fire of digestion in your stomach, as food is turned into fuel for the body. Feel the fire of electricity as messages are sent along your nerves, synapses sparking and passing on all the signals that keep your body functioning.
Move on to the water within your body. Think of the water in your saliva, in your eyes, the moisture within you. Then consider all the water in your blood and other fluids, and the water that makes up the bulk of your tissues in your body.

Now consider the earth within you, the solidity of your bones and nails, your hair and teeth, your skin. Think how earth gives you form and defines the shape you are. When you have done this for a while consider how all the elements work in harmony to create the body of your temple. By performing this visualisation and studying Qabalah you have already demonstrated the desire to make your spirit grow, and the first step to this is balancing your physical and material world.

Malkuth Temple - Visualisation

The Malkuth temple is circular and 15m in diameter. The walls are of white marble and extend up to a height of 3m. From here they become a domed hemi-spherical ceiling, which is a deep azure blue flecked with gold (lapis lazuli). The floor of the temple is made of onyx and marble squares, 1m square like a chessboard. In the centre of the temple there is a white marble double-cube altar, 1m in height and 0.5m square on the top. On the top of the altar is a small silver bowl, in which burns an undying blue flame, the flame of spirit.

In the north are two pillars, of 1m diameter each, 2m apart, rising from the floor to the ceiling, these pillars are 1m in from the wall. The left pillar is black and made of onyx, the right pillar is white and made of marble. In the wall behind and between them is visible a normal size doorframe. Two more such doorframes are visible behind the pillars in the northwest and northeast when standing between them, but are largely obscured when standing in the middle of the temple.

As you look around the temple you suddenly become aware of a large figure looming over you. You realise that it is Sandalphon, and you raise your gaze from his sandaled feet, to look at his beautiful and androgynous (though slightly feminine) face, glowing with a radiance that makes it hard to keep looking at him. He stands about 3m tall, and is wearing a simple brown tunic. Behind his back you see a large pair of white wings, folded over on themselves.

Sandalphon hands you an ear of corn with his right hand, and holds the forefinger of his left hand to his lips in a gesture of silence. You remember the saying from the ancient Greek Orphic mysteries, "In silence is the seed of wisdom gained", that was spoken into the ears of initiates as they were given an ear of corn to contemplate as you have been.
As you contemplate you remember that silence is the virtue of the element of earth, and remember the other elemental virtues, the knowing of air, the willing of fire and the daring of water. You realise you will need to cultivate all these qualities and balance them in yourself to progress on your journey, to embody the virtue of the element of spirit – becoming.

You thank Sandalphon for his guidance, and he nods to you, before disappearing, leaving you alone in the temple. You place the ear of corn on the altar next to the spirit flame, and consider the mysteries you have explored. As you look around you see the white mist starting to fill the temple, indicating it is time to return to the mundane world.

30. YESOD (ISVD) - Foundation

> *"The Ninth Path is called the Pure Intelligence because it purifies the Emanations. It proves and corrects the designing of their representations, and disposes the unity with which they are designed without diminution or division."*[81]

Yesod (pronounced *Yes-od*) is the Sephira of the Moon. Traditionally the Moon is associated with the night, and associated nocturnal activities, like dreaming and practicing magick. Hence the name Foundation, for Yesod is the foundation of magickal practice, corresponding as it does to both the astral plane and to the unconscious.

Yesod is joined to four other Sephiroth on the Tree, which provides a good analogy to the four phases of the Moon. The 32nd path from Malkuth to Yesod then brings you into Yesod through the New Moon. Opposite this is the 25th path to Tiphereth, which corresponds to the Full Moon. The 30th and 28th paths – to Hod and Netzach respectively, represent the waxing and waning Moon.

The Moon controls the tides on Earth, and Yesod is the higher aspect of Water on the Tree, as the next three Sephiroth also embody the higher qualities of the elements. This is why the elemental Archangels are also attributed to planets.

As the realm of the Moon and the astral, Yesod is also associated with ethereal creatures. The four paths connected to Yesod make it the first crossroads we encounter on the Tree. Classically the crossroads is the place of transformation, of death, spirits and ethereal creatures, ruled over by deities like the Greek Goddess Hekate, with the liminal power they possess.

Yesod poses a riddle that is sublime in its simplicity, yet so often failed by those standing at the crossroads – which path do I take from here. The correct answer is "All of them!" This answer requires the creative use of the imagination, to think outside the box, one of the main ordeals of Yesod.

The shape made by the four paths connecting Yesod is also that of the trident. This is the tool of Neptune, and implies the connection between Yesod as the Moon, which governs the tides, with the higher Sephira of Chokmah, attributed to Neptune. As Malkuth may be seen as a lower emanation of the

---

[81] *The Thirty-Two Paths of Wisdom - Joannes Rittangelius*

energies of Binah, so may Yesod be seen as a lower emanation of Chokmah. Chokmah is creative form, without force, but in Yesod it is in the transitional moment of manifestation from force into form, the creation of manifestation in Malkuth.

The description of Yesod from *The Thirty-Two Paths of Wisdom* gives more of an insight into the nature of Yesod. Yesod purifies the emanations, because it is the realm of connection between the conscious mind of man (the microcosm) and the subtle realms that permeate the universe (macrocosm).

In the downward flow of energy, Yesod puts the impulses of the higher energies into a form which man can work with. In the upward flow of energy, Yesod is the great barrier, the mirror of truth that causes most to succumb to their own ego and not strive further to the illuminating powers behind it. In the earliest drawings of the Tree of Life glyph, Malkuth was only joined to Yesod, reinforcing this position of Yesod as the purifying force and filter for the whole Tree.

Divine Name: Shaddai El Chai (ShDI AL ChI)

This name translates as "*The Almighty and Ever-Living God*". This name emphasises the creative power inherent in Yesod. Looking at the individual components of this name provides more insight. "Shaddai" adds to 314, as does Metatron, the archangel of Kether who is the voice of God. By Gematria we thus have a direct link between the primal divine force of God expressed through the creative word (Metatron) and the creative and purifying force of Yesod expressed through the divine name. Shaddai by itself is also a title used for Yesod.

"Al" is the divine name of Chesed, and simply means God, i.e. God as the divine spark that permeates all of life and all of his creation. The word for "*and there was*" (VIHI) also adds to 31, further implying the notion of the creative force. "ChI" adds to 18, as does *the serpent* (ChTA) and IAVA, which is Notariqon of "*Let there be light*". The serpent is the creative wisdom, which must be embraced with open eyes, lest deception occur. So it can be seen that this whole divine name is imbued with the essence of creative transformation.

Archangel: Gabriel (GBRIAL)

Gabriel means "*The Strength of God*". Gabriel is the angel who usually delivers messages to humanity, embodying the link between man and the universe and the divine as expressed by Yesod. Gabriel first appears in the Old Testament in the book of Daniel. It is Gabriel who first indicates the coming of a messiah to Daniel in this book. Gabriel visited Zachary to tell him his son would be called John (the Baptist) and most famously he told Mary that she was pregnant with Jesus. In Islam Gabriel is also seen as the divine messenger, it was he who delivered the Qur'an to Mohammed.

As the Archangel of the Moon and Water, Gabriel is the guide to the inner tides of our unconscious. Gabriel can help with developing the imagination and psychic abilities. He is also associated with domestic matters, especially the development of the home, or finding a new home. Gabriel is the archangel to call to if you are having problems with your menstrual cycle, as he rules the forces that influence it.

Gabriel can appear as male or female, and may be called to as either. Gabriel often appears carrying a staff topped with lilies, showing his fruitful nature and ability to help you bring plans to fruition. He is usually seen standing about 3m tall, with a beautiful face, which is more feminine than most of the Archangels. He wears a violet robe, and may bear a silver cup in his hands.

Order of Angels: Kerubim (KRVBIM)

The Angels of Yesod are the Kerubim, meaning *"The Strong"*. They are represented as having two sets of wings, one set pointing upwards and one set downwards; and have a head of one of the four elemental animals – eagle, lion, man and bull.

The Kerubim (or Cherubim) were also the guardians of the gate of Eden, embodying the creative aspects of the elemental powers. Kerubim adds to 278, the same as *the material world* (TzVLM HTVTGTz), emphasising their ability to interact with the physical as emissaries of the elemental energies. In medieval Grimoires the Kerubim correspond to the Order of Angels (and should not be taken as the Cherubim of the Grimoires, who equate to the Auphanim of Chokmah).

Heaven: Levanah (LBNH)

Levanah translates as *"the Moon"* and adds to 87. This word can also mean whiteness and frankincense. White is one of the main colours associated with the Moon, and frankincense is the great purifying scent, fitting in with the description given in *The Thirty-Two Paths of Wisdom*. The word *cup* (ASIK) also adds to 87, fitting perfectly with the cup as the elemental tool of water.

Qliphoth: Gamaliel (GMLIAL)

The name Gamaliel means *"Obscene Ass"*. This seems very peculiar until we consider the classic "forbidden kiss" of initiation found in some magickal groups over the centuries. Here the candidate would be blindfolded and told to kiss the anus of an animal (like a goat), and have to act on faith and trust to do so, only to discover afterwards that he had kissed a beautiful maiden who is swapped in at the last minute.

The Yesodic Qliphoth remind us that we have to look at the panoramic view, and not become trapped in self-delusion, otherwise we fall prey to our animal side and do not strive for the spiritual – we become the obscene ass ourselves.

Gamaliel adds to 114, the same as *gracious* (HGVQ) and *science* (MDAa), both words that imply taking a more comprehensive approach and striving for balance and a complete perception.

Titles of Yesod

Kol (All)
This title is an old name for Yesod, and refers to the genitals as the centre of creative force, for they are located at Yesod, and all creation takes place through union.

Life of the Worlds
Again, a title referring to Yesod as the centre of procreative energy as the genitals.

Lower End of the Heavens
Yesod is the last of the Sephiroth before the manifestation in Malkuth, and as the Moon is the nearest body to Earth in the heavens.

Pillar Connecting Heaven and Earth
As the next Sephira up the Middle Pillar from Malkuth, Yesod can be seen as the pillar that connects it to the heavens above.

Procreative Power
Yesod corresponds to the genitals on the human body, as this title indicates.

Seal of Truth
This title emphasises the decision to make the spiritual journey, to apply discernment and move beyond the mundane world.

Shaddai
"The Almighty" is a very appropriate title for Yesod, for without it the magickian cannot ascend the Tree and perfect himself. This title reminds us that we must always find the divine within ourselves and also in the universe around us, emphasising the interconnectedness of all life. This title also emphasises

the link between Yesod and Binah, as written in Job 32:8, *"The soul of Shaddai gives them Understanding."*

The Righteous is the Foundation of the World

This title states emphatically the essence of Yesod, that one must have right in your heart to achieve success and growth, in all things spiritual. Without righteousness you cannot build the firm foundations necessary for sustained growth, and your world will crumble without the firm foundations required.

Tzaddiq (The Righteous One)

The 25th path from Yesod up to Tiphereth is known as the Path of the Righteous, and this is reflected in this title.

Experience of Yesod

The Vision of the Machinery of the Universe

This can be seen as the opening up of the conscious mind to the influences of the more subtle realms, leading to a greater sense of ones place in the universe, enabling progress. For you cannot start a journey if you do not know where you already are!

Virtue of Yesod

Independence

As the realm of the imagination, Yesod encourages us to be independent – to think for ourselves and not accept the status quo of what we are told. Yesod forces us to challenge our notions, enabling the development of a secure foundation based on experience, from the trial and error approach that serves much more effectively than the approach of gullible belief.

Vices of Yesod

Deception

The Moon rules over illusion and deception, and the magickian must always be vigilant not to deceive himself into self-delusion, for this leads to inflation of the ego and self-importance, a deadly enemy to spiritual growth.

Idleness

Laziness is one of the great and constant challenges to the magickian. The illusory qualities of the Moon make it very easy to fool ourselves into not putting in sufficient effort to progress. When laziness sets in it sends on a downward path, back down to the inertia of Malkuth.

Colours of Yesod

King Scale: Indigo
The indigo represents the generative quality of spirit, and the psychic powers of the magickian activated. The deep blue of balance has become the indigo of the night sky, full of potential and imminent creativity, and home of the Moon in its orbit.

Queen Scale: Violet
Violet is a classical lunar colour, hence the attribution here. This violet is also made by uniting the blue of Chesed and scarlet of Geburah, forming the apex of the downward water triangle in the planetary hexagram when drawn on the Tree with Tiphereth as its centre point.

Emperor Scale: Very dark Purple
The very dark purple of the Emperor Scale unites the indigo and violet of the King and Queen Scales, to emphasise the watery quality of Yesod.

Empress Scale: Citrine, flecked with Azure
Citrine as Air of Earth (see Malkuth colours) is the aspiration to move beyond the terrestrial sphere, embodied by man's obsession with reaching the Moon. It is flecked with azure to represent the night sky, home of the moon.

Magickal Formula of Yesod

ALIM
ALIM is the formula associated with the Sephira. It means "*Gods*" and adds to 81. 81 is one of the main lunar numbers, as 9^2. The formula of Gods is one of multiplicity, and emphasises the nature of pantheism as a manifestation of monotheism. Through being able to connect with many faces of divinity, one can come to know a little the unknowable source behind all life.

81 is also the numeration of *Throne* (KSA), and emphasises the integral essence of the middle pillar as the perfected balance of the regal mage. The crown (Kether) is worn by the King (*Melek – title of Tiphereth*) who from the Foundation of his Throne (*Yesod*) rules the Kingdom (*Malkuth*).

Magickal Image

A beautiful and very strong naked man
Although the moon is considered feminine by some cultures, equally other cultures consider it masculine. The nakedness, strength and beauty of the man indicate his achievements, in that he has already perfected his control of the physical – his body (as Malkuth), and has removed all the illusions surrounding him (i.e. clothes). The naked body also recalls the skyclad

aspect of Wicca, which is largely a lunar religion, and which encourages naked ritual to honour the moon goddess and her consort.

Human Body

The reproductive organs
The genitalia are the foundation of the reproductive process (i.e. creation). In man the whiteness of the semen can also be considered lunar, and of course the female menstrual cycle is also linked through duration to the tides of the Moon.

Numbers

Yesod is the ninth Sephira on the Tree, and accordingly has the number nine associated with it. Nine is the number which always returns to itself, with all its multiples being divisible by itself, indicating the cyclic nature of nine.

The mystical number of Yesod is 45, i.e. $\Sigma(1-9)$. 45 is 9x5, the number of the Moon multiplied by the five elements. 45 is also *Adam* (ADM) and *The Fool* (AMD), linking to the magickal image of Yesod.

Yesod itself adds to 80 (ISVD), which is the same as *Throne* (KS) and *Union* (VAaD). Again the emphasis on Yesod as the key central Sephira of the Tree for magickal growth is clear.

Tarot

The four Nines are attributed to Yesod, as are the Four Princes, recalling the magickal image.

Animals associated with Yesod

Cat
The cat is traditionally associated with the moon as the traditional witch's familiar.

Dog
The dog has long been associated with the moon, both through its howling at the full moon, and also the association with lunar hunting goddesses like Artemis and Diana.

Elephant
The elephant is considered lunar largely by the crescent shape of its ivory tusks.

Ghosts
As the realm of the imagination and the night, ghosts and night terrors are naturally assigned to Yesod.

Toad
The toad lives in the water and can also live on land. It is known for the *"precious jewel in its forehead"*, implying the psychic powers and creativity, both lunar qualities. Also the toad is traditionally associated with witchcraft.

Minerals associated with Yesod

Chalcedony
By its white colour and association with lunar deities like Diana.

Ivory
Due to its white colour, and usual crescent shape. Also the ivory gate of true sleep of Morpheus is appropriate to the dream state associated with Yesod.

Moonstone
By its colour and name is lunar. The play of colour and luminescence of moonstone suggest the image of the moon's surface in the sky. Moonstone also has a long history of use for psychic work, appropriate to Yesod.

Pearl
Due to its colouring and being grown in the sea. The creation myth of the Yezidi is also appropriate, as it involves the archangel Gabriel and pieces of the giant white pearl being used to make the stars.

Quartz
By its white/transparent colour and association with the Moon. Also gold may be found within quartz, hinting at the sexual process and the path up the middle pillar through Yesod to the gold of Tiphereth.

Silver
As the planetary metal of the Moon. Silver is precious but soft and easily tarnished, requiring constant care, as does the attention of the magickian.

Plants associated with Yesod

Banyan
Banyan forms a whole ecosystem of which it is the foundation, and grows in swamps, which are the union of the waters and earth.

Mandrake
Mandrake is used in sexual magick and also bears a human shape, making it very Yesodic.

Mugwort
Mugwort for its use to aid skrying and astral travel and also its use to regulate menstruation.

Scents associated with Yesod

Camphor
Camphor by its colour and the sharp scent it produces.

Jasmine
Jasmine due to its flowery and seductive smell, making it one of the refined and rarefied aphrodisiacs of the moon.

Ylang Ylang
Ylang Ylang as a relaxant ideal for preparing the mind for astral and psychic work.

Symbols & Tools associated with Yesod

Altar
The altar as the foundation that the magickian works upon, giving a basis for actions to establish the foundation of magickal work.

Ankh
As the *"key of life"* and representative of the sexual union its form implies, as well as is watery associations and use in ancient Egypt to bless water poured through the hole in the loop.

Magick Mirror
The magick mirror is the tool par excellence of the moon, used to skry in and enable the psychic abilities of the magickian to be focused. As the moon reflects the light of the sun, so the mirror reflects the light of its environment.

Nonagram
The 9-rayed star represents the cyclic nature of the Moon, being formed by a single continuous line, or by superimposing three triangles at 40° to each other, representing the changing faces of the moon.

Perfumes
The stimulatory effect of perfumes as a bridge between the material world of Malkuth and the subtle realms of the astral make them Yesodic. Also by their use as offerings to spirits and deities, filling the air and rising to the sky.

Sandals
As the foundation the magickian walks upon, and also the shape of the Ankh being implied by the strap.

Deities associated with Yesod

Celtic
— *Arduinna* as a Moon Goddess.
— *Arianrhod* as Goddess of the Silver Wheel.
— *Nantosuelta* as Goddess of Rivers.
— *Rhiannon* as Goddess of the Fairy Realms.

Egyptian
— *Khonsu* as the Moon God.
— *Thoth* as a Lunar Deity.

Greek
— *Artemis* as the Goddess of the New Moon.
— *Hekate* as the Goddess of the Moon, of crossroads, and of the liminal.
— *Morpheus* as God of Dreams.
— *Selene* as a Lunar Goddess.

Roman
— *Diana* as the Goddess of the New Moon.
— *Luna* as the Moon Goddess.

Sumerian
— *Nanna* as the Moon God.
— *Ningal* as the Moon Goddess.

Meditations & Exercises

Heaven

Meditate on the Crescent symbol of the Moon and see what images and ideas come to mind.

Magickal Formula

Recite the formula ALIM (pronounced *El-o-heem*) as a mantra for a few minutes and record your impressions.

Magickal Image

Meditate on the Magickal Image of a very strong and beautiful naked man standing in a field at night with the full moon in the sky behind him. Vary the image so that the different moon phases are represented – new moon (crescent), half moon and dark moon (i.e. no moon) as well as the full moon, and see what difference this makes to your meditation.

Tarot

Lay out the four Nines in an equal-armed cross. Put the 9 of Disks at the top and the 9 of Wands at the bottom, the 9 of Cups on the left and the 9 of Swords at the right. Contemplate the images and see what inspiration arises

Yesod Temple - Visualisation

The Yesod temple is circular and 15m in diameter. The walls are of a swirling pattern of grey and purple semi-solid mist and extend up to a height of 3m. From here they become a domed hemi-spherical ceiling, which is a deep azure blue flecked with gold (lapis lazuli). The floor of the temple is made of marble, with a 9-rayed star in amethyst-purple spanning the whole floor. In the centre of the temple there is a white quartz double-cube altar, 1m in height and 0.5m square on the top. On the top of the altar is a small silver bowl, in which burns an undying blue flame, the flame of spirit.

In the north are two pillars, of 1m diameter each, 2m apart, rising from the floor to the ceiling, these pillars are 1m in from the wall. The left pillar is black and made of onyx, the right pillar is white and made of marble. In the wall behind and between them is visible a normal size doorframe. Two more such doorframes are visible in the northwest and northeast behind the pillars when standing between them, but are largely obscured when standing in the middle of the temple. In the south is another doorframe, back to Malkuth.

You hear a bell ring and look around. Between the pillars you see the figure of the archangel Gabriel. He stands around 3m tall, with a very beautiful feminine face. He has large white wings folded at the back and wears a violet tunic. In his left hand he bears a bunch of lilies and in his right hand is a silver chalice. He walks towards the altar and places the chalice down on it in front of you.

Gabriel gestures that you should look in the chalice, and as you look in the waters contained within it you see them mist over, so they look like the night sky with clouds rolling through. You gaze deep within the clouds and visions start to appear, of times you had forgotten, from your childhood. You keep looking and the images become of you when you are younger and younger. Then they change again and it is someone you do not immediately recognise. But as you look the figure seems more and more familiar, and you realise it is your previous incarnation on this earth.

After a while Gabriel touches you on the shoulder, and tells you that is enough for today. You can return again and look further back in the chalice of remembrance, to explore and learn from your past lives. You thank him for this gift, and with a smile he disappears. You gaze at the altar and see the chalice has also vanished. All that remains there are the white lilies he was carrying in his left hand.

You turn to the south to return back through the doorway there into the Malkuth temple, so that you can return to the mundane world.

31. HOD (HVD) - Splendour

"The Eighth Path is called the Absolute or Perfect Intelligence because it is the mean of the Primordial, which has no root by which it can cleave or rest, save in the hidden places of Gedulah, from which emanates its proper essence."[82]

Hod (pronounced *Hod*) is the Sephira of Mercury. Mercury is associated with the intellect, and the power of logic and rational thought. In terms of our existence, Hod is our thoughts and ideas. As the fastest moving planet, Mercury is entirely appropriate as the cosmic representative of this, the darting quicksilver fire of the nerve synapses firing in our brains, as ideas dart around at the speed of light.

The ability to think logically is often seen as being very cold, and the intellect as being very divorced from feeling and sensing. However this perspective tends to discount the other quality of the intellect, which is intuition. This is why the symbol of Mercury is the caduceus, or twin serpent staff. The cold logic of the mind is balanced by the intuitive flashes of inspiration that are also Mercurial in their nature – the black and white serpents of the caduceus. Communication is another Mercurial trait, and a necessary quality, for a good idea means nothing if it is not clearly communicated to others and its benefits spread.

Mythically Mercury is the psychopomp, the guide between the worlds. This role expresses the fluid quality of Mercury, the ability to adapt to ones environment and be at home in any surroundings and circumstances. This is the Splendour of the active mind, able to respond to change and adapt to better ways of functioning. Efficiency could be described as the key word for Hod, the ability not to waste your energy, but rather to use it effectively to always do everything in the best and most appropriate manner.

The other key word for Hod is flexibility. Mercury is nothing if not adaptable, able to undergo immediate changes and be ready to deal with whatever may occur. Flexibility also requires honesty and the ability to exercise clarity and discrimination no matter the circumstances.

Mercury is also associated with healing, of the mind and body. Mercury provides the knowledge and skill needed to practice healing, for the training to

---

[82] *The Thirty-Two Paths of Wisdom - Joannes Rittangelius*

be a doctor or healer is a long and arduous process, requiring the mind to be honed like a scalpel to work effectively.

The power of the mind is to give form to ideas, and Hod is a Sephira of form. The experiences of the astral and the imagination of Yesod may be given more form in Hod – through giving a framework to ideas and through being able to manipulate the subtle energies of the astral.

Divine Name: Elohim Tzabaoth (ALHIM TzBAVTh)

This name translates as *"The Gods of Hosts"*. The multiplicity of deity within this divine name emphasises the manifestation of the divine in a variety of forms. This is paralleled in Netzach with the use of the name Tzabaoth, and demonstrates that both thoughts and emotions are a plurality of experiences, providing a multitude of ways to experience the divine. The word Elohim combines a feminine noun with a masculine ending, indicating the duality of gender associated with Mercury and reminds us that the intellect is both male and female.

Archangel: Raphael (RPhAL)

Raphael means *"Healer of God"*, and he is the archangel charged with healing mankind and the earth. He is the Archangel of Mercury and the Air. Some books attribute Michael to Hod and Raphael to Tiphereth, due to Tiphereth also being associated with healing. However this alternative attribution ignores the essential airy natures of Raphael and fiery nature of Michael, which clearly indicates the correctness of attributing them as they are found here.[83]

Raphael is also the patron of travellers, often being depicted with a pilgrim's staff, and he protects those on journeys, especially air travel. As well as protecting travellers, Raphael's special charges are the young and innocent. Raphael is the archangel of knowledge and communication, and may be called to help with any related areas, such as improving your memory, learning languages, exams, dealing with bureaucracy and business matters.

Raphael was the angel who gave King Solomon the ring inscribed with the pentagram that enabled him to bind demons, and force them to build his

---

[83] *The cross-over of attributions first seems to occur in Liber Juratus (the Sworn Book of Honorius) in the thirteenth century. By the early 17th century both sets of attributions were being used by different magickians, as is illustrated by differing versions of the manuscript known as The Nine Keys. See The Keys to the Gateway of Magic: Summoning the Solomonic Archangels & Demonic Princes by Stephen Skinner & David Rankine.*

temple. He was said to have healed the earth after the Flood, and also visited Noah after the Flood to give him a book of medicine, which had belonged to the angel Raziel.

Raphael is usually seen standing about 3m tall, with a beautiful face. He wears an orange robe and sandals, and may bear a caduceus in his right hand.

Order of Angels: Bene Elohim (BNI ALHIM)

The Angels of Hod are the Bene Elohim, meaning *"The Sons of the Gods"*. Bene Elohim adds to 148, the same as AHIH IH JHVH ALHIM, one of the great names of God that combines the divine names of the three Sephiroth of the supernal triad. This shows us the importance of this order of angels, that they are the *"mean of the primordial"*, combining qualities from all the Sephiroth of the supernal triad to be the healing angels. 148 is also the total for Netzach, whose order of Angels are the Elohim (Gods), so it is appropriate that the Bene Elohim (Sons of the Gods) should be linked to that Sephira.

The original concept of Bene Elohim was the idea of the gods of the old polytheism, who became downgraded and integrated into Judaism and hence Qabalah. Psalm 29:1 reads *"Render to Yahweh, O sons of gods (BNI ALHIM), render to Yahweh glory and strength."* This is clearly a Qabalistic reference, as glory and strength are Chesed (as Gedulah – glory) and Geburah (strength). The Bene Elohim equate to the Order of Archangels in medieval grimoires.

In appearance the Bene Elohim stand about 2m tall with white wings and are very beautiful. Some of them appear more masculine, and some more feminine. They wear orange tunics.

Heaven: Kokhav (KVKB)

Kokhav translates as *Mercury* or *"Sunstar"*. It sums to 48, which is the product of 6 and 8, emphasising the link between Mercury (8) and the Sun (6). 48 is also the number for ChM, meaning heat or fire, again recalling the sun, and Gedulah, meaning *Mercy* (GDVLH), the alternative title of Chesed, which is specifically referred to Hod in the description from *The Thirty-Two Paths of Wisdom*.

Qliphoth: Samael (SMAL)

Samael means *"The False Accuser"*. Samael is sometimes described as the husband of Lilith, and it is interesting to note that he is the false accuser, i.e.

he challenges ideas to make you examine the truth of them. When you can prove the truth of something, you can dispel false accusations. So Samael can be seen as the voice of doubt that makes you question everything, and he is dispelled be the confidence of truth, which brooks no doubt for it is perfect in itself. This perception is reinforced by Gematria – Samael adds to 131, the same as *humility* (AaNVH), which is a quality gained through being true and humble.

Titles of Hod

Steadfastness
Steadfastness is a quality that is reflected by the intellect, being true to your beliefs.

Temimut (Sincerity)
Sincerity is a product of truth, and truthfulness is the virtue of Hod.

Tzaddiq (Righteous One)
Having harnessed the imagination and powers of the lunar realm, one can be righteous having conquered illusions and accepted truth.

Experience of Hod

The Vision of Splendour
This is the vision described in the first chapter of Ezekiel, of the splendour of God manifested through the Kerubim and the Auphanim (Wheels). These choirs of angels are those of Yesod and Chokmah, so literally the Foundation (Yesod) of Wisdom (Chokmah). Having had the visions of the higher self and the workings of the universe in the previous two Sephiroth, the next liminal experience is the perception of the divine within the universe, stimulating the seeker on their quest towards perfection.

Virtues of Hod

Truthfulness
The power of truth is the harshest virtue, for it forces us to face up to our faults and see things as they are. Truth implies accuracy of perception, the cold logic of Hod, which brings the binary logic of computers to mind. Truth does not allow for ambiguity, it is either yes (1) or no (0). Being truthful with yourself requires honesty and is essential to spiritual growth. Being honest with others requires integrity, as it implies a balance that does not swing towards the self-serving selfishness of the ego. This is best represented by the feather of Maat, the Egyptian Goddess of truth and harmony, against which the heart of the deceased soul was weighed on the scales of balance to

see if the person had led a good life. The French occultist Eliphas Levi beautifully summed up the value of truth with his words:

> *"Paradise exists wherever you speak the truth, and do the right; Hell is present wherever you speak that which is false, or do that which is evil. Paradise and Hell are not localities, they are states."*[84]

Humour
The ability to laugh is an essential quality for growth. We need to be able to laugh at ourselves when we behave in an arrogant or silly manner, to reach us never to become too self-important. Mercury is also the trickster, so there is an element of laughing at the misfortune of others when this is misinterpreted. The important lessons taught by the trickster are imparted with humour to bypass self-importance and ensure they strike home, not to belittle or ridicule unless it is the only way to help a person overcome stumbling blocks.

Vice of Hod

Dishonesty, Falsehood
This vice is linked to the illusory nature of unbalanced Yesodic force. For dishonesty is a knowing act, indicating a tendency to serve only the base desires of the ego, thus restricting the spirit. Being dishonest with yourself is a retrograde step that will only damage the growth of your spirit. Being dishonest with others perpetuates the energy of manipulation and using people for your own ends, which is a restriction of their will and right to grow.

Colours of Hod

King Scale: Violet-purple
The violet-purple is the product of the deep violet of Chesed with the lavender of Daath. This union of the colours emphasises the emanations which are most in tune with Hod, for Uranus (Daath) is the higher manifestation of Mercury, and Chesed (Gedulah) is the root of Hod, as described in *The Thirty-Two Paths of Wisdom*.

Queen Scale: Orange
The orange is produced by mixing the scarlet red of Geburah with the Yellow of Tiphereth, to produce the bottom point of the triangle of the right side of the body that they encompass.

Emperor Scale: Russet-red
The russet-red is formed by combining the violet-purple of the King Scale with the orange of the Queen Scale. Note also that the russet-red emphasises the

---

[84] *The Magical Ritual of the Sanctum Regnum – Eliphas Levi, 1896, p94.*

influence from Geburah above, and also subtly the influences from Tiphereth and Chesed, the yellow and blue of these Sephiroth being the other two colours that in minor quantities form russet with the dominant red.

Empress Scale: Yellowish-brown, flecked with white
The yellowish-brown is the colour of Citrine quartz, the crystal of Hod as the "Thief's Stone". The white flecks indicate the higher aspect of this, i.e. the trickster rather than simply the thief.

Magickal Formula: AZOTH

Azoth is the Mercurial Fluid, the essence. The word is made by combining the A and Z of the English alphabet (first and last) letters) with the last letters of the Greek and Hebrew alphabets, i.e. Omega (O) and Tav (Th). The nature of Azoth is clearly indicated by Gematria when looking at some of the other words that add to the same total.

Azoth sums to 414, as does *Ain Soph Aur* (Limitless Light) and *Meditation* (ThGVH). Azoth is the alchemical fluid, the essence of life that permeates all and acts as a catalyst for change and growth towards perfection. The number 8 of Hod also indicates this formula, for when placed on its side it gives us the symbol of infinity, characterising the nature of Azoth.

Magickal Image of Hod

A hermaphrodite
The hermaphrodite combines both sexes, and this echoes the combination of genders in both the divine name and the Angels (Elohim). The image of the hermaphrodite also recalls the idea of the original man as a hermaphroditic being, before the duality of gender (the first three Adams). This concept implies the divinity of balancing the genders within, and stresses the need for spiritual seekers to balance the qualities within themselves, which are commonly referred to as "masculine" and "feminine".

Human Body

The right hip and leg
The attribution of this part of the body is more based on the location of Hod on the Tree than to symbolic correspondences.

Numbers of Hod

Hod is the eighth Sephira on the Tree, and accordingly has the number 8 attributed to it. Eight is the first cube number, being 2x2x2.

The Mystical number of Hod is 36, i.e. Σ(1-8). 36 is also 6², and hints at the close relationship between Hod and Tiphereth, for Mercury is the nearest planet to the Sun, with the quickest orbit.

Hod itself adds to 15 (HVD), which is also the total for *Jah* (IH), the divine name of Chokmah. As the eighth Sephira, Hod is the lower manifestation of the energy of Chokmah, reflected through Chesed. This relationship is described through the powers of 2 and the manifestations of duality down the Sephiroth of the Tree – 4 (Chesed) is 2² and 8 (Hod) is 2³. 15 also reduces to 6, recalling again the close tie to the central Sun of Tiphereth.

Tarot

The four Eights are attributed to Hod.

Animals associated with Hod

Amphisbaena
The twin-headed mythical serpent is suggestive of the Mercurial caduceus, and hence its attribution to Hod.

Coyote
In Native American myth coyote is the trickster, which is very Mercurial.

Hummingbird
The constant activity and speed of the hummingbird is reminiscent of the quicksilver Mercurial energy.

Jackal
The jackal is sacred to Anubis, and the attribution is made for this reason.

Minerals associated with Hod

Agate
Agate is traditionally Mercurial, and was used as a protective stone for the underworld.

Citrine Quartz
Citrine is known as the Thieves Stone, and is particularly associated with Hermes as the trickster, hence its attribution to Hod.

Opal
The flashing colours within opals recall the flashes of thought within the mind. Also, as a silica gel, opal is the most fluid of the minerals referred to as crystals, containing a high percentage of water.

Mercury
As the planetary metal of mercury, with its unique quality of being fluid at the temperature range normally experienced on earth, mercury metal ideally demonstrates the fluid nature of the mental processes associated with mercury. Mercury is only found solid in nature when combined with other elements, such as sulphur to make cinnabar (Mercury Sulphide), demonstrating the need to ground thoughts to make them solid rather than uncontained fancies.

Plants associated with Hod

Moly
The black and white colouring of moly recalls the twin snakes of the caduceus, and the mythical use by Odysseus after being given moly by Hermes to transform his men back to human form after the enchantress Circe had turned them into swine.

Scents associated with Hod

Lavender
By its traditional use, as a mental stimulant and for soothing headaches, lavender is considered Mercurial.

Lemon
The stimulating and cleansing qualities of lemon are very Mercurial.

Lime
The stimulating effect of lime on the mental processes makes it a Mercurial scent.

Storax
Storax is used as a base for other perfumes, in the same way that mercury is used as the amalgam for making alloys of metals, acting as the binding material.

Symbols & Tools associated with Hod

Apron
The apron represents the craftsman or mason, and indicates the act of giving form to ideas. Also the apron conceals the "Splendour" of the person wearing it.

Caduceus
The caduceus is the magickal emblem of Mercury, as the symbol of healing and the messenger. This symbolism has been maintained by its adoption as the emblem of the medical profession.

Names
The name of an item gives it definition, and some would say restriction. When we talk about magickal names and the power they contain, the myth that first springs to mind is that of Isis tricking Ra out of his power by learning his true name. The Egyptian idea of the true name of an entity or item giving control of it is one that has become widespread in western culture, though often in an underlying way.

Octogram
The eight-rayed star represents the balanced nature of Mercury as the twin current. Likewise the octogram is formed by two squares at 45° to each other.

Deities associated with Hod

Celtic
— *Bride* as Goddess of Healing, Smithing, Poetry and Crafts.
— *Goibniu / Govannon* as Smith God and Maker of Divine Beer.
— *Gwydion* as the Magickian God.
— *Math Mathonwy* as God of Sorcery.
— *Nudd / Nuada / Nodens* as a God of Healing, Writing and Magick.
— *Ogma / Ogmios* as God of Eloquence and Writing.

Egyptian
— *Anubis* as the Psychopomp and God of Perfumery.
— *Seshat* as the Goddess of Writing.
— *Shu* as a God of Air.

Greek
— *Asclepius* as God of Healing.
— *Hermes* as the God of Magick, Communication and Healing, and as Psychopomp.

— *Iris* as a Messenger Goddess bearing the Caduceus, and also of the Rainbow, hinting at Paroketh.

Roman
— *Mercury* as the God of Magick and Messenger.

Sumerian
— *Enlil* as Air God.
— *Nidaba* as Goddess of Learning.
— *Ninlil* as Air Goddess.

Meditations & Exercises

Heaven

Meditate on the symbol for Mercury, of the equal-armed cross under a circle, surmounted with a crescent on its side. See what ideas and images come to mind.

Magickal Formula

Intone the formula of Azoth for a few minutes as a mantra and record the results you get.

Magickal Image

Meditate on the Magickal Image of a beautiful hermaphrodite. Try the meditation with the left side male and right side female, and then swap them over next time. See what difference this makes to your meditation.

Tarot

Lay out the four Eights in an equal-armed cross. Put the 8 of Disks at the top and the 8 of Wands at the bottom, the 8 of Cups on the left and the 8 of Swords at the right. Contemplate the images and see what inspiration arises.

Meditation on Words

A particularly appropriate form of meditation for Hod is the method known as *gerushin*, or meditating on verses. An inspirational phrase from the Torah was the original useage of this technique, developed in the sixteenth century CE. So a phrase such as *"I am the rose of Sharon, and the lily of the valleys"* could be used as the focus, from which you allow your mind to wander and see what course it takes. You can also use it as your focus, coming back repeatedly to the verse.

Alternatively you can use any verse that inspires you, such as Santaya's famous quote *"those who do not learn from the past are condemned to repeat it"* or Blake's *"to see a world in a grain of sand"*.

Hod Temple - Visualisation

The Hod temple is circular and 15m in diameter. The walls are of opal and extend up to a height of 3m, with flashes of red, yellow, blue and green seen in them as you walk around the temple. From here they become a domed hemi-spherical ceiling, which is a deep azure blue flecked with gold (lapis lazuli). The floor of the temple is made of Citrine quartz, inlaid with an 8-rayed silver star whose tips reach the walls. In the centre of the temple there is an opal double-cube altar, 1m in height and 0.5m square on the top. On the top of the altar is a small silver bowl, in which burns an undying blue flame, the flame of spirit.

In the north are two pillars, of 1m diameter each, 2m apart, rising from the floor to the ceiling, these pillars are 1m in from the wall. The left pillar is black and made of onyx, the right pillar is white and made of marble. In the wall between them (in the North) is visible a normal size doorframe. Four more such doorframes are visible in the northeast, east, southeast and south-southeast.

You here a bell ring and see Raphael standing before you. He is about 3m tall, with a beautiful face. He wears an orange robe and sandals, and has a caduceus in his right hand and a large flat piece of polished green crystal in his left hand. Raphael tells you that the green stone is the Emerald Tablet, and hands it to you to study.

You gaze at the Emerald Tablet, and see it is covered with strange hieroglyphs. As you look at the hieroglyphs they seem to shift in front of your eyes. The first line is now readable and says *"With certainty, that which is above is as that which is below"*.

As you continue to stare at the tablet, the words speak to you, and you realise that the truth on the Emerald Tablet is an ever-changing message that varies with the observer. Remember as fully as you can the words you read on the Emerald Tablet so you can consider them and meditate on them afterwards.

When you have finished gazing at the Emerald Tablet you offer it back to Raphael, who smiles at you. Then he bursts into laughter, claps you on the shoulder and disappears. You turn to the south-southeast to the doorway there, and walk back through it to the temple of Malkuth to return back to the mundane world.

32. NETZACH (NTzCh) - Victory

"The Seventh Path is called the Occult Intelligence because it is the refulgent Splendour of the intellectual virtues which are perceived by the eyes of the intellect and the contemplations of faith."[85]

Netzach (pronounced *Net-zack*) is the Sephira of Venus. Venus is the planet of love, and no other planet (or goddess) has inspired artists, writers and poets as much as she. Love can be experienced in a variety of ways, and this is expressed well through the Greek words for love – Agapé (*spiritual love*), Eros (*physical or sexual love*) and Filia (*brotherly or kinly love*).

The polarity of Netzach and Hod is emphasised in *The Thirty-Two Paths of Wisdom* by the use of the term *"refulgent Splendour"*, as splendour is the translation of Hod. Also the intellect is emphasised, and the balance of emotion and intellect is one of the eternal struggles experienced by mankind in seeking to develop and succeed through life.

However as Hod is a lower manifestation on the tree of form from Binah, so is Netzach a lower manifestation on the Tree of the force of Chokmah. For our emotions give force and power to our drives. It is for us to ensure that the emotional charge we create is positive, rather than negative. Negative emotions have a tendency to be stored in our bodies as blockages, and tied up energy that could be used more constructively for our growth.

Venus is of course the Morning and Evening Star, first to rise and last to set in the heavens. Originally it was perceived as being two different stars, until astronomy showed otherwise. The significance of this emotionally is to remind us that emotions have their opposites, hence the old saying *"it's a thin line between love and hate"*.

To master your emotions ensures you can channel their energy into your growth. You can recognise the futility of negative emotions and transform them into their positive counterparts. This includes self-love, though in a positive way where you acknowledge your faults and strive to correct them, not in a narcissistic way.

Always remember that in the Middle Ages and Renaissance, Venus was the one goddess who was unconquered, remaining ever-present through art, sculpture and literature. Not for nothing was Aphrodite's Girdle described as

---

[85] *The Thirty-Two Paths of Wisdom - Joannes Rittangelius*

being able to bind anything. Love is the strongest force in the universe, and it can help you realise your potential if it is present in your life in a positive way.

Divine Name: Yahveh Tzabaoth (IHVH TzBAVTh)

This name means *"The Lord of Hosts"*. This name refers to God as the victorious warrior, and expresses the transmission of the Martial force of Geburah through the balancing Solar energy of Tiphereth to the Venusian form of Victory.

Archangel: Uriel (AVRIAL)

Uriel, also known as Auriel or Oriel, is the Archangel of Venus and of Earth, and of peace and salvation. His name means *"Light of God"*, and he is often depicted with a flame or lamp in his hands. Uriel embodies the power of light as illumination and spiritual passion. Uriel is associated with magickal power, and the application of force. As such he is the angel to help cause a positive breaking of bonds when needed and overcoming inertia, being able to go with the flow of the "winds of change". He is also the patron of astrology and has been linked strongly with electricity.

Uriel is credited with being the angel who gave alchemy and the Qabalah to man. Uriel was the angel who helped inspire Abraham to lead the Jews out of Ur. As one of the most powerful Archangels, Uriel is said to be the bearer of the keys to hell, standing as guardian to that infernal realm. Uriel adds to 248 in Hebrew, the same as *in vision* (BMRAH), which is highly appropriate for the "light of God".

Uriel is usually seen standing about 3m tall, with a beautiful face. He wears an emerald green robe and carries a copper lamp in his left hand.

Some texts give Hanael or Anael as the archangel of Netzach, as he is depicted as a Venusian figure through many of the medieval texts. The attribution of Hanael to Netzach seems to start around the fifteenth century CE.

Order of Angels: Elohim (ALHIM)

The Angels of Netzach are the Elohim, meaning *"Gods"*. Elohim is also the magickal formula associated with Yesod, emphasising the strong link between the two most feminine of the planets – Venus and the Moon. As with Hod, the multiplicity of combined gender is emphasised through Elohim being a feminine noun with masculine ending.

As with the Bene Elohim, this word originally referred to other gods. In Psalm 82:1 we read *"God was standing in the congregation of El, amid the gods (ALHIM) he was holding judgement."* So the theme of the supreme god working through manifestations of deity is clearly illustrated here, a theme that runs through the Tree of Life and is one of the reasons for its versatility. The Elohim were referred to in medieval Grimoires as the Order of Principalities.

The Elohim stand about 2m tall, with white wings and are very beautiful. Some have more masculine faces and some more feminine. They wear emerald green tunics and are surrounded by an aura of beauty.

Heaven: Nogah (NVGH)

Nogah translates as *"Venus"* or *"glow"*, referring to the twilight. As the twilight is the time when the light of day shines forth into the night, so these concepts are considered to be masculine (day) and feminine (night), and twilight is a reference to the act of sexual union, when two partners unite.

Nogah adds to 64, the same as *Golden waters* (MI ZHB), emphasising the goddess of love rising from the waters. *Justice* (DIN) also adds to 64, and indicates the quality of justice as an expression of compassion – equality dispensed by the victor.

Qliphoth: The Ravens of Dispersion (AaRB ZRQ)

The raven is the carrion bird, found on battlefields. The link between love and war is here emphasised, and the inherent tendency towards both in mankind. A'arab Zaraq adds to 579, the same as *Sons of Adam* (ThAaNVGIM), i.e. mankind.

Titles of Netzach

Bitachon (Confidence)
To achieve Victory, and/or to achieve Love, and emotional balance, you need to have confidence. Confidence comes from a balanced emotional being, and represents the firm foundation of experience and self-knowledge.

Firmness
Firmness refers to our purpose – being able to maintain ones convictions and discipline without being tempted by laziness or hedonism. We need to be firm with ourselves to reach our goals, and firm in dealing with others to not allow them to manipulate us to their own ends.

Eternity

As Netzach represents the quality of love, so the nature of love is eternal. For divine love is beyond measure, and fills eternity, which is its receptacle.

Persistence

Love endures and persists, and so ultimately triumphs. Hence the use of this title, representing the persistence needed to achieve Victory.

The Lasting Endurance of God

As mentioned above for Eternity, the love of god for life is undying and eternal, the lasting endurance of his being.

Experience of Netzach

The Vision of Beauty Triumphant

This is a vision that suffuses the whole being with spiritual love, making you aware of the inherent beauty within all life, and the marvel of existence. Having this vision tends to be a life-changing experience, as it usually engenders the virtue of unselfishness in the person.

Virtue of Netzach

Unselfishness

One of the greatest qualities of love is that it removes selfishness, engendering the desire to help others. This is displayed through the love of family, friends and partner. When you help others, you radiate energy out into the world, seeking to help the species and the world grow.

Vices of Netzach

Hedonism

The pursuit of pleasure to the exclusion of all else is a downward path to the animal self. Hedonism denies the spiritual aspirations and is dangerous as it can conceal itself within the pleasures of activities you enjoy, engendering obsession. The firmness of the alternative title of Netzach must be applied to yourself to ensure you do not abandon your goals and dreams.

Lust

Lust is a vice that stems from either laziness or a tendency to objectivise. When you lust after a possession you desire something without putting in the work for it. And when you lust after a person, you are seeing them as a trophy, a status symbol that will improve your self-image through possession. Both these types of lust typify a turning away from the discipline and unselfishness needed to develop as a spiritual seeker, and for good reason do so many of the world's religions warn against them.

Colours associated with Netzach

King Scale: Amber
Amber suggests the richness of the resin, long prized as a jewel, and worn as a necklace of love, e.g. the Brisingamen of the Norse goddess Freya.

Queen Scale: Emerald
Emerald is the gemstone of Netzach, and the colour is associated with fertility, especially in ancient Egypt. Also emerald is formed by mixing the blue of Chesed with the yellow of Tiphereth, to give the bottom point of the triangle they form with Netzach.

Emperor Scale: Bright yellowish-green
Yellowish-green is formed by uniting the amber of the King Scale with the emerald of the Queen Scale.

Empress Scale: Olive, flecked with gold
Olive is formed from blue, red and yellow, with a predominance of the former. These are the colours of the three preceding Sephiroth of Chesed, Geburah and Tiphereth, with emphasis on Chesed, which is directly above Netzach on the Pillar of Mercy. Olive is also water of earth (see Malkuth), recalling the Love Goddess (implied by the golden flecks) rising out of the sea and coming on to the land, as in the myths of Aphrodite and Venus.

Magickal Formula: AGAPÉ

Agapé is spiritual love. It is unconditional and selfless, and is a demonstration of spiritual strength, that the animal nature has been overcome, and compassion and the desire to evolve can be radiated outwards to help improve the world around you. Agapé is a Greek word, and is a key term in the modern magickal doctrine of Thelema. Part of the essence of this doctrine is that in Greek Gematria Agapé adds to 93, the same as *Will* (Thelema). So love and will are expressions of the same energy – the force and the intent. Significantly the name of *Nike*, Greek goddess of Victory, also adds to 93, demonstrating the relevance of this formula to this Sephira.

Magickal Image of Netzach

A beautiful naked woman
Love is more commonly represented by a goddess than a god, and the attribution of a beautiful naked woman to represent the Venusian qualities of

love is an obvious one, again recalling Aphrodite raising from the waves. The naked woman could also be seen as the prize won by the warrior, who has achieved Victory (Netzach) and survived, and can enjoy the favour of love.

Human Body

The Left Hip and Leg
As with Hod, the attribution seems to be more based on location on the Tree than on any particular symbolic associations.

Numbers associated with Netzach

Netzach is the seventh Sephira on the Tree, and accordingly has the number 7 attributed to it. 7 has been attributed as the number of Venus since ancient times.

The Mystical number of Netzach is 28, i.e. Σ(1-7). 28 is the number of days in the lunar month, and also the average time for a woman's menstrual cycle, so the link to the feminine and the Moon are clear. 28 is also the number for *union* (IChVH) implying sexual union.

Netzach itself adds to 148 (NTzCh), the same as *Bene Elohim* (see Hod) and AHIH IH IHVH ALHIM, the great name of God that combines the divine names of the supernal triad. This can be interpreted as signifying that the manifestation of the divine power is best expressed through love, the force of Netzach, which will ultimately have the Victory.

Tarot

The Four Sevens.

Animals associated with Netzach

Dove
The dove is classically known as the bird of love, yet it will also fight fiercely if cornered.

Lynx
The lynx has a long association with Venus.

Nightingale
As the songbird associated with love and lovers, the attribution here is clear.

Peacock

The peacock is associated with love as the bird that courts through its fantastic and elaborate plumage. The fact that it is the male peacock who is the dandy emphasises the position of Netzach at the base of the masculine Pillar of Mercy. The colouring in the plumage of the peacock is caused by the large quantity of copper (the Venusian metal) which is present in its feathers.

Raven

Due to the association of ravens with battlefield, and also the name of the Qliphoth of Netzach.

Swan

The swan is considered Venusian due to its beauty and grace, and association with royalty.

Minerals associated with Netzach

Copper

Copper is the planetary metal of Venus, soft by itself but when combined into alloys producing much harder metals, as the love of two people produces a more complete whole.

Emerald

Classically associated with Venus due to its colour and value. Also the inclusions in an emerald are called the *"jardin"* (garden), recalling Venus as being goddess of gardens as well as love. Also the Holy Grail was said to be made of an emerald that fell from Lucifer's brow when he fell, and as the morning star he embodies Venus.

Jade

As a green stone associated with beauty, and by its use as a gift between lovers, Jade is clearly Venusian.

Malachite

Malachite is a copper-based crystal, used to aid with menstruation, and hence Venusian in its nature.

Rose Quartz

As a stone of beauty, love and serenity, and by its name, rose quartz is attributed to Venus.

Zoisite

By its green colour and Venusian associations.

Plants associated with Netzach

Laurel
The laurel wreath is a symbol of victory, hence its attribution here.

Rose
Rose is the flower of love, and hence its attribution to Netzach.

Scents associated with Netzach

Benzoin
Benzoin has an earthy, sensual scent associated with seduction, and is hence Venusian through all these qualities.

Rose
The scent of rose is fragrant and worn by lovers.

Sandalwood
Sandalwood is classically associated with sex, as in the suvasini (sweet-smelling woman) of Tantra.

Symbols & Tools associated with Netzach

Eight-rayed Star
As distinct from the octogram, the 8-rayed star is a motif used to represent early Love goddesses like Inanna and Ishtar.

Girdle
The girdle of Venus contains the power of love, and may bind anything, being the strongest force in the universe.

Lamp of Love
The lamp is representative of the light of love, which must be enkindled in the heart of the seeker to truly strive for the divine. Also the lamp is borne by Uriel as one of his tools.

Septagram
The seven-rayed star represents the energies of Venus as the whole spectrum of love, as seven is the number of the rainbow.

Deities associated with Netzach

Celtic
— *Aine* as a Goddess of Love and Fertility.
— *Branwen* as a Goddess of Beauty and Love.

— *The Morrigan* as a Goddess of Sex and battle, also the raven is one of her aspects (the Badb).

Egyptian
— *Bastet* as a Goddess of Pleasure.
— *Bes* as a protective Warrior God associated with love, marriage and childbirth.
— *Hathor* as a Goddess of sensuality, sexuality, and dance.
— *Sebek* as a God of Fertility and protection.

Greek
— *Aphrodite* as the Goddess of Love, often inciting lust and battle.
— *Nike* as Goddess of Victory, the name of the Sephira.

Roman
— *Lucifer* as the Morning Star.
— *Venus* as Goddess of Love and of gardens.

Sumerian
— *Inanna* as Goddess of Love and War, and representing the morning star.

Meditations & Exercises

Heaven

Meditate on the symbol for Venus, of an equal-armed cross, surmounted by a circle. Record what ideas and images come to mind.

Magickal Formula

Intone the formula of Agapé for a few minutes as a mantra and record your impressions.

Magickal Image

Meditate on the Magickal Image of a beautiful naked woman. Try varying the age of the woman in your meditations, so that she is in her twenties, thirties, forties, fifties and see what difference this makes to your meditation.

Tarot

Lay out the four Sevens in an equal-armed cross. Put the 7 of Disks at the top and the 7 of Wands at the bottom, the 7 of Cups on the left and the 7 of Swords at the right. Contemplate the images and see what inspiration arises.

Netzach Temple - Visualisation

The Netzach temple is circular and 15m in diameter. The walls are of white marble and extend up to a height of 3m. From here they become a domed hemi-spherical ceiling, which is a deep azure blue flecked with gold (lapis lazuli). The floor of the temple is made of rose quartz, with a 7-rayed star in green spanning the whole floor. Within the centre of the seven-pointed star is a red 7-petalled rose. In the centre of the temple there is an emerald double-cube altar, 1m in height and 0.5m square on the top. On the top of the altar is a small copper bowl, in which burns an undying blue flame, the flame of spirit.

In the north are two pillars, of 1m diameter each, 2m apart, rising from the floor to the ceiling, these pillars are 1m in from the wall. The left pillar is black and made of onyx; the right pillar is white and made of marble. In the wall behind and between them is visible a normal size doorframe. Four more such doorframes are visible in the northwest, west, southwest and south-southwest.

A bell rings and you see Uriel standing before you. He is about 3m tall, with a beautiful face. He wears an emerald green robe and carries a lit, polished copper oil lamp in his left hand. Uriel places the lamp on the top of the altar and bids you gaze into the flame.

You contemplate the flame, and see white, yellow and red dancing in the flame. As you see these colours you become more aware of the emotional tides within your own being. Then you become aware of the surrounding blackness around the flame. At this point you feel how your emotions are sometimes negative, and how jealousy, spite and other negative emotions hold you back.

As you keep gazing at the blackness around the flame, you perceive a sky blue colour in the blackness around the flame, and your spirit resonates to this, reminding you that you can be so much more than you are now, and that when you are in total harmony your emotions they do not drain your energy and slow your progress down.

You become aware of Uriel's presence again as he steps to the altar and takes up the lamp. You thank him and spend a couple of minutes just contemplating, allowing your emotional, spiritual and mental beings to harmonise before you leave the temple.

You now head to the doorway in the south-southwest to return back to the Malkuth temple, so you can return to the mundane world.

33. TIPHERETH (ThPhARTh) - Beauty

"The Sixth Path is called the Mediating Intelligence, because in it are multiplied the influxes of Emanations; for it causes that influence to flow into all the reservoirs of the blessings with which they themselves are united."[86]

Tiphereth (pronounced *Tif-er-et*) is the Sephira of the Sun. As the sun is the centre of our universe, and the heart is the centre of the body, so Tiphereth occupies the centre of the Tree of Life. Long before astronomy accepted a heliocentric view of the universe, the Tree of Life was predicting this with its central attribution of the sun to Tiphereth.

Tiphereth represents the true will of the individual, the living fire of divine spirit that burns in the heart and is flamed by the intent of truth and spiritual devotion. This is why it is called the *"Mediating Intelligence"*, for it is the point of balance in man, receiving the flow of the universe and directing it in a harmonious manner with his personal genius attached to it.

Tiphereth is also the lower reflection of the unknowable divine of Kether, as the manifest divinity. It represents the divine child, the manifestation of deity. As such it is the point of illumination, the revealing of the mysteries to bring forth Wisdom (Chokmah) and Understanding (Binah). Hence the attribution of gods of light and the sun, as those who illuminate the day.

Another key to the role of Tiphereth is that it is the point of balance between force and form. The higher energies of the Tree find their expression through the centre, and those energies can then manifest into form lower down on the Tree.

The role of the illuminating energy of Tiphereth is to engender growth and evolution. In nature we see this through the sunlight being used for photosynthesis in plants, and the effects of sunlight on humans. Lack of sunlight can result in insufficient production of vitamin D under the skin, and for many people a malaise of the spirit (SAD or Seasonal Affectiveness Disorder). The solar light makes life more pleasurable and bearable.

You will see that Tiphereth is unique amongst the Sephiroth in having several magickal images and experiences associated with it. This is because this is the level of spiritual maturity. To achieve the beauty and perfection of

---

[86] *The Thirty-Two Paths of Wisdom - Joannes Rittangelius*

Tiphereth requires several rites of passage, it is a prize that needs much toil, but is well worth the labour.

Divine Name: Yahveh Eloah va-Daath (IHVH ALVH VDAaTh)

This name is usually translated as *"God made Manifest in the Sphere of the mind"*. This name may seem curious when the attribution of the heart to Tiphereth is considered. It must be recalled though that in the ancient world the heart was seen as the place of the soul and centre of understanding, hence e.g. the weighing of the heart in the Egyptian underworld. Tiphereth is also associated with the will, and the will is a mental quality.

Further, the true will is the path of evolution and correctness for an individual, when they are doing what is right for them and going with the flow of the universe. In this sense the individual can be said to be performing the divine will, as they are on the path of right action, and are ascending the path of spiritual growth. Hence by performing their true will, they are manifesting God in the sphere of the mind.

Archangel: Michael (MIKAL)

Michael was the first angel created, and is often seen as the leader of the angels or "first among equals". His name means *"He who is like God"*. He is usually shown wielding a sword or lance, and sometimes the scales of justice. As with the other Archangels, Michael should be visualised standing about 3m tall, and he wears a golden yellow tunic.

Michael is the archangel of Fire and the Sun, and helps those who call him to achieve goals and destinies. Amongst the achievements especially sacred to Michael are marriage and music. If you are seeking to achieve a legitimate goal, or in need of protection, Michael is the angel you should call to, as he is the defender of the just and is also known as the Merciful Angel.

Michael appears a number of times in the Bible. Michael was the archangel who appeared to Moses as the fire in the burning bush. He also rescued Daniel from the lion's den and informed Mary of her approaching death. Michael appears in Revelations as the leader of the celestial host that defeats the antichrist. He is the prayer-leader in the Heavens in Islam.

There has been much debate about the attribution of Michael (and Raphael) to Tiphereth or Hod. Since the twelfth century different Grimoires, and even copies of the same Grimoires have attributed both these Archangels to both these Sephiroth. The biblical symbolism of fire, lion, leader of the celestial host are all clear indications that Michael should be attributed to Tiphereth rather than Hod.

Order of Angels: Malachim (MLKhIM)

Malachim means *"Kings"*. The Sun is the ruler of our solar system, and so it is not surprising that the quality of rulership should be associated with the angels of Tiphereth, who are governed by the first of the Archangels, Michael. The Malachim equate in medieval Grimoires to the Order of Virtues.

In appearance the Malachim stand about 2m tall, and are very beautiful. They have white wings, and wear golden tunics and have golden crowns on their heads. All around them there is an intense aura of nobility and grace.

Heaven: Shamash (ShMSh)

Shamash means *"The Sun"*. This term in Hebrew is probably derived from the name of the ancient Sumerian sun god. It should be mentioned that solar gods are usually associated with healing, i.e. the balancing of the energies of the body, as Tiphereth balances the energies of the Tree.

Qliphoth: Thagirion (ThGRIRVN)

Thagirion means *"The Disputers"*. In this context the Thagirion can be seen as the forces that seek to unbalance the impetus of the seeker from his true will. For the true will is not a steady path, but requires constant vigilance. There is no task more difficult than consistently practicing the true will, for it means always acting with grace and considering the flows around you, and avoiding personal gain and egotism.

Titles of Tiphereth

Adam
This title links the Tree of Life to the first Adam, the hermaphroditic being who contained both male and female before being split into the duality of gender. In the same way Tiphereth balances the energies of the female and male pillars in its unifying harmony.

Clemency
In this context clemency is the mildness and gentleness of compassion and reconciliation. It is the positive benevolence of the balanced person.

Gate of Righteousness
Tiphereth is at the top of the Path of Righteousness, the 25th path. To this end it is the Gate of Righteousness.

Green
Green is known as the colour of life and fertility, due to its massive presence throughout nature (as chlorophyll in plants). In ancient Egypt the term *"to do good things"* referred to good actions, and the attribution of green here may be seen in the same way, as a representation of life-affirming and positive energy and action.

Harmony
As the centre of the Tree of Life, Tiphereth is the place of Harmony within it. At this point energies are balanced and reflected.

Husband of Malkah
This title indicates the union of Tiphereth with Malkuth to produce the divine union of Sun and Earth.

King (Melekh)
This title is based on the quality of rulership associated with the Sun, which is the planet of kingship. It also emphasises the angels of Tiphereth – Kings.

Rachamin
This name, meaning *Compassion*, is used in early Qabalistic texts as an alternative title for Tiphereth. It indicates the need for compassion in a spiritually developed person, recognising their interconnectedness with all other life. It also recalls the line from The Book of the Law: *"Compassion is the vice of Kings."*

Reconciliation
Tiphereth is known as the *"Reconciler of the Tree of Life"*, as it reconciles the energies of the higher Tree with those of the lower Tree.

The Lesser Countenance (Zair Anpin)
This title is a complement and reflection of Kether as The Greater Countenance. It implies the manifest power of the sun, which has been the subject of so much worship by different cultures through history as the source of life. It also refers to Jesus as the Son of God, physically manifesting his countenance in human form.

It may also be translated as *"The Impatient One"*, indicating the desire of the Bridegroom (Tiphereth) to be united with his bride (Malkuth).

The Man
This title also refers to Adam, but here it is as Adam Kadmon, man perfected, and emphasises the microcosmic attribution of the Tree of Life to the human body.

The Reflecting Mirror
Tiphereth reflects the light of the divine countenance of Kether, manifesting it as the light of the sun.

The Son
As with the Lesser Countenance, this title refers to Jesus as the Son of God.

Experience of Tiphereth

The Vision of the Harmony of Things
The imagination, intellect and emotions have all been brought into harmony, enabling the seeker to realise their true will, and perceive their place in the universe and the greater flow of life.

Knowledge and Conversation of the Holy Guardian Angel (HGA)
This expression is frequently quoted without explanation, but what is it? Tiphereth is the centre of the Tree and point of balance, connecting the upper and lower halves. Knowledge and Conversation of the HGA is another way of saying that a person has reached a point of balance, where they have harmonised their emotions (Netzach), intellect (Hod) and Imagination (Yesod), so that they are in control of the material existence (Malkuth).

This point of balance is the discovery of the true will (Tiphereth), or correct path for the individual to be taking to fulfill their spiritual evolution. By being balanced they have a clearer access to the messages of the unconscious (Yesod) and their superconscious (Kether), and act accordingly. So essentially if the HGA is considered the interface between the conscious mind and the divine part of the self, achieving knowledge and conversation of it is the process of being able to draw from the divine genius inherent in the soul.

The Vision of the Mystery of the Crucifixion
This is an appreciation of the symbolism of selfless sacrifice as a path to liberation. In the case of Jesus this has been perceived as an act of redemption, but it equally applies to figures like Buddha, and might equally be called *"The Vision of the Mystery of the Boddhisattva"*, as any individual reaching this stage of spiritual evolution who chooses to stay there and help others to also reach their level is acting out of compassion and selfless love of life.

Virtues of Tiphereth

Devotion to the Great Work
The balance engendered through reaching Tiphereth produces an ineffable desire to achieve perfection of the self and help others to achieve the same – this is the Great Work.

Compassion

Compassion is the desire to help others without thought of reward or self-aggrandisement. Compassion travels hand in hand with devotion to the Great Work, and the two virtues are inseparable. When you lose one, you lose both.

Vice of Tiphereth

Pride

Pride is one of the most difficult vices to deal with. Whilst there is nothing wrong with being pleased with your achievements, it is a very small step into pride, which can lead to feelings of arrogance and superiority. As soon as these creep in, all the work you have done to balance yourself starts to slip away. It is an essential aspect of spiritual development never to assume you are better than others, but rather to accept that everyone has different paths that they travel at different paces. To think otherwise will inevitably lead you to slip backwards on your path, causing you to waste energy that could be better spent on continuing to move forwards.

Colours associated with Tiphereth

King Scale: Clear Pink Rose

This represents the colour of the sky at dawn as the sun rises, affirming the birth of the sun and the beginning of the new day.

Queen Scale: Yellow (Gold)

The golden yellow of the sun itself.

Emperor Scale: Rich Salmon

The salmon pink is made by adding the clear pink rose of the King Scale to the Golden Yellow of the Queen Scale.

Empress Scale: Gold Amber

The colour of the harvest, implying the earthing and transmutation of the solar rays. Also amber, which was thought in ancient times to be formed from solidified sunlight.

Magickal Formulae

IHShVH

This magickal formula is that of divine manifestation. On the one hand it is the name of Jesus, as God Incarnate. However it is also the unpronounceable name of Tetragrammaton (IHVH); which can be seen as representing the four elements, with the letter Shin, corresponding to Spirit, in the centre. So it is a formula of the elements in perfect balance, manifesting spirit by their harmony.

INRI

INRI was the Notariqon written above Jesus on the cross, representing the sentence *"Jesus of Nazareth, King of the Jews" (Jesus Nazaraeus Rex Judaeorum)*, so in that instance it represents sacrifice as previously discussed. However as has been pointed out by Crowley, it could also be used to represent other relevant phrases, such as *"All of nature is renewed by fire" (Igni Natura Renovata Integra)*, describing the positive quality of fire in enabling various forms of plant to germinate and continue. In this instance it then represents the highest aspect of Fire, as does Tiphereth itself. Another interpretation of INRI is the message of Christ, *"Intra Nobis Regnum del"*, or *"the kingdom of God is within us"*.

Magickal Image of Tiphereth

A Majestic King

The majestic king is the strong ruler, which is a clear embodiment of the principles of Tiphereth as the solar regent. It also recalls the images of the king from alchemy as the seeker undergoing spiritual transformation.

A Child

The child represents the aspect of Tiphereth as the child of Chokmah and Binah, and can be seen as representing the child of promise, the solar rebirth at the winter solstice. This formula expresses the cyclic nature of the relationship between the sun (Tiphereth) and the earth (Malkuth), for the child may grow up to become the adult ruler, married to the Bride (Malkuth).

A Sacrificed God

This represents the formula of self-sacrifice as expressed through the myth of Christ, and the Buddha, where the good of the whole is put before the good of the individual. This formula is also seen in modern paganism in the harvest myth of the slain corn king at Lughnasadh, whose body feeds his people.

Human Body

The Heart

The heart is traditionally attributed to the sun, as the centre of the body, responsible for the well-being of the whole body by circulating the blood, as the sun is responsible for the planets orbiting it.

Numbers associated with Tiphereth

As the sixth Sephira on the Tree, the number of Tiphereth is 6. Six is unique in that it is the only number that can be formed by multiplying its factors and also by adding them, i.e. 1+2+3 = 6, as does 1x2x3.

The mystic number of Tiphereth is 21, i.e. Σ(1-6). 21 is also the number of AHIH, the divine name of Kether, *"I am"*. This once again indicates the position of Tiphereth as the reflection of Kether, manifesting the unknowable divine into the knowable divine. The word for *innocence* (ZChV) also adds up to 21, showing the purity associated with Tiphereth.

Tiphereth itself adds to 1081, which is Σ(1-46). This number is of such a size that no other obvious significant words add to the same total, although this in itself could be considered significant.

Tarot

The four Sixes.

Animals associated with Tiphereth

Leopard
The speckled coat of the leopard is considered to be solar, and big cats generally are attributed to the Sun.

Lion
As the "king of the beasts", the lion is an obvious attribution to Tiphereth.

Phoenix
As the bird that regenerates itself through fire, the phoenix is obviously solar by nature.

Spider
Tiphereth sits in the centre of the web of the Tree like a spider, also it is connected by eight paths to eight of the Sephiroth, corresponding to the eight legs of the spider.

Tiger
The tiger is unmatched amongst the big cats, making it another solar creature.

Minerals associated with Tiphereth

Amber
The golden colour of amber and its beauty have made it highly prized through the centuries, and also by the ancient belief that is was made from solidified sunlight.

Gold
As the king of precious metals, and by its colour, gold has long been seen as the planetary metal of the sun. Also the almost universal use of gold to make crowns and items of royal jewellery.

Sunstone
By its name and the sparkles of light it reflects, sunstone is another solar stone.

Topaz
The golden colour of topaz is very solar.

Plants associated with Tiphereth

Acacia
Is associated with resurrection, and hence linked to the concept of the sacrificed god associated with Tiphereth.

Bay (Laurel)
Bay is attributed to Tiphereth for its association with solar gods, such as Apollo.

Daisy
By its love of the sun, opening at dawn and closing at dusk, leading to its original name of *"Day's Eye"*. Also the yellow centre with white petals tinged pink is very solar.

Oak
Oak is traditionally solar and is considered the ruler of the trees. Consider also the mystery of the mistletoe being collected by the Druids from the oak tree with gold sickles.

Sunflower
The sunflower is a symbol of the Sun by its appearance and love of the Sun.

Scents associated with Tiphereth

Cinnamon
The spicy heat of cinnamon has resulted in its long association with the sun.

Frankincense
Frankincense is associated with spirituality, purity and the will. It was also used as a symbol of Ra in ancient Egypt, linking it to solar worship.

Ginger
The warm spicy aroma of ginger and its stimulating effects on the body are very solar.

Juniper
Juniper is traditionally solar.

Rosemary
Another traditional attribution.

Symbols & Tools associated with Tiphereth

Calvary Cross
This is attributed to Tiphereth as a symbol of the mystery of the sacrificed god, and also due to its being made of six parts (four vertical, with two more horizontal) when being seen as comprised of squares. In fact in this form it can be seen as an opened up cube.

Cube
The cube is 6-sided, and implies the balance of Tiphereth through its equality of edges and faces. Also it has eight corners, corresponding to the eight paths coming off Tiphereth.

Hexagram
The hexagram is the 6-pointed star, which naturally associates it with Tiphereth. It embodies the balance of the upward and downward flowing energies in a central harmony. It is also the symbol of the universe, reflecting the central position of the sun in the universe and the Tree of Life.

Lamen
The lamen is worn on the chest over the heart, giving it Tipherethic attributions. Also it is worn as an act of will to attract positive and harmonious forces, and so represents an expression of the will.

Rose Cross
The Rose Cross represents the magickal expression of the whole through the central point, i.e. Tiphereth.

Sword

The sword represents the will of the magickian. Some attribute it to Geburah due to its being made of iron and used for war, but this misses the point of the use of the sword in magick, to direct and where necessary control.

Deities associated with Tiphereth

Celtic

— *Belenus / Bel / Beli / Bile* as the Sun God and Lord of Light.
— *Gwyn Ap Nudd* as Lord of Light and Ruler of the Otherworld.
— *Lugh / Lleu* as Lord of Light.
— *Mabon* as the Child of Promise who brings Health or Sickness to the Land.
— *Mog Ruith* as the Sun God in his bronze chariot flying through the sky.
— *Sulis* as a Solar Goddess.

Egyptian

— *Horus* as the conquering Solar Child.
— *Nefertem* as the Child of the Dawn.
— *Osiris* as the Sacrificed God.
— *Ra* as the Sun God.
— *Sekhmet* as the fierce midday sun and manifestation of Re's wrath.

Greek

— *Apollo* as the Lord of Light.
— *Dionysus* as the Liberator.
— *Eos* as Goddess of the Dawn and Sister of Helios.
— *Helios* as the Sun God.

Roman

— *Aurora* as Goddess of the Dawn.
— *Sol Invictus* as the Conquering Sun.

Sumerian

— *Dumuzi* as the Dying and Resurrected God.
— *Utu* as the Sun God.

Meditations & Exercises

Heaven

Meditate on the symbol for the Sun, of a circle with a dot in the centre, and record what ideas and images come to mind.

Magickal Formula

Intone the formula of IHShVH (Ye-hesh-u-ah) for a few minutes as a mantra and record your impressions.

Magickal Image

Meditate on the Magickal Images of Tiphereth. For the majestic King you can try meditating on him standing and seated on a throne, to see if you receive any differences. For the child try visualising the child as a boy and as a girl, the age should be in the 4-7 range. For the sacrificed God you can visualise Christ on the cross, and Buddha being eaten by a tiger.

Tarot

Lay out the four Sixes in an equal-armed cross. Put the 6 of Disks at the top and the 6 of Wands at the bottom, the 6 of Cups on the left and the 6 of Swords at the right. Contemplate the images and see what inspiration arises.

Breath Meditations

Make yourself comfortable, and sit cross-legged on the floor (or sit on a chair if this is a problem, but keep your back straight). Concentrate on your nostrils, on the breath entering and leaving. Do not try and control your breathing initially, it is good to practice this meditation for a week or so before moving onto breath control.

Whenever your find your attention has wandered as a result of boredom or fatigue, or thoughts intrude, gently but firmly return your attention to your nostrils. Do not be disturbed by this in any way as it is inevitable, simply return your attention to the nostrils and continue.

The frequency with which the attention wanders merely highlights how little we focus our minds, and regular practice of meditation helps us become more aware of ourselves, and able to concentrate without being distracted. Do not be distressed by the frequency with which thoughts may intrude at first, keep returning the concentration to the nostrils, eventually you will find your internal voice shuts off and all is still.

This process of *"shutting off the internal dialogue"* can take time to master completely, but the time will come when you can shut the dialogue off at will, and focus easily without too much distraction. This is a great benefit to magickal work and shows a major level of progress. This state is known as *mochin de-gadluth* ("mentality of adulthood") indicating that the seeker has reached an advanced level of mental control, as compared to the usual state where the internal dialogue chatters on, known as *mochin de-katnuth* ("mentality of childhood").

After a week or so, move to inhaling to a count of four, holding the breath to a count of four, and then exhaling to a count of four. This technique will accustom you to regulating your breath. With practice it becomes automatic so you do not have to concentrate on your breath when meditating, and you can control your breath automatically whilst meditating using another focus.

For relaxation inhale to a count of four and exhale to a count of eight. This can be increased with practice, but the exhalation should always be longer than the inhalation, preferably double the length.

With experience (say after a few months), retention of the breath for longer periods is a powerful technique. Inhale to a count of four, hold for a count of sixteen, and exhale to a count of eight. With practice this can be increased, but it should be in equal increments, such as to six (inhale), twenty-four (hold), twelve (exhale). This is known as north-south breathing.

Tiphereth Temple - Visualisation

The Tiphereth temple is circular and 15m in diameter. The walls are of tiger's eye and extend up to a height of 3m, with veins of amber, brown and black shades running through them. From here they become a domed hemi-spherical ceiling, which is a deep azure blue flecked with gold (lapis lazuli).

The floor of the temple is made of sunstone, inlaid with a gold hexagram whose tips reach the walls. Within the centre of the hexagram is a golden sun design, with six larger rays reaching out to touch the points of the inner hexagon. In the centre of the temple standing on the centre of the sun design there is a topaz double-cube altar, 1m in height and 0.5m square on the top. On the top of the altar is a small gold bowl, in which burns an undying blue flame, the flame of spirit.

In the north are two pillars, of 1m diameter each, 2m apart, rising from the floor to the ceiling, these pillars are 1m in from the wall. The left pillar is black and made of onyx, the right pillar is white and made of marble. There are eight normal size doorframes, in the north, north-northeast, northeast, southeast, south, southwest, northwest and north-northwest.

You hear the sound of a bell and a harmony, like a chorus of angels. As you look around the temple you see the archangel Michael. He holds an unsheathed sword in his right hand, and a sword in a scabbard in his left hand. As with the other Archangels, Michael stands about 3m tall, and he wears a golden yellow tunic. His face is beautiful but seems to radiate light and power, making it almost impossible to look directly at his face.

Michael offers you the hilt of the scabbarded sword, and you pull the sword out of its scabbard. As you hold it the sword seems to sing, and you feel a connection with the blade. You realise this sword represents your will, your determination, clarity and discrimination.

Michael reminds you that the sword of will is double-edged, and that you should exercise a clear mind and true purpose when you wield this sword. You thank him, taking the scabbard off him and resheathing the sword. You know that you will always be able to call this sword to your hand whenever you need it for magickal work. For know though you have connected with your sword, so you place it on the altar and thank Michael again for his help.

You then move to the south of the temple to the door to Yesod to return to the Malkuth temple, and from there back to the mundane world.

34. GEBURAH (GBVRH) - Strength

> *"The Fifth Path is called the Radical Intelligence because it resembles Unity, uniting itself to Binah, Understanding, which emanates from the primordial depths of Chokmah, Wisdom."*[87]

Geburah (pronounced *Ge-voor-ah*) is the Sephira of Mars. It is associated with power and energy. The power of Geburah must be directed by the true will, to be power with, or it can turn into the domineering power of control over others. The only power over we need to be interested in is power over ourselves, the ability to control our actions and keep them in harmony with our true wills as manifestations of the divine will.

War and violence are associated with Mars, and these are examples of power being used to control – the *"might is right"* syndrome. Yet ultimately violence is futile, for deeds built on unnecessary violence will always come undone as they lack a natural balance. As Sun Tzu said, *"If you have to resort to violence you have already lost."*[88]

Within nature of course violence is a function of life and the food chain, hence the expression *"nature is red in tooth and claw"*. But the violence in nature is based around killing for food, or to establish hierarchies to breed the healthiest young. It is instinctual violence as part of animal behaviour. Humans have established patterns of behaviour (ethics and laws) to reduce the need for violence. In a social structure violence is usually anti-social.

The art of the warrior, which can be seen as part of the lessons of Geburah, is about control. Many people do not realise this. A good warrior will be assertive rather than aggressive. This is known as *"showing the sword"*. By establishing clear boundaries and showing you will not be dominated, much of the time you can avoid conflict. Sometimes conflict is unavoidable, then a warrior will do the minimum necessary to resolve the situation.

So the power of Geburah is the power to do what needs doing, under the direction of the will. As soon as the violence becomes uncontrolled and unnecessary, the individual undoes all the hard work they have put in to rise that far on the Tree of Life. Man's history is littered with negative martial energy, showing that as a species we have a very long way to go!

---

[87] *The Thirty-Two Paths of Wisdom - Joannes Rittangelius.*
[88] *The Art of War – Sun Tzu.*

Divine Name: Elohim Gibor (ALHIM GBVR)

This divine name means *"The Strong Gods"*, and emphasises the martial quality of this Sephira. It sums 297, as does *"fortified castle"* (ARMVN), indicating the associations with combat and security.

Archangel: Khamael (KhMAL)

Khamael (or Samael or Camael) is the archangel of Mars, and is one of the seven Archangels who stand in the presence of god, which is emphasized by the meaning of his name, *"he who sees God"*. Khamael is a warrior who represents divine justice, and is the head of the order of Angels called Seraphim.

In appearance Khamael stands about 3m tall with a beautiful face and fiery red hair. He appears as a warrior, with a scarlet red tunic, green plates of armour, an iron helmet and a sword. He has large green wings.

Khamael is said to grant invisibility and rules over martial qualities like power and invincibility. Khamael is the ideal angel to call upon to help you take personal responsibility and to develop self-confidence. He will help you deal with the consequences of your actions and to find justice, but only if you stick to the truth. Many writers have put Khamael forward as the angel who wrestled with Jacob. He is also thought to have been the other angel who appeared with Gabriel to comfort Jesus during his agony in the garden of Gethsemane.

Khamael is the angel who guards the gates of heaven, chief of the twelve thousand fiery Angels of destruction who guard the gates. Khamael is also the angel who holds Leviathan in check until Judgement Day, when he will swallow the souls of sinners. Other duties of Khamael are as patron Angel of all those who love God, governing the heavenly singing, and to bring the gift of godliness to mankind, helping them find the holiness that exists within but is rarely fully released.

Order of Angels: Seraphim (ShRPhIM)

Seraphim means *"Fiery Serpents"*, and adds to 630, the same as *"The Holy Spirit"* (DVChA QRIShA). The first of the Seraphim was Lucifer, who fulfilled the divine will by ensuring the departure of man from Eden.

In appearance the Seraphim are very beautiful angels, around 2m tall with who have three pairs of white wings on their backs, in scarlet tunics, whose auras are filled with flames that surround them at all times. They are described in Isaiah 6:2 in his vision of God. These angels are highly significant as they can be seen as bringers of divine change of great magnitude, embodying the Holy Spirit. The Seraphim equate in the medieval Grimoires as the Order of Powers or Potestates (not to the Seraphim in the grimoires, who are confusingly equated to the Chaioth haQadosh of Kether).

Heaven: Madim (MADIM)

Madim means *"Mars"* and *"redness"*. Mars is known as the red planet, and the red of blood and danger is classically associated with this planet and Sephira.

Qliphoth: Golachab (GVLChB)

Golachab means *"The Burners"*. The Golachab present the challenge of using power without burning yourself or others by lack of focus or harmony in the wielding of that power. It is all too easy to get your fingers burned when in a position of power, and the Golachab ensure that this will happen unless you keep to the path of your true will.

Titles of Geburah

Fear (Pachad)
Fear may seem a curious title, until we appreciate the positive aspects of fear. Fear is a motivating force. On an emotional and mental level fear of failure will make you strive harder to succeed, and to be as good as you can at something. On a physical level it floods the body with adrenaline, ready to act, through *"fight or flight"*. And of course there is the *"fear of God"*, the awe and terror that can permeate the being when realising a fraction of the magnitude of the incomprehensible.

Justice (Din)
Justice indicates the martial energy being balanced into control without violence, demonstrating a positive side to power.

Red
Red is the traditional colour attribution for Geburah, as red and gold. As with Chesed being white, it is significant that red is the colour of the female in alchemy.

Experience of Geburah

The Vision of Power
This vision shows us what we are capable of, the power that we can wield by doing our will. Yet it also reminds us of the old saying *"Absolute power*

corrupts absolutely". Unbridled power becomes domination, and leads to abuse of power. This is why the mercy of Chesed is needed to balance power with compassion and temperance.

Virtues of Geburah

Courage
Courage can manifest in being brave when there is danger, and overcoming fear, or standing up for what is right and having the *"courage of your convictions"*. Both instances are noble behaviour, as they demonstrate the best of being human, a desire to do what is right, i.e. uphold the divine will through positive action.

Energy
By following your true will you act efficiently, which means you have more energy to do things. People tend to be very inefficient in their lives, and waste a huge amount of energy. But the more you practice Qabalah and develop the qualities of the Sephiroth, the more you strive to be efficient and direct all your energy positively and usefully, so that you are as effective as possible.

Vices of Geburah

Cruelty
When might is unbridled it becomes cruelty. Cruelty is forcing people to do things that are hurtful or damaging to them, and taking pleasure from it. To engage in cruel behaviour indicates a conscious decision to exercise power over others, and shows the path of evolution has been ignored for the path of self-aggrandisement. There can be no excuse for cruel behaviour; it shows a lack of spiritual awareness and compassion.

Destruction
When energy is directed into destruction, it results in the wasting of all the positive energy of construction that went into the destroyed thing. This is destruction for the sake of it, not the constructive destruction of say, a forest fire. To take pleasure from destruction for its own sake shows a malaise of the spirit that indicates a person has chosen to cut themselves off from not only the spiritual source, but also the society they live in.

Colours associated with Geburah

King Scale: Orange
Orange suggests the pure fiery nature of Mars, and also the colour of Mars when observed in the night sky.

Queen Scale: Scarlet Red
The scarlet red of Mars, associated with blood and martial activities.

Emperor Scale: Bright Scarlet
The orange of the King Scale mixed with the scarlet red of the Queen Scale to give a bright scarlet.

Empress Scale: Red, flecked with black
The martial red, not as bright as scarlet to reflect its more physical nature, is tinged with the black of Binah to show the influence it receives from above.

Magickal Formula: AGLA

AGLA is Notariqon for the phrase *"Ateh Gibor Le-olahm Adonai"* (You are strong forever O Lord), and its use as the magickal formula of Geburah emphasises the strength associations of Mars.

Magickal Image of Geburah

A mighty warrior in his chariot, armed and crowned
It is significant to note that the warrior is crowned, implying he is of royal blood and in a position of authority. This then suggests that he is leading, and wielding power as he might a weapon. This is the formula of the warrior, ready to act where necessary, but only where necessary.

Human Body

The right arm and right hand
As 90% of the population are right-handed, this association makes sense as the right hand is the part of the body most associated with action – the doing of things requiring tools or weapons.

Numbers associated with Geburah

Geburah being the fifth Sephira, 5 is its number. We have 5 digits on each hand and each foot, and man is associated most with this number, for it is also the pentagram representing the limbs and senses of man.

The mystical number of Geburah is 15, i.e. $\Sigma(1-5)$. 15 is also the total for *Hod*, showing the influence of Geburah onto the Sephira below it; and *Jah*, the Divine Name of Chokmah, indicating that the energy of Geburah needs to be tempered with wisdom.

Geburah itself adds to 216which is 6^3. 216 is also the total for *fear* (IRAH) and *anger* (RVGZ), both of which are concepts associated with this Sephira. 216 is also the number of letters in the names of the 72 angels of the Shemhamphorash.

Tarot

The four Fives.

Animals associated with Geburah

Basilisk
Martial by its fiery gaze that turns other creatures to stone.

Wolf
Wolves are associated with Mars through the creation myth of Rome, with Romulus and Remus being suckled by the she-wolf, and founding the very Martial Roman Empire.

Wolverine
As the tenacious fighter that will tackle opponents irrespective of size.

Minerals associated with Geburah

Bloodstone
By its name and high iron content, bloodstone is associated with Mars. Its other name is heliotrope, as it was believed to turn sunward, indicating the link between Geburah and Tiphereth.

Garnet
The garnet is a fiery red in colour, and was believed to be formed from the solidified eyes of dragons, giving the fiery connection with the breath of the dragon, who also presented the challenge to the warrior – win or die (unless he was clever enough to use his wits and win by riddling).

Haematite
As an iron-based crystal, and its use as an ore for extracting iron.

Iron
Iron is the planetary metal of Mars, and is used for making weapons and tools, hence its attribution here.

Magnetite
Another iron based crystal; magnetite also attracts iron by its magnetic qualities, showing its martial nature.

Ruby
Ruby is the classic martial stone by its colouring and hardness. Also ruby has long been considered to have blood-purifying qualities.

Spinel
Spinel was often mistaken for ruby, and is of a similar martial red in its colour and qualities.

Plants associated with Geburah

Hickory
The hardness of hickory is the reason for its attribution.

Nettle
The sting of the nettle on its underside and its non-stinging smooth upper side indicate the Martial nature of the nettle perfectly.

Rue
Is traditionally associated with Mars

Tobacco
The smoke of tobacco is said to be martial in its qualities.

Scents associated with Geburah

Basil
Is associated with spiritual courage, and hence a positive Geburic scent.

Black Pepper
The violent effect of black pepper and its fiery qualities make it eminently martial.

Oponax
The fiery scent of opoponax is stimulating and encourages action, as appropriate to Mars.

Symbols & Tools associated with Geburah

Chain
The chain is made of iron, and was used to control rebellious spirits in evocatory magick. The use for discipline is Geburic.

Pentagram
The pentagram as the 5-pointed figure is Martial by the number of points.

Scourge
The scourge is a sign of severity and is used to impose discipline, hence its association with Geburah.

Spear
As a tool the spear can only really be used to fight, and so it is eminently martial in its qualities.

Deities associated with Geburah

Celtic
— *Andraste* as a possible War Goddess.
— *The Morrigan* as Goddess of Battle.

Egyptian
— *Horus* as a God of War.
— *Seth* as a God of violent forces, and the sacredness of red to him as a colour of power and danger.

Greek
— *Ares* as the God of War.
— *Eris* as Goddess of Discord, unbalanced Martial energy.
— *Nemesis* as Goddess of Divine Retribution.

Roman
— *Bellona* as a War Goddess.
— *Discordia*, as Goddess of Discord who preceded Mars' chariot into battle.
— *Mars* as the God of War.

Sumerian
— *Inanna* as Goddess of War.

Meditations & Exercises

Heaven

Meditate on the symbol for Mars, of a circle with an equal-armed cross coming out at the 1.30 position on the clock.

Magickal Formula

Intone the formula of AGLA for a few minutes as a mantra and record your impressions.

Magickal Image

Meditate on the Magickal Image of a mighty warrior armed and crowned in a chariot. Try varying the age of the warrior, and what weapons he is armed with, and see what difference this makes to your meditations.

Tarot

Lay out the four Fives in an equal-armed cross. Put the 5 of Disks at the top and the 5 of Wands at the bottom, the 5 of Cups on the left and the 5 of Swords at the right. Contemplate the images and see what inspiration arises.

Geburah Temple - Visualisation

The Geburah temple is circular and 15m in diameter. The walls are of garnet and extend up to a height of 3m. From here they become a domed hemispherical ceiling, which is a deep azure blue flecked with gold (lapis lazuli). The floor of the temple is made of marble, inlaid with an iron pentagram whose tips reach the walls. In the centre of the temple there is a ruby double-cube altar, 1m in height and 0.5m square on the top. On the top of the altar is a small iron bowl, in which burns an undying blue flame, the flame of spirit.

In the north are two pillars, of 1m diameter each, 2m apart, rising from the floor to the ceiling, these pillars are 1m in from the wall. The left pillar is black and made of onyx, the right pillar is white and made of marble. In the wall between them (in the North) is visible a normal size doorframe. Three more such doorframes are visible in the east, southeast and south.

You hear a bell ring and see Khamael appear in front of you. He stands about 3m tall with a beautiful face and fiery red hair. He is dressed as a warrior, in a scarlet red tunic, green plates of armour, an iron helmet and a sword. He has large green wings.

Khamael tells you to call your sword to your hand, which you do. As you hold your sword in your hand you feel a flow of orange energy from your sword. It surrounds you and fills your aura, creating a visible egg of orange energy around you. You feel the strength of Mars permeating your being, filling you with power.

A sense of your own ability to achieve your goals fills you, and strengthens the aura around you. As it grows stronger, you realise that you do not have to allow anyone else to drain your energy with their behaviour if you keep your boundaries clear and firm. You know that all your energy can be put into achieving the goals that matter to you.

Khamael tells you that you have learned the lesson he was showing you, and you thank him and bow to him. He smiles and disappears. You spend some time contemplating this and then move to the south of the temple to return to the Hod temple, and from there back to the Malkuth temple and then to the mundane world.

35. CHESED (ChSD) - Mercy

> *"The Fourth Path is called the Cohesive or receptive Intelligence because it contains all the Holy Powers, and from it emanate all the spiritual virtues with the most exalted essences. They emanate one from another by virtue of the Primordial Emanation, the Highest Crown, Kether."*[89]

Chesed (pronounced *Hes-ed*) is the Sephira of Jupiter. Jupiter is traditionally associated with rulership, and success. It is the planet associated with religion, but the mysteries contained within a religion rather than the exoteric form or structure. Jupiter embodies the benevolent ruler, dispensing justice with mercy, tempered with authority. Jupiter teaches obedience to the higher cause, when service becomes a pleasure and not just a duty, for the relevance and rightness of the actions can be seen, as well as the benefits of the consequences of such actions.

Chesed is the first reflection of Chokmah, and represents the highest level that form can take before being transmuted to pure force. Chesed is linked with the highest aspects of water, which can be seen as the force that overcomes all. Hence the Pillar of Mercy is also known as the Pillar of Water.

The divine essence of Kether is likened to dew, and this finds its first expression below the Abyss in Chesed. This is why the *Thirty-Two Paths of Wisdom* says, *"They emanate one from another by virtue of the Primordial Emanation, the Highest Crown, Kether."* This is also why the entrance to the sixth palace (Chesed) is described as *"thousands upon thousands of waves of water ... yet there is not a single drop of water there, only the radiance of the marble stones with which the palace is furnished."*[90]

Jupiter is also associated with ascendancy, and gaining a superior position. This includes such areas of life as good bodily health, as well as mental, emotional and spiritual health. Chesed represents the holistic balance of all aspects of the self. Without this balance you cannot cross the Abyss, for it will result in destruction of the self due to lack of integrity.

---

[89] *The Thirty-Two Paths of Wisdom - Joannes Rittangelius.*
[90] *Hekhalot Rabbati.*

Divine Name: Al (AL)

This name means *"God"*, and adds to 31. It is sometimes written as El rather than Al. The suffix *–el* is found in the majority of archangelic names, and in Sumerian was associated with the *"shining ones"*, a particularly appropriate term regarding angels. 31 is also *LA*, meaning *"not"*, implying the formula of reversal, as expounded by Frater Achad[91] in his works in the 1930s.

This formula encourages the individual to think outside of the box, looking at the different possibilities contained within an idea or situation, a state worth being in when wielding the benevolent authority of Chesed. The word meaning *To Go* (HVK), also adds to 31, and implies the quality of action, which is particularly appropriate to Chesed, as the final impetus to leap into the Abyss to cross over to the Supernal Triad.

Archangel: Tzadkiel (TzDQIAL)

Tzadkiel, who is also known as Zadkiel, Satqiel, Zedkiel and Zachiel, is the archangel of Jupiter, and of benevolence, memory and mercy. His name means *"Righteousness of God"*, and he is often depicted with a dagger in his hand. However this dagger represents the power of the intellect, and also his role in saving Abraham's son. Tzadkiel is a comforter, and he is associated with invocation and prayer. He is hence the archangel to help overcome despondency, and to help you forgive others for their negative deeds.

Through prayer and invocation he is also a channel to help you attune yourself with divinity in the way you perceive and experience it. As archangel of Jupiter, Tzadkiel can also be appealed to for help with financial matters and for achieving justice in a situation. Tzadkiel is the angel who prevents Abraham from sacrificing his young son Isaac to God, which is where his associations with the dagger and mercy come from.

Tzadkiel is the chief of the order of angels known as the *"Brilliant Ones"* (Chasmalim). He is one of the two standard bearers (along with Zophiel) who follow directly behind Michael as he enters battle. Tzadkiel is described as one of the seven Archangels who preside next to God.

Tzadkiel is usually seen standing about 3m tall, with a beautiful face, wearing a blue tunic and bearing a dagger in his left hand.

---

[91] *The magickian Charles Stansfield Jones, whom Aleister Crowley regarded as his magickal child.*

Order of Angels: Chasmalim (ChShMLIM)

Brilliant Ones
The Chasmalim or *"Brilliant Ones"* stand about 2m tall, and are extremely beautiful, with white wings. They wear sapphire blue tunics, and give off an aura of intense light that makes it difficult to look at them.

Chesed is unusual in that the total for its angels, the Chasmalim is 428, the same as the total for its Qliphoth. The Chasmalim equate in medieval Grimoires to the Order of Dominions or Dominations.

Heaven: Tzedeq (TzDQ)

Tzedeq (or Tzedek) means *"Jupiter"*, which is the planet of expansion. It can also mean righteousness, and is used as a title for lower Sephiroth which represent lower manifestations of the energy of Chesed.

Qliphoth: Gha'aghseblah (GAaShKLH)

Gha'aghseblah means *"Smiters"* or *"Breakers-in-Pieces"*. This is in opposition to the positive creative aspect of Jupiter, which is benevolent rulership.

Titles of Chesed

Compassion
This title, like Love, refers to the benevolent and nurturing aspect of the developed spirit at Chesed. This title is also used for Tiphereth, indicating the first stage at which compassion can be sustained.

Glory (Gedulah)
Glory represents the expression of the divine essence. It demonstrates the manifestation of the inner radiance, as an outer glory.

Grace
This title indicates the method of behaviour that should be automatic and natural for someone who has reached Chesed on the Tree. To have developed this far, a person must be living in a state of grace.

Love
This refers to the highest aspect of love, of unconditional love for all things, demonstrating the readiness for crossing the Abyss.

Majesty
Chesed is the highest ruler below the Abyss, representing the Jovial ruler, and the positive quality of that rulership, i.e. majesty.

Mercy
Chesed is the centre of the Pillar of Mercy, and embodies the benevolent qualities of that Mercy.

White
This is due to the traditional attribution of white and silver as the colour of Chesed. However it is interesting to note that white is the colour of the male principle in alchemy, balancing the female red of Geburah.

Experience of Chesed

Vision of Love
The type of love referred to here is unconditional spiritual love (Agapé). It is the love of all life that characterises the divine impetus to grow and evolve. This vision is the true *"religious experience"*, of the type that will totally affect the recipient's life, and cause them to devote their whole life to the development of humanity on a spiritual basis, which is the next evolutionary step.

Virtue of Chesed

Obedience
Being able to obey others requires the discipline learned earlier on the path. In this instance it refers to obedience to the divine will through the true will. It is the unswerving obedience to the cause of the Great Work, which consumes the magickian with the undying flame of spirit.

Vices of Chesed

Bigotry
The negative side of religion is intolerance, which is expressed through bigotry. Bigotry is the expression of a closed mind, unable to accept or value the input of others, and is a reflex of arrogance and egotism. When bigotry is expressed, the fall will be swift.

Gluttony
Chesed stresses the health of the body, so self-indulgence through gluttony is a vice to be avoided. Gluttony may result from the desire to feel more grounded and connected to the physical, as at Chesed the seeker is one step away from abandoning everything to jump into the abyss. Hence gluttony may manifest as a last-ditch attempt by the ego to keep the body firmly rooted to the physical.

Hypocrisy

By not being true to what you believe in you become a hypocrite. Hypocrisy is a betrayal of the self, of the values you uphold, and of the people you are hypocritical too. It is a reflex of abuse of power, when the corruption of power has permeated the being and turned the path of the true will into the gratification of the ego, ensuring the seeker slides back down to the bottom of the Tree of Life.

Tyranny

When the benevolent compassion of the wise ruler, as expressed by Chesed, becomes abused by the desire to dominate, tyranny follows. Tyranny is the refusal of the ruler to recognise that she or he is also a servant.

Colours associated with Chesed

King Scale: Deep Violet

The deep violet of Chesed combines the blue of Chokmah and the crimson of Binah, demonstrating the first manifestation of the divine energies below the Abyss. Also violet is widely associated with royalty and episcopal matters.

Queen Scale: Blue

The blue of the sky (air) and Jupiter is here used to demonstrate the elemental and planetary attributions of Chesed.

Emperor Scale: Deep Purple

Deep purple is formed by uniting the deep violet of the King Scale with the blue of the Queen Scale, again demonstrating the principles of royalty and religion.

Empress Scale: Deep Azure, flecked Yellow

The deep azure flecked yellow recalls the colouring of lapis lazuli, the stone of Chesed. It also indicates the sky as the stars in the firmament.

Magickal Formula: IHVH

Tetragrammaton, the unpronounceable name of God, is assigned here as the magickal formula, and with very good reasons. Firstly it is the fourfold name, corresponding to the number of the Sephira. Secondly Chesed is the first Sephira below the abyss, representing the highest that man can aspire whilst in physical form, so this formula is one of transformation, of moving beyond the physical.

It is said that if IHVH is correctly pronounced it will destroy the universe, but this could be interpreted as destroying the universe of the adept, i.e. moving him or her beyond the physical into the abyss and on towards godhead. Also

Chesed is referred to as containing "all the holy powers", and everything is contained within the Tetragrammaton (see the earlier chapter on the *Unpronounceable Name of God*).

Magickal Image of Chesed

A mighty crowned and throned king
This image represents the height of achievement below the Abyss – rulership. It is also a classic Jupiterian image, as the Ruler of the Gods.

Human Body

Left arm and hand
The left side of the body is associated with the "passive" qualities of compassion and benevolence of Jupiter in contrast to the dynamism and "active" nature of Mars on the right side.

Numbers associated with Chesed

As the fourth Sephira, 4 is the number of Chesed. Four is a number of stability, being 2². It represents solidness, and this is the physicality of form beginning to manifest below the abyss.

The mystic number of Chesed is 10, i.e. $\Sigma(1-4)$. 10 is also a number of solidness, representing the physicality of Malkuth. This emphasises that all the spiritual impulses in Chesed find their expression in the physicality of Malkuth, if we have eyes to see.

Chesed itself adds to 72. 72 is a highly significant number, as it is associated with the Shemhamforash, the 72-fold name of God which gives the name of 72 angels. The Shemhamforash is seen as an expansion of IHVH, which is the magickal formula of Chesed.

Tarot

The four Fours.

Animals associated with Chesed

Eagle
The eagle is classically associated with Jupiter as king of the birds.

Horse
The horse has airy associations due to its speed, and is hence linked to Jupiter. Also in the ancient world horses were status symbols, demonstrating the power and importance of the rider.

Pegasus
As a combination of the horse and the wings of air, the pegasus expresses the energy of Chesed as the highest aspect of air.

Unicorn
The unicorn is a symbol of purity, demonstrating the perfection of the self needed to move beyond Chesed.

Minerals associated with Chesed

Lapis Lazuli
A classically Jupiterian stone, Lapis Lazuli also symbolises the vault of heaven.

Sapphire
By its colour and associations with purity and mystical states, sapphire is distinctly Jupiterian.

Sodalite
Sodalite is Jupiterian by its blue colouring and associations with serenity.

Tin
Tin is the planetary metal of Jupiter.

Turquoise
As the "Horseman's Stone" and by its colour, turquoise is a Jupiterian stone.

Plants associated with Chesed

Shamrock
The four leaves of shamrock make its symbolism Jupiterian, as does the association with luck.

St John's Wort
Due to its use in purification and exorcism, St John's Wort is associated with Jupiter.

Scents associated with Chesed

Cedar
Cedar is traditionally one of the most religious of scents, used both as an incense and to make temple furniture. The scent of cedar inspires the mind to the purity of purpose demanded by Chesed.

Hyssop
Another traditional religious herb, hyssop is a fumigatory herb used for exorcism. It reminds us that purification is always important, hence its use in the temples to keep away negativity.

Symbols & Tools associated with Chesed

Crook
Symbolising the role of the ruler as the "shepherd" of his people, both spiritual and material.

Equal-armed Cross
The balance within the cross, and the four arms, both make it an appropriate symbol of Chesed.

Orb
The orb symbolises the world, and is another emblem of authority and rulership.

Pyramid
By its four sides and majesty the pyramid is a symbol of Chesed. Also it hints at the City of Pyramids in Binah.

Sceptre
Another symbol of rulership, and also benevolence, as the sceptre is a symbolic tool and not a practical one.

Tetrahedron
As the balanced four-sided figure the tetrahedron embodies Chesed.

Wand
The wand represents the will of the magickian harmonised with the universe, so it has no edge or need to command, merely to direct.

Deities associated with Chesed

Celtic
— *Taranis* as the "Thunderer", God of Storms.

Egyptian
— *Amun* as the Ruler of the Gods

Greek
— *Themis* as Goddess of Justice.
— *Zeus* as the Ruler of the Gods.

Roman
— *Jupiter* as the Ruler of the Gods.
— *Justitia* as the Goddess of Justice.

Sumerian
— *An* as the Sky God.

Meditations & Exercises

Heaven

Meditate on the symbol for Jupiter, an equal-armed cross with a leftward facing crescent attached to the top of the left-hand arm of the cross, and see what ideas and images come to you.

Magickal Formula

Intone the formula of IHVH (Yah-veh) for a few minutes as a mantra and record your impressions.

Magickal Image

Meditate on the Magickal Image of a mighty throned king. Vary the age of the king and see what a difference this makes to your meditations.

Tarot

Lay out the four Fours in an equal-armed cross. Put the 4 of Disks at the top and the 4 of Wands at the bottom, the 4 of Cups on the left and the 4 of Swords at the right. Contemplate the images and see what inspiration arises.

Blue Sapphire Meditation

For this meditation (derived from a traditional Kabbalistic meditation) you need a piece of sapphire, or another pure blue stone that is a single shade of blue. Hold the crystal in your hand and say:

The sapphire[92] is blue;
The blue is the colour of the sea;
The sea is the colour of the sky;
And the sky is the colour of the Throne of Glory.

Visualise the sea for a couple of minutes, and then visualise the sky for a similar time. Then hold the crystal to your brow, to the position of the third eye, and focus on opening your psychic senses, and try to visualise the sapphire throne of God. If you can see this then see a mighty throned king on the throne. Practice this meditation to help develop your psychic sensitivity.

Chesed Temple - Visualisation

The Chesed temple is circular and 15m in diameter. The walls are of white marble and extend up to a height of 3m. From here they become a domed hemi-spherical ceiling, which is a deep azure blue flecked with gold (lapis lazuli). The floor of the temple is made of lapis lazuli. In the centre of the temple there is a sapphire double-cube altar, 1m in height and 0.5m square on the top. On the top of the altar is a small tin bowl, in which burns an undying blue flame, the flame of spirit.

In the north are two pillars, of 1m diameter each, 2m apart, rising from the floor to the ceiling, these pillars are 1m in from the wall. The left pillar is black and made of onyx, the right pillar is white and made of marble. In the wall between them (in the North) is visible a normal size doorframe. Three more such doorframes are visible in the south, southwest and west.

You hear a bell and see Tzadkiel standing before you. He is about 3m tall, with a very beautiful face, and a large pair of wings on his back. He wears a sapphire blue tunic and bears a dagger in his left hand. He steps to one side and you see a throne has appeared behind him.

The throne is carved from a single piece of lapis lazuli, and is deep blue with gold flecks running through it. Tzadkiel gestures to the throne and you go and sit in it. As you sit there you feel a tremendous sense of peace, and visions of successes you have achieved and good deeds you have performed fill your mind. You realise that your uniqueness contributes to the ongoing flow of life that you are part of.

A blue glow emanates from the throne and surrounds you, bringing a sense of love and healing with it, and filling your aura with the peace and reflection of Chesed. You enjoy this sensation for a while, and then Tzadkiel gestures that you should stand again. You do so and the throne disappears. You realise it is now time to leave the temple so you thank Tzadkiel and bow to him.

---

[92] *Or name of other crystal if using a different type.*

You then turn to the south to go through the doorway to the temple of Hod, where you pause for a short while to contemplate your experiences, and then continue down to the temple of Malkuth and back to the mundane world.

35. DAATH (DaaTh) - Knowledge

Daath (pronounced *Da-art*) is the interface between the Supernal Triad and the lower Tree. The dew of Kether passes through Daath to fertilise the rest of the Tree, as is recorded in Proverbs 3:20, *"By his knowledge the depths are broken up, and the clouds drop down the dew."*

Daath is considered to be the first child of Chokmah and Binah, which did not come to manifestation. It is a paradox, being the *"Sephira that isn't"*. The Sepher Yetzirah makes it very clear that Daath is not a Sephira – *"Ten Sephiroth of Nothingness, ten and not nine, ten and not eleven"*.[93]

Some modern writers claim that Daath is a relatively new concept, however references to Daath are found throughout the important texts, such as the Torah and magickal works such as *Sepher Raziel Hemelach* (*The Book of the Angel Raziel*). Indeed the latter work refers to Daath in the first paragraph of its first book.[94]

As a result Daath can be seen in some respects like a Zen koan. Trying to make sense of Daath unless one is experiencing Daath is nonsensical. The only way to really appreciate Daath is from direct experience.

Daath is also intimately connected with the legend of the Fall, for it is the *"Tree of Knowledge (Daath) of Good and Evil"* which Eve and Adam eat the fruit of. Daath then becomes the bridge between the perfection of the Supernal Triad, and the lower Tree, which strives for the lost perfection (of Eden).

Divine Name: Ruach ha Qadosh

This name means *"Spirit of Holiness"* and is often used in connection with the transmission of the divine energy and purpose from Kether, sometimes as the ability to prophesy. The attribution of this name to Daath is one from Kabbalah, as modern Qabalah does not make such an attribution. Modern sources mostly repeat the Divine Name of Binah (IHVH Elohim), which is lazy and not entirely appropriate.

---

[93] *Sepher Yetzirah 1:4.*
[94] *"It is decreed, the holy and pure are filled with secret wisdom [Chokmah]. The knowledge [Daath] is the result of understanding [Binah]." Part 1, Sepher Hamelbosh (Book of the Vestment).*

The name comes from Exodus 31:3 and refers to the fulfillment of sanctity to work in the Tabernacle: "*And I have filled him with the Spirit of Holiness, in wisdom, and in understanding, and in knowledge*". The whole of the Knowledge Triad is referred to in this line – wisdom (Chokmah), understanding (Binah) and knowledge (Daath). To utter the holy name (Tetragrammaton) the throat and indeed whole being would have to be pure and the rites known, hence this Divine Name is highly appropriate for Daath.

Archangel: Mesukiel (MSKIAL) / the Four Archangels

Different sources make different suggestions about the attributions for Daath. Some sources suggest Mesukiel, whose name means "*The Veiler of God*", whereas other modern sources give Raphael, Michael, Gabriel and Uriel as guardians of this liminal point.

Mesukiel should be seen in a similar form to the other Archangels – around 3m tall, with large wings on his back (though the wings are black) and a grey-white tunic. His face is very beautiful, but is difficult to see clearly, as if there is a translucent veil in front of it.

Order of Angels

There is not an order of Angels assigned to Daath.

Heaven

Some attribute the planet Uranus to Daath, as the planet of revolution and breaking down of old form. Sirius is also suggested by some modern writers, as the brightest and most significant star in the heavens.

Qliphoth: Choronzon (ChVRVNZVN)

Choronzon is another name for Satan, i.e. the adversary. This is not the devil in the modern Christian sense of the word, but rather the entity that will seek to confound you and destroy the development that you have achieved. Choronzon is not evil, he is simply the ultimate force of reduction, which will destroy that which has not been made strong enough through persistence and strong foundations.

Abaddon ("*the Destroyer*") as the angel of the bottomless pit (Revelations 9:11) could also be attributed here. In this context Daath is interpreted as the bottomless pit, and thus Abaddon is the necessary destruction of physicality and anything which holds the pure spirit back from ascending higher up the Tree.

Titles of Daath

Science
Science seeks to bring truth through understanding, and hence the attribution of this title to Daath.

The Bridal Chamber
As the place of union of the Father and Mother (Chokmah and Binah), and also of the bride and groom (Malkuth and Tiphereth).

The Hidden or Invisible Sephira
Daath's influence is definite and can be felt, but it is not a complete Sephira as we understand them. For this reason it is the Hidden Sephira or Invisible Sephira, detectable more by its effects.

The Midnight Sun
Many myths (like the Egyptian) have the idea of the sun passing through the underworld, being lost to human sight during the hours of darkness. At such times it is referred to as the Black Sun or the midnight sun. Hence Daath is the midnight sun, as it is concerned with the transmission of energy between the divine source (Kether) and the sun (Tiphereth) in the darkness (Daath).

The Mystical Sephira
The energy of Daath is about transformation, leaving behind the last flaws and becoming pure energy, hence it is the Mystical Sephira.

The Sephira that is not
The *Sepher Yetzirah* is very clear about the fact that there are ten Sephiroth. So although in some respects Daath is treated as a Sephira, it is also not one. It is like a Zen koan!

The Upper Room
Daath is known as the Upper Room because it is the highest point on the Tree of Life that can be entered by humans.

Experiences of Daath

Dark Night of the Soul
This is the sense of futility and desperation that fills the seeker, blotting out the light of illumination and hope and replacing it with the darkness of failure. Mystics have recorded their experiences of this state, which can actually strike at any time, not just in Daath. The Dark Night of the Soul is an extreme challenge to all you have learned and experienced, to overcome the negative emotional state and journey on through to the illuminating light of the radiant dawn, trusting in your purpose and not being dragged down.

Vision across the Abyss

The Abyss is the place of transformation. As Nietzsche said, *"And when you stare persistently into the Abyss, the Abyss also stares into you."* The vision across the abyss gives the enticement to leave behind the physicality of form, to experience the transformation it brings.

Virtues of Daath

Confidence
By the time you have climbed high enough up the Tree of Life to jump into the Abyss, one virtue you will have developed is confidence!

Detachment
Daath also brings about a detachment from the physicality of form, as it is the bridge between the pure force of the Supernal Triad with the manifesting form of the lower Tree.

Vices of Daath

Cowardice
Like a horse that stops at a hedge and refuses to continue, so Cowardice can rear its head and try to entice the seeker to remain in the pleasures of the flesh, rather than evolve higher up the Tree. This is a subtle and insidious form of cowardice that can strike as swiftly as a venomous snake.

Doubt
Another sudden assailant at the Abyss is doubt. Suddenly any insecurities that have not been resolved lower down the Tree suddenly become magnified and seize hold of the seeker, bringing doubt and loss of confidence.

Hubris
Whilst pride in your achievements is not a bad thing, when it becomes outright hubris it is a problem. This suggests an excess of Geburic force, making the seeker feel over-proud and not allowing the detachment needed to let go of the last ties to the physical.

Isolation
Whilst preparing to jump into the Abyss it is very easy to isolate yourself in the belief that it will make it easier. This is not the case, as you need to have fully appreciated people and things to really be able to let go of them. Simple isolation is a means of allowing ego to creep in, and self-delusion shines into the seeker's spirit from the Yesod-Daath Mirror.

Colours associated with Daath

King Scale: Lavender
Lavender as the emanation of the energy of Uranus, expressed through Daath.

Queen Scale: Grey-White
The Grey of Chokmah is tinged with the White of Kether, showing the transmission of energy via the Pillar of Mercy.

Emperor Scale: Pure Violet
This attribution refers to the Yesod-Daath mirror. The dark purple of Yesod is reflected via Tiphereth into Daath, and then lightened by the white brilliance of Kether into Daath from above.

Empress Scale: Grey, flecked Gold
The grey of Binah is flecked with the gold of Tiphereth, indicating the flow of energy from the Mother to the Son.

Magickal Formula: AUMGN

As the sound of the universe, expressing the creative divine, Aumgn (or Om as it is written in brief) is appropriate to Daath, which corresponds to the throat and is the gateway between the divine supernal triad and the rest of the Tree.

Silence
The formula of silence is the one used to overcome the guardian of the Abyss, Choronzon. Choronzon causes the seeker to doubt everything, and befuddles with a seamless blend of lies and truth, so the only defence against this is to ignore him and not interact, thereby robbing him of his power. Thus this silence is not merely that of not speaking, but also of a still mind untroubled by internal dialogue. By this point on the Tree the seeker should be able to shut off the internal dialogue at will, and needs to do this at Daath.

Magickal Image

There is no magickal image associated with Daath.

Human Body

Throat
The throat is the place of creation, in the sense of uttering the sacred words and names. Also the absence of sound (silence) is the formula for overcoming Choronzon.

Numbers associated with Daath

Daath is sometimes considered the eleventh Sephira on the Tree, so if it has a number it is 11.

The mystic number of Daath would thus be 66, or $\Sigma(1\text{-}11)$. The Divine Name ALHIK (referring to Deuteronomy 4:24, "*The Lord thy God is a consuming fire*") also adds to 66. This appropriate name gives a measure of the process of refinement and transcendence called for to pass through Daath.

Daath itself adds to 474, the same as the plural of *wisdom* (ChKMVTh), indicating the diverse nature of Daath, refracting the higher energies from above into rays and fragments to assail and test the seeker.

Tarot

No cards are specifically attributed to Daath.

Animals associated with Daath

No specific animals are attributed to Daath. However the images of the bizarre fish and creatures that live in very deep seas come to mind as being appropriate symbolic representations for Daath.

Minerals associated with Daath

Rainbow Quartz
The prismatic effect of rainbow quartz, displaying all the colours within the colourless medium of quartz is indicative of Daath.

Plants associated with Daath

Pennyroyal
This is associated with Daath due to its use as an abortificant, linking it as the aborted child.

Scents associated with Daath

An absence of smell would be more appropriate for Daath, as it is a place of leaving the traces of the physical behind.

Symbols & Tools associated with Daath

Prism
The prism takes white light (Kether) and refracts it into the seven colours of the rainbow (the seven Sephiroth below the Abyss).

Web
The web indicates the interconnectedness of diverse points, making a form of perfection out of diversity, that is peculiarly appropriate to Daath.

Deities associated with Daath

Egyptian
— *Apep* the chaos serpent, as challenging the sun god Re (Tiphereth).
— *Heka* as Lord of Ka's (souls) and being the primal force of magick.
— *Khephri* as the beetle pushing the sun in a dung ball through the blackness.
— *Serket* the scorpion goddess, as *"she who causes the throat to breathe"*.
— *Set* as a deity of chaos.

Greek
— *Erebus* as the Primordial Darkness fathering Hypnos (Sleep) and Thanatos (Death).
— *Prometheus* as Benefactor of mankind, stealing the fire from heaven.

Roman
— *Janus* as looking down to the physical and up to the ethereal.

Sumerian
— *Tiamat* as the Goddess of the Primal Waters of Chaos.

36. BINAH (BINH) - Understanding

"The Third Intelligence is called the Sanctifying Intelligence, the Foundation of Primordial Wisdom; it is also called the Creator of Faith, and its roots are in Amen. It is the parent of faith, whence faith emanates."[95]

Binah (pronounced *Bee-nah*) is the Sephira of Saturn. It is also the Sephira of the Great Mother, the Divine Feminine. This is expressed in Proverbs 2:3, *"For you shall call Understanding (Binah) a Mother."* Binah is located at the head of the Pillar of Severity and completes the Supernal Triad.

Until the eighteenth century Saturn was perceived as being the outer planet, and as such represented a boundary to man. Beyond Saturn was the vastness of the infinite, which is why Binah is seen as the beginnings of form. Saturn marked the boundary, the moment of transition between force and form.

There is a saying in modern science that *"evolution occurs at the boundaries"*, and from a magickal perspective we can see a lot of sense in this. The coastline where the sea and the land meet, or hilltops where air and earth meet are classic examples of places perceived as being imbued with force and good natural spots for performing magick.

However from a more individual perspective, we can say that evolution takes place at the boundaries of our consciousness. We need to discover our boundaries, our limits, before we can transcend them and take another step towards perfection.

Although Binah may be seen as being unattainable as a continuous state of being in human form, being representative of the beginning of a pure energy state, nevertheless we can draw inspiration from the deep panoramic understanding that Binah has to offer. This is why Binah is also known as the *"City of Pyramids"*. Although pyramids were places to preserve the dead, they also provide a panoramic view from the top, and the top can only be reached by a long ascent from a very large base.

Saturn used to be associated with death, as the end of existence. In the sense of the loss of physical form at the Abyss to continue the journey up the

---

[95] *The Thirty-Two Paths of Wisdom - Joannes Rittangelius.*

Tree to Binah, in one sense this is true. However it is not death of the pure soul, rather it is the lesser death of form, of the body.

Binah is described as having *"its roots in Amen"* because this is a title of Kether, and it reminds us that Binah is the beginning of the roots of Kether, the first flowering into form of the divine impetus which sustains the whole Tree.

Binah is one of the great keys to the Tree of Life. The more you meditate on the symbolism of Binah, the more you may find yourself able to manipulate your own life and energies in a more positive manner, as you become more aware of the greater web of life around you.

Divine Name: Yahveh Elohim (IHVH ALHIM)

This name translates as *"Lord Gods"*. The multiplicity of the *Parzufim* ("faces") as expressions of the divine impetus in Elohim is made clear by being united with the ultimate force of Tetragrammaton. This formula encapsulates the power of Binah as the place of the beginning of form, and as such, the womb of creation, being the head of the Black Pillar. All of the Divine Names on this pillar contain the name Elohim, indicating the multiplicity of the nature of form.

Archangel: Tzaphkiel (TzPhKIAL)

Tzaphkiel means *"Beholder of God"*. He is also known as Jophiel, whose name means *"Beauty of God"*. Tzaphkiel is one of the seven Archangels who stand in the presence of God. He is known as the Angel of Paradise because of his role in the Garden of Eden, and in modern times is the patron of all those who fight pollution and love and protect nature.

He is also the patron of artists, bringing illumination and inspiration to those who seek to create beauty in the world. He is usually seen as a beautiful male angel standing about 3m tall, wearing a black tunic, with white wings, and bearing a flaming sword in his right hand.

He is the first angel mentioned in the Bible, though not by name, being the guardian of the Tree of Life, and it was he who drove Adam and Eve from the Garden of Eden after they had eaten the forbidden apple, and bars the return of man, standing at the gates bearing the flaming sword. Tzaphkiel is one of the chiefs of the choirs of the Cherubim, who are assigned the task of watching the four gates to Eden. He is also a Prince of the Angelic Order of Thrones. Tzaphkiel is said in Jewish lore to be especially good friends with Metatron, the archangel of Kether.

Order of Angels: Aralim (ARALIM)

Aralim means the *"Strong and Mighty Ones"*. They are referred to in medieval Grimoires as the Order of Thrones. In appearance the Aralim stand about 2m tall, with beautiful though somewhat severe faces. They wear black tunics and gold crowns. They have white wings on their backs, and rainbows play about them at all times.

Heaven: Shabathai (ShBThAI)

Shabathai means *"Saturn"*, and this is the first planetary attribution on the Tree of Life. Saturn is the giver of form, which can be seen as both restriction of energy into the physical, and the means of establishing creation, i.e. as the womb of creation.

Qliphoth: Satariel (SAThARIAL)

Satariel means *"Hiding"*. This is in opposition to the energy of Binah as being given form and made manifest. So everything that should become clear with the understanding of Binah is hidden and confused.

Titles of Binah

Bright Fertile Mother (Aima)
This title refers to Binah as the Sephira of the Divine Feminine, balancing the Masculine energy of Chokmah that she carries within (as the Yod).

Dark Sterile Mother (Ama)
This title indicates Binah as the Sephira of the Divine Feminine without the fertilising energy of Chokmah.

Great Sea (Marah)
The waters of the womb have often been linked to the primal waters of creation, e.g. in Egyptian myth, and this is a similar such attribution to Binah as the birthplace of form.

Jerusalem Above
This title refers to the Greater Shekinah, as the idealised holy place, in contrast to the Lesser or Exiled Shekinah in Malkuth.

Throne (Khorsiya)
This title demonstrates the qualities of Binah as the lowest Sephira of the World of Briah, supporting the energies of the other Supernal Sephiroth above it, as this world is known as the Throne of God from visions such as those of the Merkavah tradition.

Upper Mother
This is another title that contrasts Binah with Malkuth, again emphasising the link between these two Sephiroth.

Experience of Binah

Vision of Sorrow
The Buddhist experience of all as sorrow is particularly appropriate at Binah, as it is the ultimate crossroads between force and form. As both states will always strive for the other, sorrow is the inevitable consequence until transcendence is achieved.

Virtue of Binah

Silence
This refers to the silence of the mind that has shut off its internal dialogue, not simply the absence of speech. The silence of speech of Malkuth has reached its highest aspect in Binah as the silence of mind.

Vice of Binah

Avarice
This is the avarice or greed for that which a person does not have, referring to an absence of balance – the unfertilised Ama.

Colours associated with Binah

King Scale: Crimson
Crimson as the colour of rich oxygenated blood indicates the menstruum of the fertile woman, indicating the feminine nature of Binah.

Queen Scale: Black
The black indicates the absorption of all colours, showing the Saturnian nature of Binah as the devourer of time. Also black as the colour of mourning indicated by the Vision of Sorrow.

Emperor Scale: Dark Brown
The Saturnian dark brown is formed by adding the crimson of the King Scale to the black of the Queen Scale.

Empress Scale: Grey, flecked Pink
The grey of Chokmah indicates its fertilising influence on Binah, expressed through the flecks of pink, which hint at Tiphereth, the child of their union.

Magickal Formula: IAO

IAO was a derivative of Tetragrammaton (IHVH), making it a pronounceable word that could be used in magickal work. In this way the uncontrollable force of Tetragrammaton (and Chokmah) is given form (Binah), enabling it to be used as a formula of transformation and growth.

Magickal Image of Binah

A Mature Woman, A Matron
This image classically represents the feminine energy of Binah, and particularly the Shekinah.

Human Body

The Right side of the Face
The image of God was usually shown in profile, displaying only the right side of the face, as the full face with both eyes open was thought to destroy the universe. The right side is the side where the glimpse of God, i.e. the form of Binah, can occur.

Numbers associated with Binah

Binah is the third Sephira of the Tree, and hence its number is 3. The impetus of the line as direction, the energy of Chokmah, is given form in the triangle, the first manifestation of solidity through the creation of a plane. Although 2-dimensional the transition is clearly indicated by the figure, hence its use as the place of manifestation.

The mystical number of Binah is 6, or $\Sigma(1-3)$. As the number of Tiphereth is 6, we can also see a reference to the child as the product of the mother. In one sense Tiphereth represents the child born from Binah (after her fertilisation by Chokmah).

Binah itself adds to 67, which is the same as the letter *Zain* spelt in full. Zain is attributed to the 17th path, which leads from Binah to Tiphereth, and is hence particularly appropriate. Zain means sword, and represents the sword of intent, which is the will of Tiphereth guided by the understanding of Binah.

Tarot

The four Threes.

Animals associated with Binah

Bee
The bee as a symbol of the soul and the great goddess is appropriate to Binah as a symbol of the Neshamah. Also of course a Queen bee rules the hive.

Woman
Some sources (e.g. Crowley) give woman as appropriate to Binah as the ultimate representation of the feminine.

Minerals associated with Binah

Coral
By its creation as the external form of the polyp, and also the association of Binah with the ocean.

Jet
Jet is traditionally a stone of mourning, and also formed from fossilized wood, showing a transformation of form, giving the symbolism of Binah.

Lead
As the planetary metal of Saturn.

Obsidian
As a symbol of life and death obsidian is Saturnian, and also by its black colouring indicating the colour of Binah in the Queen Scale. Also obsidian may be flecked with brown indicating the colour of Binah in the Emperor Scale, or white or grey, recalling the influx of energy emanating from Kether and Chokmah.

Smoky Quartz
The brown of Binah in the Emperor Scale is recalled by the colouring of smoky quartz.

Star Ruby
This gem is attributed here as the colour of Binah in the King Scale, with the star of Chokmah contained within it. It is also the highest aspect of the Geburic ruby, the pinnacle of the Pillar of Severity.

Plants associated with Binah

Cypress
Cypress is a traditionally Saturnian tree and is hence appropriate here.

Lotus
The lotus represents the beauty of the Shekinah, rising from the waters (Binah) and is a classical symbol of feminine energy.

Opium Poppy
The bright red of the poppy flowers represents the colour of Binah in the King Scale, and hints at the dark power within.

Scents associated with Binah

Civet
As musk is a scent of male attraction, so civet is produced by the female civet cat to attract males, and is hence appropriate to Binah.

Myrrh
Myrrh is associated with sorrow, hence its association with the vision of sorrow.

Symbols & Tools associated with Binah

Scythe
The scythe reaps the harvest and is traditionally Saturnian as the shift between states.

Sickle
The sickle harvests plants for their medicinal and magickal qualities to be used in the sacred rites, hence its association here, linking form with change.

Triangle
The triangle is used to constrain and give form to spirits, and so is entirely appropriate to Binah as the beginnings of form. Also the triangle has three sides, the number of Binah.

Yoni
As the ultimate symbol of the feminine, and symbolically depicted by the triangle of manifestation. Likewise the womb as the source of creation is appropriate.

Deities associated with Binah

Celtic
— *The Cailleach* as the Sterile Mother aspect of the Goddess.
— *Danu /Anu / Don* as Mother of the Gods and Goddess of Wisdom.

Egyptian
— *Heket* as the divine midwife at the primeval creation.
— *Isis* as the Mother Goddess, and by her name meaning throne.
— *Mut* as the wife of Amun and Primal Mother.
— *Neith* as the Primal Goddess who gives birth to Re and Apep.
— *Nephthys* as the Dark Fertile Mother.
— *Sia* as perception, forming a triad with Hu and Re.
— *Tefnut* as the Goddess of the waters and Eye of Re.

Greek
— *Cybele* as the Dark Mother who wields the sickle.
— *Hera* as the Queen of the Gods.
— *Rhea* as the partner of Kronos and mother of the Titans.
— *Tethys* as the Sea Goddess embodying the Great Sea (Marah).

Roman
— *Fortuna* as Goddess of Fate.
— *Juno* as the Queen of the Gods.

Sumerian
— *Nammu* as goddess of the watery deep.

Meditations & Exercises

Heaven

Meditate on the symbol for Saturn, of the equal-armed cross connected to a crescent pointing horns down and see what images you get.

Magickal Formula

Intone the formula of IAO (Ee-ay-o) for a few minutes as a mantra and record your impressions.

Magickal Image

Meditate on the Magickal Image of a mature woman. Try varying the age of the woman, and the richness of her garments, and see what difference this makes.

Tarot

Lay out the four Threes in an equal-armed cross. Put the 3 of Disks at the top and the 3 of Wands at the bottom, the 3 of Cups on the left and the 3 of Swords at the right. Contemplate the images and see what inspiration arises.

Visualisation – The City of Pyramids

You are standing in an endless desert. Beneath you the sand is white, tiny pieces of quartz eroded by the passing of untold millennia. Above you the stars fill the black sky. You gaze up at the stars, seeing the millions of silver specks of light. As you continue to stare you realise that they are not all silver, and start to make out other colours, like blue and red, amongst the silver.

A cold wind blows, chilling your body to the bones, and you are distracted from your star-gazing. You look around you, at the rolling dunes that stretch on to the horizon in every direction. Then you notice something in the distance, off to your left. At the very edge of your vision you see something rising out from the endless sands. It is only a tiny speck on the horizon and you decide to find out what it is. You start walking, as flying and other magickal means of travel do not work here in this desert.

You walk for what seems like hours, always keeping the speck on the horizon in the centre of your field of vision. Eventually you have walked for miles, and you can make out the speck a little bit more clearly now. You realise it is a whole series of pyramids. They are massive, reaching hundreds of metres from the floor, and made entirely of black stone. As you stare at these mammoth constructions, brilliant white light discharges from their peaks, and shoots off into space.

You cannot see if there is anything living amongst the pyramids for they are too far away, but you can see that there is a whole city of pyramids, stretching off behind the front ones. You realise that this city is of the dead and the living. The dead are the physical forms left behind by the living spirits, who have transcended the flesh and become beings of pure energy. As you realise this, the white mist rolls in on the cold desert winds and surrounds you.

37. CHOKMAH (ChKMH) - Wisdom

"The Second Path is called the Illuminating Intelligence. It is the Crown of Creation, the Splendour of Unity, equalling it. It is exalted above every head, and is named by Qabalists the Second Glory."[96]

Chokmah (pronounced *Hok-mah*) is traditionally the Sephira of the fixed stars, in more recent times often attributed to Neptune. It is the place where the divine essence begins to be expressed. This is made clear in Proverbs 4:7 *"The beginning is Wisdom: Acquire Wisdom."*

Chokmah is the first emanation from Kether, and begins the process of differentiation, bringing duality onto the Tree of Life. Chokmah is considered the masculine impulse, as Binah is the feminine, both emanating from the androgynous energy of Kether. It is situated at the head of the Pillar of Mercy.

The outer limits of our perception are marked by the stars, which represent Chokmah. Chokmah is the creative impulse of the divine will, and as such mirrors that intent of the will in us as humans. This is well expressed in The Book of the Law, in the lines *"Every man and every woman is a star."* (AL I.3). We all have the divine spark within us, which is symbolically represented by the stars in the heavens.

On a physical level our bodies are made of atoms and molecules that may once have been parts of stars. So the interconnectedness of everything in the universe, all energy, is perfectly expressed in this statement. It also encapsulates our aspirations to fulfill our potential and realise the divine spark within us more fully into manifestation.

This is why Chokmah is the *"Illuminating Intelligence"*, because it shines light into every area of life and the universe. By the light of Chokmah, the pure will permits the template of creation to be unfolded, the perfection and truth of the divine becomes visible to all.

It is the *"Crown of Creation"* because the energy of Kether has begun its journey to manifestation, and this is expressed in the vastness of the stars, which we can see crowning the earth each night and reminding us of our connection to the rest of the universe.

---

[96] *The Thirty-Two Paths of Wisdom - Joannes Rittangelius.*

Divine Name: Jahveh (IHVH) or Yah (IH)

The unpronounceable name of Tetragrammaton that is the creative utterance of God is the beginning of the expression of his wisdom and creativity. It is significant that the paths on this pillar (the 16th and 21st) have the letters attributed to them whose total is 26 (Vav:6 + Kaph:20), the same as IHVH. We may also note that the four letters may be permuted into twelve combinations, echoing the twelve signs of the Zodiac, which is attributed to Chokmah. For more on this Divine Name see the earlier chapter *The Unpronounceable Name*.

Yah is also sometimes given as the divine name of Chokmah. This name is also known as the "*Inner Chamber*", being comprised of the first two letters of Tetragrammaton. It adds to 15, but when the letters are spelt in full it adds to 30, showing a doubling effect, as can be seen by moving from 1 (Kether) to 2 (Chokmah). 15 is also the total for Hod, the eighth Sephira, demonstrating the link between these two Sephiroth, for Hod (8) is the expansion of Chokmah (2) through Chesed (4), the scale of two increasing.

Archangel: Raziel (RTzIAL)

Raziel means "*Herald of God*". As the archangel associated with wisdom (Chokmah), we can see why Raziel is given as one of the two possible Archangels who transmitted knowledge of the Kabbalah to Adam.

Raziel is usually seen standing about 3m tall, with a beautiful face, wearing a grey tunic and sandals. Stars seem to twinkle and shine about his head as he moves, like an ever-changing diadem of constellations.

Order of Angels: Auphanim (AVPHNIM)

Auphanim means "*Wheels*". The Wheels are described in Ezekiel 1:15-18, as being like a huge wheel, of beryl colour (i.e. aquamarine), with many eyes on the rims of the wheel. In medieval Grimoires they are called the Kerubim.

Heaven: Masloth (MSLVTh)

Masloth means "*The Zodiac*" or "*Fixed Stars*". The Fixed stars represented the ultimate to man, the absolute boundary of his perception. The first swirlings of Kether are removed by time and space and are unknowable, but the wisdom of Chokmah can be aspired to.

In modern magick Neptune is sometimes attributed to Chokmah, probably due to the Kabbalistic attribution of the Mother letter Mem, corresponding to water, to Chokmah.

Qliphoth: Ghagiel (AaVGIAL)

Ghagiel means *"Hinderers"*. The Ghagiel serve to hinder the free flow of energy from Chokmah to further down the Tree of Life.

Titles of Chokmah

Ab/Abba
Meaning Father, referring to Chokmah's function as the masculine principle.

First-born of Elohim
This title refers to Chokmah as the first emanation of Kether.

Inner Chamber
This title refers to the divine Name of Chokmah, Yah, as the first two letters of Tetragrammaton or the alternative divine name.

Only Begotten Son
As the only Sephira emanating directly from Kether. Although Chokmah is considered to be the father (Ab), in relation to Kether it is the son, showing the way relativity is always a factor on the Tree.

Power of Tetragrammaton
From the attribution of IHVH as the Divine Name of Chokmah, also indicating the pure will of Atziluth, which is attributed to Chokmah.

Power of Yetzirah
The creative energy of Chokmah as the Father is reflected in the Son, Tiphereth, which is the centre of the Lesser Countenance, expressing the World of Yetzirah.

Primordial Torah
This is the Torah that existed before manifestation, the wisdom (in potential) waiting to be revealed.

Revelation
As the first knowable aspect of the Divine, and the beginning of the unfolding of creation.

Yod of Tetragrammaton
This title is straight from the attribution of the first letter of the four-fold name to Chokmah.

Experiences of Chokmah

Tetragrammaton
The correct pronunciation of this name is said to destroy the universe. Hence the experience of Tetragrammaton can be likened to the final destruction of individuality, preparing the soul for re-union with the ultimate divine.

The Vision of God face to face
This experience is the final vision or "revelation" of the ultimate before reunion with it. This is often described in spiritual traditions as an experience that you cannot survive, and in some respects this is true. Language can be deceptive though, and it should be made clear that the destruction referred to is that of self before becoming part of the unified and eternal all.

Virtue of Chokmah

Devotion
This represents the final devotion, to the ultimate divine, the unified and eternal all that represents everything. The devotion described is the devotion to perfection, which overcomes any other priorities.

Vice of Chokmah

No vices can be associated with this level of perfection.

Colours associated with Chokmah

King Scale: Pure soft Blue
The pure soft blue represents the panorama of the heavens (i.e. the stellar firmament) as perceived through the sky.

Queen Scale: Grey
The grey colour indicates the transmission of energy through the Supernal Triad – from the white brilliance of Kether to the blackness of Binah.

Emperor Scale: Iridescent pearl-grey
The iridescent pearl-grey is formed by adding the pure soft blue of the King Scale to the grey of the Queen Scale. Also this colour is that of Labradorite, the stone of Chokmah.

Empress Scale: White, flecked with Red, Blue & Yellow
The creative energy is finding its first expression, hence the three primary colours of red, blue and yellow fleck the white potential symbolising Kether.

Magickal Formula: IH

Yah (IH) is known as the Inner Chamber, for it is the first two letters of Tetragrammaton, containing the first and highest point, which is the Yod.

Magickal Image

A bearded male figure

As the image of Binah indicates the divine feminine, so this image represents the divine masculine, mature and able to demonstrate this (through the beard).

Human Body

The left side of the face

This is the concealed side of the face, where the divine wisdom is still unknowable due to being too far outside the realm of human experience.

Numbers associated with Chokmah

As the second Sephira on the Tree, the number of Chokmah is 2. Two represents the line, connecting two points. This is then indicative of motion, as it gives direction, and indicates energy in action. The straight line is the shortest distance between two points, and hence represents the emanation of energy from Kether to Chokmah.

The mystical number of Chokmah is 3, or $\Sigma(1\text{-}2)$. This hints at the completion to come when Chokmah has become full and sent forth the emanation of energy that forms Binah, thus completing the Supernal Triad.

Chokmah itself adds to 73, which is the same as the letter *Gimel* spelled in full. This is interesting as Gimel is attributed to the 13th path, from Kether to Tiphereth. This path is from the divine essence to the son, and Chokmah represents the father. As the father manifests through the son, this equation shows the way the unified energy manifests through diverse expressions.

Tarot

The four Twos.

Animals associated with Chokmah

None attributed, though some sources (e.g. Crowley) give Man as the masculine principle.

Minerals associated with Chokmah

Aquamarine
Due to its watery associations and hence to Neptune.

Beryl
As the colour of the Auphanim.

Labradorite
Due to its iridescent pearl-grey, as Chokmah in the Emperor scale, with flashes of blue indicating the King Scale.

Star Sapphire
As the higher aspect of the Chesedic sapphire, being the pure blue of Chokmah in the King Scale, with the star of Chokmah within.

Plants associated with Chokmah

Amaranth
Is attributed here as the flower of immortality, as symbolic of the Chayah.

Mistletoe
As the ultimate symbol of the Druids, growing on the oak (Chesed), with its white berries symbolising semen, mistletoe is a potent symbol of male potency and Chokmah.

Olive
As sacred to Athena as the fruit of wisdom.

Scents associated with Chokmah

Musk
Musk is a scent of sexual attraction produced by male musk deer.

Symbols & Tools associated with Chokmah

Line
The straight line as both a phallic symbol and also the indication of energy moving.

Lingam

The erect male phallus as the ultimate symbol of male creativity is appropriate to Chokmah.

Deities associated with Chokmah

Celtic

— *Bran* as the wise oracle.
— *Lir / Lyr* as the Sea God for Neptunian attributions.
— *Mannanan Mac Lir / Manawydan / Mannan* as the God of Magick and the Sea

Egyptian

— *Atum* as the speaker of the logos and first from the primal waters.
— *Hu* ("*creative utterance*") as the magickal power of words and as "*he who spoke in the darkness*".
— *Khnum* as the Creator God giving form.
— *Nuit* as the cosmos.

Greek

— *Athena* as the Goddess of Wisdom, sprung from her father's head.
— *Metis* as the original Goddess of Wisdom.
— *Poseidon* as the Sea God for Neptunian attributions.

Roman

— *Coelus* as God of the Sky and the Heavens.
— *Janus* as the twin-faced God of Time, looking forward and backwards, and representing duality.
— *Minerva* as the Goddess of Wisdom, sprung from her father's head.
— *Neptune* as the Sea God for Neptunian attributions.

Sumerian

— *An* as God of the Heavens
— *Enki* as God of Wisdom and Magick.

Meditations & Exercises

Heaven

Meditate on the symbol of a cluster of stars and see what images and ideas you get.

Magickal Formula

Intone the formula of IH (Yah) for a few minutes and record your impressions.

Magickal Image

Meditate on the Magickal Image of a bearded man. Try varying the age of the mean, and correspondingly the beard colour, and see what a difference this makes to your meditations.

Tarot

Lay out the four Twos in an equal-armed cross. Put the 2 of Disks at the top and the 2 of Wands at the bottom, the 2 of Cups on the left and the 2 of Swords at the right. Contemplate the images and see what inspiration arises.

Meditation on the Stars

Meditating on the stars can induce profound shifts in consciousness. To perform this meditation you need to be somewhere away from a big city, so light pollution will not block out the beauty of the night sky.

Lay out a blanket and lie on the ground, gazing at the stars overhead. Contemplate the stars, and recite the phrase "*Ribbono shel Olahm*" or its English equivalent "*Lord of the Universe*" as a mantra.

38. KETHER (KThR) – The Crown

"The First Path is called the Admirable or Hidden Intelligence because it is the Light giving the power of comprehension of the First Principle, which hath no beginning. And it is the Primal Glory, because no created being can attain to its essence."[97]

Kether (pronounced *Ket-er*) is the Sephira of the first swirlings, which could be equated with the "*Big bang*" as the beginning of the manifestation of the unmanifest as expressed through the veils of negativity. In modern times it is usually equated to Pluto. Kether is located at the head of the Middle Pillar, at the apex of the Supernal Triad.

Kether is the unknowable divine; the creative essence and impetus that infuses all the deities that are manifestations of the energy of the universe. Hence it is the crown, because it is worn on the top of the head, representing that which is beyond the comprehension of the mind.

Kether contains within itself the plan of the entire Tree of Life. All the Sephiroth are within Kether in potential, undivided and unexpressed, in a harmony of unity. This is why the *Zohar* describes it as "*the principle of all principles, the Secret Wisdom*[98], *the Most Exalted Crown, with which all Crowns and diadems are adorned.*"

In its position in relation to the rest of the Sephiroth, Kether is the shining point of unimaginable brilliance, for it is entirely positive, emanating all the other principles from its essence. However in respect of the veils of negativity it is a point of contraction, through which the limitless light (*Ain Soph Aur*) crystallises part of itself into the physical universe.

The Yechidah ("*unique essence*" or "*unity*"), representing the highest aspect of the Neshamah, can be seen as corresponding to the divine and immortal spark of the soul that is eternal and is symbolised by Kether. It is the most ephemeral and transcendental part of the soul, where the highest essence of man unites with the divine.

However within the divinity of Kether is a vital lesson to remember, which is that it is reflected in Malkuth – "*Kether is in Malkuth, and Malkuth in Kether,*

---

[97] *The Thirty-Two Paths of Wisdom - Joannes Rittangelius.*
[98] *The term Chokmah Nesethrah (secret wisdom) is frequently used to describe the whole Tree of Life.*

but after a different fashion". This recalls the whole notion of man being created in God's image, which is another way of saying we all have a divine spark within us. This union within each of us with the divine spirit with the physical emphasizes the fact that matter is also sacred, and not something to be reviled or despised, as many have declared. Denial of the flesh may be a way to holiness, but there are ways which enable us to experience the fullness of life as well as pursue our spiritual path, and this is vital in our modern age.

Divine Name: AHIH (Eheieh)

This name means "*I am*", and can be seen as the affirmation of existence by the divine. The phrase "*I am*" is one of the most widely used in language, as it qualifies the actions of the individual. It is also used to commence any affirmations.

AHIH adds to 21, which is the mystic number of Tiphereth, demonstrating the potential of the unknowable divine to express itself through the manifest beauty of Tiphereth. 21 is also the total for "*purity*" (ZChV), expressing the essential quality of the first manifestation, and "*deep meditation*" (HGIG), implying looking deep within to find the connection to the divine.

An expanded version of this Name is also sometimes used, which is AHIH AShR AHIH, "*I am that I am*". This is also sometimes translated as the alternative title of Kether, "*Existence of Existences*".

Archangel: Metatron (MTTRVN)

Metatron (or Methratron) is the *"Voice of God"*. The force of God's voice is perceived as being too great for any living being, that it would destroy them through its power. Hence Metatron acts as the voice of God, enabling that force to be expressed in a manner that does not overcome. Enoch is said to become Metatron, raised to the highest rank due to his piety, becoming transformed into a being of pure fire.

Metatron is described as being one of the oldest of the Archangels. He is also called Jahoel and the Lesser Jao[99]. The Kabbalistic scholar Gershom Scholem gives evidence to suggest that Metatron was originally the secret name of Michael, and that this tradition survived until the fourth century CE. This connection shows the bond between Kether and Tiphereth as Father and Son, Great and Lesser Countenance.

---

[99] *This is clearly a form of IAO as a derivative of IHVH, indicating his power as the first archangel of God.*

Similarly it seems likely that the secret name of Metatron (i.e. the archangel of Kether) was Akhtariel, which was always written followed by Yah YHVH.

Metatron always wears a crown (indicative of Kether), the brilliance of which makes it impossible to look at his head directly. When visualizing him he usually seen seated on a throne, or standing about 3m tall, with an incredibly beautiful face, which is more masculine than most of the Archangels. He wears a brilliant white robe, and rainbows seem to fill the air all around him when he moves.

Metatron adds to 314, the same as *remote* (RChVQ), which fits with Metatron's place as one of the seven Archangels in god's presence, and as archangel of Kether. 314 is also *Shaddai*, a title of Yesod and Divine Name, showing the role of that Sephira as described in *The Thirty-Two Paths of Wisdom*, to *"dispose the unity ... without diminution or division"*. Metatron is the archangel referred to in Exodus 23:21 *"Take heed of him, and hearken unto his voice; be not rebellious against him; for he will not pardon your transgression; for My name is in him."*

Order of Angels: Chaioth ha Qadosh (ChIVTh HQDSh)

This name translates as *"Holy Living Creatures"*, and they are also known as the *"guardians of the Throne"* (Merkavah). They are described in Ezekiel 1:6-13, as having the body of a man, with four faces, of the four elemental creatures of Man (Air), Lion (Fire), Eagle (Water) and Bull (Earth). Each one has two pairs of wings, and their feet are described as being like the sole of a calf's foot, and of burnished bronze. The angels appear joined in a circle, with wings linked on either side, and with an amber-coloured fire between them, from which shoots forth lightning. They are referred to in medieval Grimoire texts as the Seraphim.

We can see that the faces are those of the animals corresponding to the fixed or so-called Kerubic signs of the Zodiac, i.e. man (Aquarius), lion (Leo), eagle (Scorpio) and bull (Taurus). In this the beginning of the unfolding of the Tree is hinted at, by showing part of what is to come, the whole wheel of the Zodiac and time.

Heaven: Rashith ha-Gilgalim (RAShITh HGLGLIM)

The First Swirlings, the Primum Mobile
This was used as a term to describe the *"Milky Way"*, also known as the *"Encompassing Serpent"*, and can be seen as the completion of the Path of the Serpent on the Tree of Life, having ascended through all the paths and finally reached Kether.

Qliphoth: Thaumiel (ThAVMIAL)

Thaumiel means *"Twins of God"*, who by their nature imply division into duality of the original unity, denying its fundamental integrity and wonder.

Titles of Kether

Amen
Apart from the use of this title which is Notariqon of *"The Lord and faithful King"* to end prayers, revealing the addressing of the prayer to the divine, this title has interesting Gematria associated with it as well. Amen adds to 91 (AMN), which is Σ(1-13), being the full expression of Unity (AchAD = 13). 91 is the total for *Angel* (MLAK), showing that God is the source of all the angels. 91 is also the total for *Daughter* (MLKA), a title of Malkuth, showing the link between these two Sephiroth once more.

Ancient of Ancients
The nature of Kether as the first source is stressed by this title.

Ancient of Days
This classical title showing the pre-eminent nature of the divine essence of Kether.

Arik Anpin – Long of Face
Kether is "long of face" because of the vastness of the divine countenance. This may also be translated as the *"Patient One"* and indicates the pure compassion of the divine.

Chokmah-illa-Ah – Heavenly Wisdom
In older texts Kether is thus described, and the appendage of heavenly distinguishes it from Chokmah, whilst also making the emanation of that second Sephira from Kether obvious.

Concealed of the Concealed
So called because the light of Kether is unknowable to man and any being in physical form.

Divine Thought
As the title implies, Kether corresponds to the divine essence expressing itself as thought.

Existence of Existences
Kether is the energy that permeates all the different levels of existence. This is an alternative literal translation of AHIH AshR AHIH, which can also be translated as *"I am that I am"*.

He

Implying the unity of the divine first cause. If we considered this as being representative of the Hebrew letter Heh, when spelt in full it adds to 10 (HH), implying the energy of all the Sephiroth is contained within Kether.

Holy Ancient One

As the primal cause, Kether is the ancient one, and holy for it represents the pure divine essence.

Inscrutable Height

This title reminds us that the height of the divine countenance is considered vast, and would take centuries to view if traveling constantly, were its full scale appreciated.

Long of Nose

This title is linked to Arik Anpin, "*Long of face*", and refers to the vastness of the divine countenance. It is not a reference to the divine having a particularly big nose!

Long Suffering

The journey towards perfection, redeeming all the lost light from the "*Breaking of the Vessels*" is one that will take a vast span of time, hence Kether is long-suffering waiting fro that return to perfection.

Lux Interna

The "*internal Light*" or "*Light within*" recalls the illuminating power of Kether as the first manifestation of the divine from the veils of negativity, and recalls the thread of light in Tzim-Tzum.

Lux Occulta

As the "*hidden light*", Kether is the unknowable illuminating divine energy.

Lux Simplicissima

This could be read as the "*Single Light*" or the "*Simplest Light*". Both of these are appropriate, for Kether is indeed the single light of unity, and it is also the simplest light, as it has not divided and is thus simple and not complex.

Macroposopos

This title refers to the fact that Kether contains the potential and template of all the other Sephira contained within it.

Mirum Occultum

This translates as "*hidden wonder*", again referring to the unknowable and divine nature of Kether.

The Head which is Not
This title hints at the link between Kether and the first of the veils of negativity, the Ain, which is the not of not-existence.

The Most High
This title refers both to the divine power within Kether, and also its place at the top of the Tree of Life.

The Point within the Circle
As the point of manifestation of the divine essence, the circle being the outward radiation of the creative energy as the perfect shape, without beginning or end.

The Primordial Point
Again referring to Kether as the place of the initial manifestation of the divine essence.

The Profuse Giver
Kether is the source from which the rest of the Tree of Life springs, so it is the giver of profuse amounts of energy into the universe that it creates.

The Small or Smooth Point
Refers to the initial moment of transition, where the formless became the point, which was small as it was contained within the limitless light of Ain Soph Aur.

Zair Anpin - The Vast Countenance
Implying both the position of Kether on the Tree of Life, and the magnitude of divinity.

The White Head
This title refers to the position of Kether on the Tree of Life, and the association with the colour white, as containing all the other colours within it.

Experience of Kether

Union with God
The ultimate aim of the Great Work is to return to the divine source, i.e. achieve union with god. This experience may occur briefly in moments of meditation when the state of divine bliss (i.e. Samadhi) is achieved, but can only be achieved fully by the dissolving of the identity back into the ultimate.

Virtue of Kether

Attainment – Completion of the Great Work
By completing the Great Work the magickal experience is automatically experienced. As a goal to strive for this is a wonderful thing, for it sets us an ultimate target. In reality we can only achieve this by moving past the physical and existing as pure energy.

Vice of Kether

None - Perfection does not have any vices.

Colours associated with Kether

King Scale: Brilliance
The indescribable luminosity of the divine is expressed through light beyond colour. All the colours of the spectrum are contained within it, but they are undifferentiated at this point, which is that of undifferentiated purity.

Queen Scale: Pure White Brilliance
The luminosity of the King Scale is now expressed through white, which contains all the colours within it, as Kether contains the potential of all the lower Sephiroth.

Emperor Scale: Pure White Brilliance
Pure white brilliance is formed by adding the Brilliance of the King Scale to the pure White Brilliance of the Queen Scale.

Empress Scale: White, flecked Gold
The all-containing white is flecked with gold, expressing the purity of the metal most associated with divinity. The potential for the expression of the father (Kether) through the child (Tiphereth) is also hinted at by the gold flecks.

Magickal Formula: ARARITA

Ararita is Notariqon for the phrase Achad Resh Achudohtoh Resh Yechidotoh Temurahtoh Resh, which translates as "*One is his beginning, One is his individuality, His permutation is One*". This formula emphasises the divine as the inherent creative force present in all life. Though we are all separate, yet we are all interconnected, forming part of the greater whole that is the desire to evolve.

ARARITA sums to 422 (when the T is taken as *Teth*), which is the same as "*The Vast Countenance*" (ARIK ANPIN), a title of Kether, demonstrating further the relevance of this formula for this Sephira. If the "T" in ARARITA is taken as a Tav, it adds to 813 (ARARIThA) the same as Genesis 1:3 – "*And God said Let there be Light, and there was Light*", which expresses the first illumination of Kether.

Magickal Image of Kether

An ancient bearded King, seen in profile
This image recalls titles of Kether like the "*Ancient of Days*" and "*Ancient of Ancients*". It indicates the wisdom, understanding and knowledge that come from experience. The ancient king has done it all and reached the zenith, being able to go no further.

Kether was also represented as the giant head of a bearded ancient king (the "*Vast Countenance*"), rising in profile from an endless sea, indicating the primal nature of Kether. The images are in profile to indicate that Kether can only be glimpsed and never truly known.

Human Body

The crown of the head
The very top of the body as Kether is the top of the Tree of Life. Also the crown sits on the top of the head and represents rulership, as the Divine Creator is seen as the ruler of all creation.

Numbers associated with Kether

Kether is the first Sephira on the Tree, and unsurprisingly its number is 1. Magickally one is the undivided totality, the interconnectedness of all.

The mystical number of Kether is also 1, as it is the source, and does not have any preceding numbers to add to it.

Kether adds to 620, as does "*The Doors*" (ShAaRIM), implying its position and role as the point where the unmanifest energies of the veils of negativity become manifest as the primal essence, which then permeates the rest of the Tree with its divinity. 620 is also the total of the words *Chokmah Binah Daath* (ChKMH BINH VDAaTh), the first descending triad of the Tree, and shows that the divine essence can also be expressed through its separation into the duality of male and female and the resulting product of their union, expressed as a product of thought rather than a physical child (which is Tiphereth).

Tarot

The four Aces are attributed to Kether. The Aces are the roots of the powers of the Elements as expressed in the subsequent numbers from 2-10, the unfolding of the potential power of the Elements through their manifestations.

Animals associated with Kether

Serpent Ouroboros
The ouroboros serpent with its tail in its mouth symbolising both eternity and making the glyph of zero is appropriate to Kether, particularly as it also implies the veils of negativity beyond Kether, which Kether manifests.

Swan
The swan is attributed to Kether due to its colouring and regal nature, and ability to live in the three environments of air, water and earth. It is also suggested that this attribution is made due to the linking of the swan with the Sanskrit word Aumgn, which represents the creative impulse of the universe.

Minerals associated with Kether

Diamond
Diamond is the hardest of minerals, formed of one substance only, carbon, which is necessary for all life. The beauty of diamond, and the way it refracts light, as well as its ability to amplify energy and its incredible value all make it a symbol of Kether. Also diamond takes its name from the Greek *adamas* meaning unconquerable, and this also hints at the creation of Adam Kadmon and the manifestation of man.

Zircon
Zircon is usually white or colourless, yet can be tinged with all the other colours, showing the potential of all the Sephiroth within Kether.

Plants associated with Kether

Almond in flower
The almond is associated with the Rod of Aaron, and represents the whole of the Middle Pillar. The flowering almond at the top of the plant thus symbolises Kether at the top of the Middle Pillar.

Scents associated with Kether

Almond
The scent of almond is attributed to Kether for the same reasons given above, as the emanation of the flowering plant.

Ambergris
Ambergris enhances the fragrance of any smell it is mixed with, so it brings out the best of them, expressing the Kether aspect.

Symbols & Tools associated with Kether

Crown
The crown is worn as a symbol of authority and the divinity we all strive for, and is appropriate for this reason, as well as being the meaning of Kether and corresponding to its position on the head.

The Lamp of Illumination
Providing the light for the seeker to work by, and also illuminating the eternal and unknowable nature of ultimate divinity.

The Point
The point represents the first manifestation, indefinable and intangible yet still manifest, as is Kether.

The Swastika
As a symbol of the swirling of energy, beginning to move.

Deities associated with Kether

Egyptian
— *Amun* as the Creator God, forming order from the primaeval chaos.
— *Re* as the Creator God, bringing the universe into being.
— *Ptah* as the Creator God who brings the universe into being through the "thoughts of his heart and the words of his mouth".

Greek
— *Aether* as the first manifestation of Deity from the endlessness of Nox, referred to as the place from whence all souls emanate.
— *Ananke* as Goddess of destiny and Mother of the Fates.
— *Zeus Hypsistos* as the ultimate deity, of whom all others are perceived as aspects.

Roman
— *Theos Hypsistos* as the ultimate deity, of whom all others are perceived as aspects.

Sumerian
— *Apsu* as the God of the Sweet Waters of Creation.

Meditations & Exercises

Awareness Mantra & Meditation

This meditation draws on the power of the Divine Name of Kether – AHIH (Ee-hay-ya). As this name means "*I am*", this English translation is used to prefix the declarations of awareness meditation. You then use the phrase repeatedly, until you have exhausted your awareness and alter a state of bliss.

So e.g. you might start "*I am aware that it is warm in here; I am aware that I am wearing a blue top; I am aware that a car alarm is going off outside; etc.*" When you have stopped being able to think of anything, silence and bliss enter your mind. The moment that you start to be aware of yourself as an individual again and your internal dialogue starts up, loudly vibrate the expanded divine name AHIH AShR AHIH (Ee-hay-ya Ash-er Ee-hay-ya) meaning "*I am that I am*".

Heaven

Meditate on the symbol of a spiral for the first swirlings.

Magickal Formula

Intone the formula of Ararita for a few minutes and record your impressions.

Magickal Image

Meditate on the Magickal Image of an ancient bearded king seen in profile. Try varying this by using the image of just the king's head in profile, huge in size, rising out of the ocean, and see what a difference this makes.

Tarot

Lay out the four Aces in an equal-armed cross. Put the Ace of Disks at the top and the Ace of Wands at the bottom, the Ace of Cups on the left and the Ace of Swords at the right. Contemplate the images and see what inspiration arises.

Flame Meditation

This meditation can be done with a beeswax candle, but ideally should be done with a small oil lamp, with olive oil and a linen wick. Olive oil burns with a flame that is particularly clean. The lamp (or candle) should be placed at least a metre (just over 3 foot) from the wall, and there should be no other light source in the room, curtains should be drawn.

Contemplate the flame, and see the white, yellow and red. Then become aware of the surrounding blackness around the flame. After a while you may perceive a sky blue colour in the blackness around the flame. Concentrate again on the darkness in the room, and see it as a deep velvety darkness, that seems to enclose the flame. Return your attention to the flame and perceive it as the light of Kether surrounded by the Ain Soph.

PART IX

RITUAL TECHNIQUES

39. Pathworking

Pathworking is a form of creative visualisation. Its name is descriptive of its purpose – literally to "*work the paths*" of the Tree of Life. The term is now used to describe guided visualisations generally, but its original purpose was for exploration of Qabalistic symbolism, and through this greater understanding of the self and the universe.

Performing Pathworking

A number of pathworkings for Temples of the Sephiroth and other Locations have been given earlier in this book. To experience these fully, you may find it helpful to tape yourself reading the descriptions given. Tape them slowly, leaving gaps, to allow yourself to clearly visualise the details when you perform them. Experience will soon show you the optimum spacing for you. Generally pathworkings are most effective when they last for 10-20 minutes.

To begin a pathworking, ensure that you are sitting comfortably. You may lie down, but this is not recommended as it can result in you falling asleep! Close your eyes and focus on your breathing, making sure you have a comfortable breathing rhythm.

In your mind's eye visualise the room you are in.[100] See the walls around you, the floor below, the ceiling above, the furniture. As you visualise yourself sitting in the room, see it start to fill with a white mist. The mist becomes more and more dense, filling the room, obscuring everything from sight, until all around you is white mist; you are floating in a sea of white mist.

Then the white mist starts to disperse, rolling back and thinning out, and you find yourself in the [insert description of location here].

You take a last look around at your surroundings[101], and as you do so, the white mist starts to form again, coalescing, becoming more and more dense, filling the space all around you, until once again you are surrounded by white mist. And the white mist begins to disperse, thinning out and rolling back. As it does so you see your surroundings all around you – the floor beneath you,

---

[100] *If you are making a tape, this is a good place to begin. Read this slowly and clearly, and then move on to the description of the temple you are journeying to. Use the "Pause" button on the tape player to avoid sudden clicks from the "Stop" button that may distract you during your pathworking.*
[101] *This section should be read at the end of the pathworking, for your return to your normal surroundings.*

ceiling above, walls and furniture around. Take a couple of deep breaths and open your eyes. You have returned from your journey.

Travelling Between the Temples
Pathworkings to the Sephirotic temples and on the paths of the Tree of Life always start from and end in the Malkuth temple. As a result the Malkuth temple will become a very familiar place to you on your path. To travel to one of the temples that connect to Malkuth you draw the appropriate planetary symbol in front of the door to that temple, and vibrate the divine name of the Sephira (e.g. to move to the Yesod temple you would draw a crescent moon and vibrate the name Shaddai El Chai). You then see the stone of the wall in the doorframe disappear to be replaced by a shimmering wall of light of the appropriate colour for the temple you are travelling to. Walking through this curtain of light then takes you into the temple.

When you are moving into a temple, you draw the planetary symbol of that temple in front of the door of the temple you are currently in, and conversely when you close the door in a temple, you draw the symbol of the temple that you are currently in. To reach the higher temples on the Tree of Life you obviously have to pass through several of the lower temples first. This is good practice, as it helps you strengthen your connections with these temples, and ensures that you always work on the corresponding elements of your psyche that form the foundations of your growth.

Temple	Entry from	Symbol to Open Door	Divine Name
Yesod	Malkuth	Lunar crescent	Shaddai El Chai
Hod	Malkuth, Yesod	Mercury	Elohim Tzabaoth
Netzach	Malkuth, Yesod, Hod	Venus	IHVH Tzabaoth
Tiphereth	Yesod, Hod, Netzach	Sun	IHVH Eloah va-Daath
Geburah	Hod, Tiphereth	Mars	Elohim Gibor
Chesed	Netzach, Tiphereth, Geburah	Jupiter	El

A Note on Visualisation

In regards to visualisation, it should be mentioned that there are references to the techniques of visualisation in the classic Kabbalistic literature. There are two terms used, which are *chakikah* (engraving) and *chatzivah* (hewing or carving).

Engraving refers to the process of fixing the image in the mind's eye so it is firm and does not waver or change shape or colour. The phrase "*burned in my thoughts"* is a good analogy to this, for you literally engrave the image in your mind.

Carving or hewing refers to the removal of unwanted aspects of the visualisation you are performing. So for instance if you were visualising letters you remove all other imagery leaving a blank wall of colour behind it. The analogy here is to hewing a gemstone out of the surrounding matrix of rock, and chipping away any extraneous bits of material to leave the desired gem.

This pair of words are found repeatedly in verses of the *Sepher Yetzirah*, relating to the letters of the Hebrew alphabet.

40. Vibratory Formula & Divine Names

Certain of the Divine Names are considered incredibly powerful, and even speaking them is said to begin processes of change. The best known of these is the unpronounceable name of God, Tetragrammaton (IHVH). Many of the divisions on the Tree of Life revolve around this formula, and of all words it could be said to be the one that represents the power of the universe as expressed through the Tree of Life.

Another major Divine Name is Elohim. There is a teaching that the ten Sephiroth became reconstituted as five Parzufim (faces) when the divine "*breaking of the vessels*" took place. The five Parzufim correspond to the five letters of Elohim (ALHIM) and to Tetragrammaton, and are as follows:

Arik Anpin – Greater Countenance, Kether - Point of Yod
Abba – Father - Chokmah - Yod
Aima – Mother - Binah - Heh
Zair Anpin - Lesser Countenance – Son - Chesed through to Yesod - Vav
Nukva - Daughter – Malkuth - Heh

Vibration of Names

The words of power in Qabalah should be vibrated rather than spoken. This means that when you use Divine Names, Archangels, Angels or Heavens, the name should be vibrated. When you vibrate a name you must breathe properly. This may sound obvious, but most people breathe shallow breaths.

To vibrate a word you need to breathe from your diaphragm, and prolong the duration of the syllables. You will know when you have found the right pitch for your vibrations, as you will literally feel your rib-cage, and possibly the rest of your body, vibrate with the power of the word you are uttering.

Before you inhale to pronounce the words, visualise the name in the air in front of you in its appropriate colour in the correct Colour Scale. It is preferable to visualise the name in Hebrew (and remember Hebrew is written right to left), but if you find this too difficult visualise the name in the Roman letters normally used for the English alphabet.
In addition to focusing your breath, you also need to focus your mind. When you inhale the breath before vibrating the words of power, you should visualise the breath being the colour associated with the Sephira to which the

name belongs, and in the appropriate Colour Scale. Feel the energy of the Sephira entering your body and suffusing your being.

E.g. if you were vibrating the Divine Name of Yesod, Shaddai El Chai, you would visualise the name and the inhaled air being indigo in colour, as the Sephirotic colour of Yesod in the King Scale. However if you were vibrating the name of the Archangel of Yesod, Gabriel, then the name and the inhaled air would be visualised as Violet, the Sephirotic colour of Yesod in the Queen Scale.

By breathing properly and vibrating words, and focusing your mind through the use of the correct colours, you will notice it is easier to achieve altered states of consciousness. You will be more aware of both the energy you generate, and also the energies around you. Try with the Tetragrammaton as *Yah-veh* (IHVH), seeing the name and the air you inhale as a pure soft blue. Practice until you can feel your body vibrating as you intone the syllables, drawing them out so that each syllable takes 5-10 seconds to vibrate.

This practice should be performed for each of the Sephira on the Tree in turn, to help attune you to their energy. It can also be used with appropriate divine names before performing meditations and pathworkings to help focus and empower you for the work to come.

Sephira	Divine Name	Colour of Name and Air
Kether	Ahih	Brilliance
Chokmah	Yah or Yahveh	Pure soft Blue
Binah	Yahveh Elohim	Crimson
Chesed	Al	Deep Violet
Geburah	Elohim Gibor	Orange
Tiphereth	Yahveh Eloah va-Daath	Clear Pink Rose
Netzach	Yahveh Tzavaot	Amber
Hod	Elohim Tzavaot	Violet Purple
Yesod	Shaddai El Chai	Indigo
Malkuth	Adonai ha-Aretz or Adonai Melekh	Yellow

41. Magickal Images & Assumption of Deity

The magickal images associated with the Sephiroth represent different perfected qualities of humanity. They contain both male and female, and a variety of ages. Such images can be very useful for working on aspects of the self that need developing or balancing.

Perform a rigorous and honestly critical examination of your self. Look at your good and bad points (*virtues* and *vices*), and see what you feel you need to work on to move forward at this time. Now see which Sephira this vice corresponds to and make a note of the divine name associated with this Sephira.

Visualise yourself as the magickal image for this Sephira. If you do not feel you live up to the ideal of this image, visualise a stylised image of how you would like to look. If the image is of the opposite gender to you, then consider it to be your feminine/masculine side, and picture it how you think you would look. Hold this image in your head and vibrate the divine name of the Sephira for several minutes. Repeat this daily for as long as you feel it takes to transform the vice into an appropriate virtue that works for you.

You may like to perform this practice with your hands raised and your fingers spread out in the position of the Priestly Blessing.

E.g. you have a tendency towards idleness, the vice of Yesod. So prepare your ritual space as described subsequently. Then visualise yourself as a beautiful naked man, and vibrate Shaddai El Chai for several minutes, remembering to visualise the name and air you breathe in as indigo. Whenever you feel prone to idleness, use the time instead to do something that helps develop you, making you more independent and less reliant on others.

42. Magick of the Hands

A very obvious correspondence exists between the ten fingers of our hands and the ten Sephiroth. This link is described in the *Sepher Yetzirah* 1:3: "*Ten Sephiroth of Nothingness in the number of ten fingers, five opposite five.*" Now as the Sephiroth are divided into the three columns of the pillars this might seem troublesome, but there is a system in place that has existed for many centuries in Kabbalah.

The five "*masculine*" Sephiroth are referred to as the five Loves (Chasadim), and include all the Sephiroth on the Pillar of Mercy, and the five "*feminine*" Sephiroth are referred to as the five Strengths, and include all the Sephiroth on the Pillar of Severity.

Now as the modern magickal perspective has shifted the perception of man on the Tree so that the feminine side is seen as the right side of the body rather than the traditional Kabbalistic view of it as the left, the attributions have to be swapped. Interestingly this swap gives Tiphereth as the attribution for the wedding ring finger, a classic association that emphasises the energy channel from this finger to the heart (Tiphereth).

Masculine Loves	Left Hand	Feminine Strengths	Right Hand
Kether	Thumb	Binah	Thumb
Chokmah	Forefinger	Geburah	Forefinger
Chesed	Middle Finger	Hod	Middle Finger
Tiphereth	Ring Finger	Yesod	Ring Finger
Netzach	Little Finger	Malkuth	Little Finger

Using the Hands for Qabalistic Mudras

When you are meditating on a Sephira, you can emphasise the energy of that Sephira by having all your fingers closed except the one attributed to it. E.g. if you are meditating on an aspect of Yesod, you have all your fingers closed (as in a fist) except the ring finger of your right hand.

Using the Fingers for Anointing

If you are anointing yourself with an oil corresponding to a particular Sephira that you are working with, this can also be reinforced by using the appropriate finger to perform the anointing with. E.g. the ring finger of the left hand for Tiphereth or the middle finger of the right hand for Hod.

Blessing Position

Raise your hands with the palms upwards and spread your fingers out. This is the position of the Priestly Blessing.

43. The Banishing Ritual of the Pentagram

Before you perform rituals one of the most important actions is to prepare the space you are in. By creating a "sacred space" you help prepare yourself mentally for the work you are about to perform, and also removes any unwanted energies from the space. This ensures that any psychic or emotional charge that may have built up in the space is removed, and will not influence your ritual in any way.

The Lesser Banishing Ritual of the Pentagram (often shortened to LBRP) is an extremely effective way of not only preparing your space but also helping to prepare you as well.

The LBRP is one of the most basic foundations of western magick, and has been worked very effectively by a lot of people over a long time period, gaining a natural "*flow*" when worked and having a lot of inherent energy from regular and repeated use. It was created in 1887-88 CE by Samuel Liddell MacGregor Mathers as part of the corpus of the Hermetic Order of the Golden Dawn, and draws its wording largely from traditional Jewish prayers and sources.

The Pentagram Ritual combines voicework, visualisation, telesmatic imagery and bodywork. With practice will come proficiency in a very useful ritual that can be used at any time. The Pentagram Ritual should be performed before performing any pathworkings or magickal work, as it will clear any negative influences and energies from the space you are in, leaving it balanced, pure and fit for you to perform your meditations and magick in.

You do not have to perform the gestures and intonations out loud. It is a very good act of mental discipline to visualise yourself performing the ritual in your mind's eye and vibrating all the appropriate names in your head. This can also be done in places where it would be awkward or impossible to perform the ritual without causing problems.

The ritual is in four parts – the Qabalistic Cross, the Pentagrams and Divine Names, the Archangels, and the Qabalistic Cross again. When performing the Qabalistic Cross, you are essentially affirming your place at the centre of your own universe, in a state of balance. You are standing in a state of grace, balanced and ready to give full rein to your spirit in its quest for growth and wisdom. The Qabalistic Cross can be performed by itself as a simple balancing exercise whenever you feel the need to calm and balance yourself.

The second part of the ritual is the inscribing of the pentagrams and intonation of divine names. Pentagrams have an almost universal useage as symbols of protection, and also the balance of the elemental forces under the unifying principle of spirit, which corresponds to the top point of the pentagram. By combining the protective power of the pentagram with the divine names that affirm the power of the divine about and within you, you create a magickal shield about you that nothing can pass through without your permission.

The third part of the ritual is the calling of the Elemental Archangels, who act as guardians for your space, ensuring that you are totally safe, and also that pure elemental energy from each of the four elements can enter your space to energise and be balanced within your work.

By performing the Qabalistic Cross again at the end of the ritual, you reaffirm yourself as the centre of your universe, which is now more balanced and focused, a sacred space ready for you to work in.

1. The Qabalistic Cross

Face east and see yourself growing and rising up to the heavens with your feet firmly on the earth, growing until the earth is a globe supporting your feet, with space all around you. See a column of blinding whiteness descending from above but not touching your head. Trace with your preferred hand (with first two fingers straight and other two fingers folded with thumb folded onto them) a line of energy down through your crown to your third eye, touch the third eye with your hand and vibrate:

ATOH (Ah-toh)

This means *"thou art"*, as you say it imagine that you can hear it echoing throughout the universe.

Move the hand down along your body and touch at the pubic bone. As you do this see the energy continue down through the body until it reaches your feet on the earth, and continues off to infinity below. As you do this vibrate:

MALKUTH (Mal-koot)

This means *"the kingdom"*, again the phrase echoes through the universe.

Next visualise a horizontal beam of brilliant white energy coming from infinity to your right. Draw this light across with your preferred hand, touching the right shoulder with your hand and feeling a reservoir of energy activating on the right side, as you vibrate:

VE-GEBURAH (Ve-geh-vur-ah)

This means "*and the power*", as before the name echoes throughout the universe. Now move your hand across the body tracing a line of energy through the heart centre and touch the left shoulder, again feeling a reservoir of energy activating, this time on the left side. See the beam of energy continue off to infinity on your left, and vibrate:

VE-GEDULAH (Ve-geh-du-lah)

This means "*and the glory*" the name echoes throughout the whole universe as before.

Bring your hands together in front of the heart, as in prayer, and vibrate:

LE-OLAHM, AMEN (Le-oh-lahm, amen)

This means "*to the worlds, Lord and faithful King*", as you say it see the cross now formed within your body, equilibriating you as the centre of your magickal universe, with the cross-point being your heart centre, the centre of balance. Vibrate with the words and hear them echoing throughout the universe, as before.

2. Setting the Circle and Inscribing the Pentagrams

Facing east inscribe a pentagram in front of you starting with your hand at a position corresponding to your left hip and moving up to the top point of the pentagram (which is approximately level with the top of your head), then continue on to complete pentagram. As you inscribe the pentagram see it forming in the air in front of you, in blue flame. With the pentagram flaming in front of you stamp forward into the Sign of the Enterer (see illustration) pushing the pentagram to infinity and intone:

YHVH (Yah-veh)

This divine name is the creative word of divinity, combining the masculine and feminine divine energies, a manifestation of the ultimate Unpronounceable Name. It should be visualised in pure soft blue, as should the breath you inhale before vibrating the name.

Return to a standing posture in a flowing movement, seeing the pentagram returning from infinity and remaining at the edge of your space, keeping your preferred hand extended in front of you. Then from the east with your hand extended out in front of you, turn to the south, see a circle of flame starting to be formed around you as you turn to the south. Now facing south inscribe a pentagram in front of you in the manner described above except that as you push the pentagram, intone:

ADNI (Ah-doh-nye)
This means *"Lord"*, and this divine name can be seen as referring to the higher self, the divine within you. Both the divine names of Malkuth have the word Adonai within them, and hence this name should be visualised in yellow, as should the breath you inhale before vibrating the name.

Now from the south turn to the west, again with hand outstretched, and see the circle of flame continuing to be formed. In the west inscribe another pentagram as previously described, intoning:

AHIH (Eh-heh-yay)

The first emanation *"I am"*, divine name of Kether and the affirmation of creative divine power, linking the divine without to that within, embodying the principle of *"As above, so below"*. It should be visualised in brilliant white, as should the breath you inhale before vibrating the name.

Turning to the north still with your hand outstretched, seeing the circle of flame continuing to be formed. In the north inscribe another pentagram in the same manner and intone:

AGLA (Ah-glah)

An abbreviation of *"Ateh Gebor Le-olahm Adonai"* – *"You are strong for the world O Lord"*, referring to the physical manifestation of divinity. It should be visualised in orange, as should the breath you inhale before vibrating the name.

Now finish inscribing the circle of flame by turning to the east with hand outstretched and finishing at your starting point.

3. Calling the Archangels

Facing east again, stand with arms outstretched to either side, and say:

Before me RAPHAEL,

As you intone the Archangel's name visualise him before you inside the circle - at least 3m tall, his face almost too bright to see, very beautiful and androgynous. He wears a yellow robe, and there are flashes of purple about his form, he holds a sword and the air element enters the circle from the east. You may feel a flow of air like gentle breezes blowing past Raphael into the circle. You should visualise the name Raphael and the air you inhale as being orange in colour.

Still facing east remaining in the same posture say:

Behind me GAVRIEL,

This time as you intone the Archangel's name visualise him behind you inside the circle, again at least 3m tall, his face blindingly bright, again beautiful but slightly feminine. Gabriel wears a blue robe and holds aloft a silver chalice, around his form there are flashes of orange. You may also visualise a waterfall behind Gabriel, and from behind you in the west you feel cool moisture as the element of water enters the circle. You should visualise the name Gabriel (pronounced Gavriel) and the air you inhale as being violet in colour.

Still facing east and holding the posture say:

On my right hand MIKHAEL,

As you intone the Archangel's name visualise him to the right of you inside the circle with the same towering height, same blinding visage as the others though slightly masculine, his robe is bright red and there are flashes of green around him as he holds a wand. Flames dance around Michael's feet, and from the right of you in the south you feel the heat as the element of fire enters the circle. You should visualise the name Michael (pronounced Mikhael) and the air you inhale as golden yellow.

Continuing to face east and hold the posture say:

On my left hand URIEL,

Intoning the Archangels name visualise him to the left of you outside the circle towering and bright like his brothers, his robe of green, with flashes of red about him. He holds a pentacle and stands in front of a field of corn with woods behind. You sense the impending strength and stability of earth, and from the north to your left you feel the element of earth enters the circle. You should visualise the name Oriel and the air you inhale as being emerald green in colour.

Now say:

For about me flame the pentagrams, and in the column shines the six-rayed star.

As you say this see the four pentagrams that you inscribed around you and yourself in a column of brilliance with a hexagram shining above your head and below your feet.

4. The Qabalistic Cross

Repeat Section 1.

Notes

By performing this ritual in a slightly different way it can be used as an invoking ritual to bring the elemental energies into your space, rather than simply as a cleaning of the space.

Instead of performing banishing pentagrams you should use invoking ones. In section 2 when banishing the pentagram is inscribed starting from a point in front of you corresponding to the position of the left hip and moving up to the topmost point and then continuing on to complete the pentagram. For invoking the pentagram is begun from a point in front of you at the level of your forehead, then moving down to the point corresponding to the position of your left hip and then continuing on to complete the pentagram.

In section 3 when each form of elemental energy enters the circle, for the banishing it should pass through you take away any '*staleness*' of that element in you. For the invoking as each element enters the circle it should fill you with its force.

Further Comments & Notes

A traditional Jewish prayer said at night before retiring contains the words:

In the name of IHVH The God of Israel: At my right hand Michael At my left Gabriel Ahead of me Oriel Behind me Raphael Above my head the Shekinah of God!

This is clearly the origin of the "*Calling of the Archangels*" part of the LBRP, though the directional attributions have been changed to make them fit the Golden Dawn attributions. Likewise the use of the Shekinah (presence) of God is something that modern seekers may wish to revive.

So the line "*And in the column shines the six-rayed star*" could be replaced with "*And in the column shines the Shekinah of God*". This obviously has the benefit of introducing a female component to the energy of the ritual, which is not insignificant or to be ignored. Experience has shown that this modification transforms the whole ritual and makes it very good as a balancing in addition to its other qualities. Try both ways and see what differences you find, and use the version you prefer.

44. The Middle Pillar Exercise

Before doing any active magickal work, it is always a good idea to ensure your energies are balanced and you feel energized and ready for the work in hand. The Middle Pillar is an extremely useful preparation for working with the Tree of Life and any Qabalistic ritual, as it energises you and leaves you balanced and focused on the Tree.

Different sources present somewhat different forms of this exercise. The version I am giving here may seem different to the forms you have come across before. This is because all the printed versions of this ritual contain a very obvious error.

The colours I give here are different to those usually given, because I am using the King Scale, which is the highest of the Colour Scales, and the one that the Divine Names are associated with. As we aspire to the highest, it is most appropriate to use the highest Colour Scale, which is the correct one to use as we are invoking the divine names that are of the World of Atziluth.

I have also included a further modification I have made to the Middle Pillar exercise that has proven to be very effective. Instead of using the Divine Name and Colour of Binah for Daath that are normally given, the Daathian attributions are used to promote a better fluency of energy flow. This means that at the throat centre the Divine Name "*Ruach ha Qadosh*" is vibrated. The translation of the sequence of Divine Names vibrated is thus:

AHIH *"I am"*
RVCh hQDSh *"The Spirit of Holiness"*
YHVH Eloah Va-Daath *"God made manifest in the sphere of the mind"*
ShDI AL ChI *"The Almighty and Ever-living God"*
ADNI hARTz *"Lord of the Earth"*

Simply reading through this sequence of names and their translations demonstrates what a powerful affirmation of personal union with divine force this combination of names creates.

As elsewhere, when you vibrate names you should use the vibratory formula, another detail that is left out in the other printed versions of this key ritual. The appropriate colours for visualising the name and the breath you inhale before vibrating the name are given accordingly.

The spheres on the body that the energy passes down through correspond to the Sephiroth of the Middle Pillar of the Tree of Life. So the energy is passing down from Kether (*crown*) to Daath (*throat*) to Tiphereth (*heart*) to Yesod (*genitals*) to Malkuth (*feet*). When the energy is circulated back to the crown you are emphasising the integrity of your aura and ensuring you are in a good state for magickal work. The energy being accumulated at the heart at the end is because the heart centre is the point of balance in our bodies, and balance is what we always strive for in our magickal work and spiritual growth.

The circulation of energy up the sides of the body back up to the crown is connecting you with the two pillars you have already visualised, the Black and White Pillars that represent the two opposing polarities of energy within you. By sending the energy back in this manner you create a circuit of complete balance of all the energies within your aura.

The Exercise

Face east and imagine yourself standing between two large pillars. The pillars should be at a distance that you would just be able to touch them if you stretched your arms out to the horizontal. On your right is a pillar 60cm in diameter and 2m high, made of black onyx. On your left is a pillar of the same size (i.e. 60cm diameter and 2m height) made of white marble. You are thus the Middle Pillar between the Black and White Pillars.

Above your head visualise a sphere of brilliant white light about 30cm in diameter, almost touching the top of your head. When you can feel the energy of the brilliant sphere clearly, visualise the energy descending as a line of white light, and as it touches the top of your head see the divine name *AHIH (Ee-hay-ya)* in front of you in brilliant white, visualise the air you inhale in that same brilliant white, and then vibrate the divine name.

See the white ray of light continue to descend straight through your head down to your throat. At your throat see a second sphere of the same size form, this time of brilliant lavender energy, enclosing your entire throat. As this occurs see the divine name *RVCh hQDSh (Roo-ach ha Ka-dosh)*[102] in front of you in brilliant lavender, visualise the air you inhale in that same brilliant lavender, and then vibrate the divine name.

See the white ray of light descend further, down to your heart. At your heart, see a third sphere of the same size form, of rose pink, enclosing your heart. As this occurs, see the divine name *YHVH Eloah Va-Daath (Yah-veh El-o-ah Va-Da-art)* in front of you in rose pink, visualise the air you inhale in that same rose pink, and then vibrate the divine name.

---

[102] *Traditionally the attribution YHVH Elohim (Yah-veh El-o-heem) is used here, but I have changed this for the reasons explained previously.*

See the white ray continue to descend down to the region of your genitals. See a fourth sphere of the same size form here, of deep indigo, enclosing this region. As this occurs, see the divine name *ShDI Al ChI (Sha-dai- El Ky – as in sky)* in front of you in deep indigo, visualise the air you inhale in that same deep indigo, and then vibrate the divine name.

Finally see the white ray continue down to the soles of your feet, where it forms a similar size sphere upon which the feet stand, bright yellow in colour. As this occurs, see the divine name *ADNI H'ARTtz (Ah-don-ai ha Ah-retz)* in front of you in bright yellow, visualise the air you inhale in that same bright yellow, and then vibrate the divine name.

Now visualise the white energy flowing back up your aura up the sides of your body and back to the brilliant sphere above your head. Repeat this a few times, and then see the energy flowing back up your front and back up to the brilliant sphere above your head, repeating this several times. (This section may be extended for several minutes if you wish). When you are ready to finish, see the energy accumulating at your heart centre, making it shine extremely brightly.

You may now begin your magickal work, or if you wish perform the Qabalistic Cross to re-establish yourself as the energised centre of your temple and your universe.

45. The Lightning Flash Affirmation

This exercise is an affirmation of your body as the Tree of Life in miniature. It is designed to energise your body and emphasise your connection to the universe about you and the flow of divine creative energy through you, and may be used by itself or as part of a ritual.

To perform this exercise you visualise each of the spheres in turn at the corresponding part of your body. As you do this, you vibrate the divine name associated with that Sephira. A similar exercise is given by Israel Regardie in his work *The Middle Pillar*, however this works exclusively with white light and has a different final component.

The Lightning Flash

Above your head visualise a sphere of brilliant (white) light about 30cm in diameter, almost touching the top of your head. When you can feel the energy of the brilliant sphere clearly, visualise the energy descending as a line of white light like a flash of lightning, and as it touches the top of your head vibrate the divine name *AHIH (Ee-hay-ya)*, seeing the name in front of you and the air you inhale as brilliant white.

See the white lightning flash descend to the left side of your face, activating a 20cm sphere of pure soft blue light, which touches your left cheek. As this occurs, vibrate the divine name *IH (Yah)* seeing the name in front of you and the air you inhale as pure soft blue.

See the lightning flash shoot horizontally through your mouth to the right side of your face, activating a 20cm sphere of crimson light, which is touching your right cheek at the same level as the previous sphere. As this occurs, vibrate the divine name *IHVH ALHIM (Yah-veh El-o-heem)* seeing the name in front of you and the air you inhale as crimson.

See the lightning flash pass diagonally left through your throat. At your throat see a 20cm sphere size form, this time of brilliant lavender energy, enclosing your entire throat. As this occurs vibrate the divine name *RVCh hQDSh (Roo-ach ha Ka-dosh)* seeing the name in front of you and the air you inhale as brilliant lavender.

See the lightning flash continue from your throat to your left shoulder, where you see a 20cm sphere of deep violet light form. As this occurs, vibrate the divine name *AL (Al)* seeing the name in front of you and the air you inhale as deep violet.

See the lightning flash shoot horizontally across your shoulders to your right shoulder, where you see a 20cm sphere of orange light form. As this occurs, vibrate the divine name *ALHIM GIBVR (El-o-heem Gi-boor)* seeing the name in front of you and the air you inhale as orange.

See the lightning flash pass diagonally down through your heart towards the left hip. At your heart, see a sphere of the same size form, of rose pink, enclosing your heart. As this occurs, vibrate the divine name *IHVH Eloah Va-Daath (Yah-veh El-o-ah Va-Da-art)* seeing the name in front of you and the air you inhale as rose pink.

See the lightning flash reach your lift hip, where you see a 20cm sphere of amber light form. As this occurs, vibrate the divine name *YHVH TzBAOTh (Yah-veh Tza-va-ot)* seeing the name in front of you and the air you inhale as amber.

See the lightning flash horizontally across your body to your right hip, where you see a 20cm sphere of violet-purple light form. As this occurs, vibrate the divine name *ALHIM TzBAOTh (El-o-heem Tza-va-ot)* seeing the name in front of you and the air you inhale as violet-purple.

See the lightning flash diagonally to the left to the region of your genitals. See a sphere of the same size form here, of deep indigo, enclosing this region. As this occurs, vibrate the divine name *ShDI Al Chl (Sha-dai- El Ky – as in sky)* seeing the name in front of you and the air you inhale as deep indigo.

Finally see the lightning flash continue vertically down your legs to the soles of your feet, where it forms a similar size sphere upon which the feet stand, bright yellow in colour. As this occurs, vibrate the divine name *ADNI MLQ (Ah-don-ai ha Me-lek)*[103] seeing the name in front of you and the air you inhale as bright yellow.

When you have done this, feel the Tree of Life within yourself. Feel all the parts of your body connected by the Lightning Flash, from your crown to the left side of your face, across to the right side, diagonally down to the throat and then to the left shoulder. From the left shoulder it continues horizontally across to the right shoulder, then diagonally down through your heart to your

---

[103] *This divine name is used for Malkuth to emphasise the divine nature of the practitioner.*

left hip, then horizontally across to your right hip. From your right hip it travels diagonally down to your genitals, and then vertically down to your feet.

Now raise your hands with the palms upwards and spread your fingers out. This is the position of the Priestly Blessing, with the ten fingers corresponding to the Sephiroth. Feel the energy of the heavens in your hands for a few seconds. Then move your hands over your heart, with your dominant hand on your heart, and the other hand over the top of it. Take a couple of deep breaths and then relax.

46. The Structure of Qabalistic Ritual

To really get the most out of pathworking and Qabalistic ritual, it is worth putting in the preparation to make sure everything goes just right. To this end I have included a suggested structure to follow for performing Qabalistic ritual to ensure you get the most from your practical work.

1. Bathing

Before performing ritual, have a ritual bath (called *mikveh* in Hebrew). You may add oils or herbs to the bath appropriate to the nature of the work you are going to perform. These can be gained by looking at the correspondences for the Sephiroth.

2. Space Purification

Perform the Lesser Banishing Ritual of the Pentagram, to totally cleanse the space you are going to work in of any negative psychic energy. This also has the benefit of establishing you as the centre of your magickal universe.

On a practical level, ensure you telephone is unplugged or turned off, and switch off your mobile or pager. If you live and work in a noisy region, you may wish to invest some time in finding ritual music that you can play to drown out any annoying background noise if you find this disturbing your practices. The album *"Ambient 4"* by Brian Eno is particularly good for this.

You may prefer to time your ritual so the energies are most conducive to your ritual. See the section in part X on *Planetary days and hours*.

3. Balancing Your Aura

Perform the Middle Pillar exercise to ensure your energies are in balance and flowing smoothly. You might also perform the Lightning Flash affirmation as well after the Middle Pillar, or as an alternative to it.

4. Magickal Work

Any work you wish to perform may now be done. This would include invocation, pathworking, consecration of talismans, meditation, vibratory work, divination, and healing.

5. Grounding

If you feel your energies are not at the balanced level you desire before finishing your ritual, perform the Middle Pillar exercise again to re-harmonise yourself. You may also wish to eat some simple food like bread and have a drink of water to help ground yourself. Some people find smelling a very earthy scent such as patchouli or vetivert helps to ground them, so this is something else you can try.

6. Opening Your Temple

Perform the Lesser Banishing Ritual of the Pentagram again to neutralise any residual energy and leave your space cleansed.

7. Record

Always write up your experiences immediately afterwards while they are fresh in your mind, in as much detail as you can. Take time to do this, do not hurry off to do something else or put the television or your mobile phone on!

PART X

QABALAH & TALISMANS

47. Kameas & Sigilisation

The use of protective amulets and talismans to attract particular forces was a major component of the Merkavah tradition of Kabbalah, as has already been discussed. Within the use of Qabalah in the western Mystery Tradition a particular set of talismanic attributions based on the planetary kameas[104] of the seven classical planets, and their associated Spirits and Intelligences, has arisen. The planetary kameas are given in Appendix 2.

Sephira	Planet	No	Spirit	Intelligence
Binah	Saturn	3	Zazel	Agiel
Chesed	Jupiter	4	Hismael	Yaphiel
Geburah	Mars	5	Bartzabel	Graphiel
Tiphereth	Sun	6	Sorath	Nakhiel
Netzach	Venus	7	Kedemel	Hagiel
Hod	Mercury	8	Taphthartharath	Tiriel
Yesod	Moon	9	Schad Barschemoth ha-Shartathan	Malkah be-Tharshisim ve-ad Be-Ruachoth Shechalim

The talismans are usually made on a piece of card or paper of the colour of the Sephira in the Emperor Scale, this being the one used for Planetary Spirits and Intelligences. The writing is written in the complementary colour to this, so it has the greatest impact. The talisman generally has a number of sides equal to the number associated with the Sephira.

Hence a Jupiterian talisman would be on a square piece of blue card, with orange writing on it. Glyphs usually included on talismans are the astrological sign of the planet, the Divine Name, the name of the Archangel, the name and/or sigil of the Planetary Spirit or Intelligence, and any other appropriate symbols the magickian desires.

---

[104] *This is the name given to magick number squares.*

Sephira	No. of sides	Colour	Lettering Colour
Binah	3	Black	White
Chesed	4	Blue	Orange
Geburah	5	Red	Green
Tiphereth	6	Gold	Purple
Netzach	7	Green	Red
Hod	8	Orange	Blue
Yesod	9	Violet	Yellow

48. Aiq Beker

The standard method of creating sigils on the kameas uses Hebrew letters, based on what is called *Aiq Beker* or the *Qabalah of Nine Chambers* (this takes its name from the letters attributed to the first two numbers, i.e. Aleph, Yod, Qoph to 1 – AIQ, then Beth, Kaph, Resh to 2 – BKR). This system reduces the numbers attributed to the letters to a numerical value in the range 1-9, ignoring the zeros of tens and hundreds.

The "Qabalah of Nine Chambers"

1	2	3
Aleph (1)	Beth (2)	Gimel (3)
Yod (10)	Kaph (20)	Lamed (30)
Qoph (100)	Resh (200)	Shin (300)
4	5	6
Daleth (4)	Heh (5)	Vav (6)
Mem (40)	Nun (50)	Samekh (60)
Tav (400)	Final Kaph (500)	Final Mem (600)
7	8	9
Zain (7)	Cheth (8)	Teth (9)
Ayin (70)	Peh (80)	Tzaddi (90)
Final Nun (700)	Final Peh (800)	Final Tzaddi (900)

The first step in creating the sigil is to take the word and reduce it to a sequence of single digit numbers, as attributed in the Qabalah of Nine Chambers.

The sigil is always begun with a small circle in the middle of the square containing the number that the first letter is attributed to. This is joined by a straight line to the middle of the square the number attributed to the next letter is in. This process is repeated until the line is drawn to the middle of the square containing the number to which the last letter is attributed, where a small cross-bar is drawn to end the sigil. This method hence only uses the squares containing the numbers 1-9, the rest of the squares in the kamea are ignored.

If two consecutive letters are attributed to the same number, and hence the same box in the kamea, this is indicated by a small loop (U-shape) before continuing as a straight line to the box containing the number attributed to the next letter. If a third or fourth letter were also attributed to the same box, an extra loop would be added for each extra letter in the word that has the same numerical attribution.

Here are two examples of this technique:

Azrael is written AZRAL in Hebrew.

A + Z + R + A + L
1 + 7+ 200 + 1 + 30

Using Aiq Beker, the zeroes are removed from the R (200 becomes 2) and the L (30 becomes 3), giving the numerical sequence 1 – 7 – 2 – 1 – 3
If we now draw this on the Saturn kamea (see Appendix 2 for numerical attributions to the boxes in this kamea), we get the following sigil.

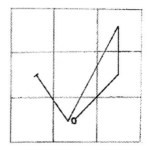

If however we were to draw the sigil for a word where there is more than one consecutive number of the same value, such as Satariel, the Qliphoth of Binah, it would give the sequence 6 – 1 – 4 – 1 – 2 – 1 – 1 – 3, i.e. Samekh = 6(0), Aleph = 1, Tav = 4(00), Aleph = 1, Resh = 2(00), Yod = 1(0), Aleph = 1, Lamed = 3(0).

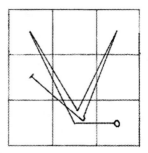

49. Planetary Hours and Timing

Each of the days of the week is associated with one of the classical planets, so these days are obviously preferable for performing magick associated with their energies. Likewise each day is divided into planetary hours appropriate to the energy of the different planets.

So for the days we would work as follows:

Kether – First Swirlings – Any, though Saturday or Sunday may be preferred
Chokmah – Zodiac – Any, though Saturday or Sunday may be preferred
Binah – Saturn - Saturday
Chesed – Jupiter - Thursday
Geburah – Mars - Tuesday
Tiphereth – Sun - Sunday
Netzach – Venus - Friday
Hod – Mercury - Wednesday
Yesod – Moon - Monday
Malkuth – Earth – Saturday

The planetary hours are not the same as the sixty-minute hours beginning at midnight that we use for normal timekeeping. The planetary days are divided into twenty-four planetary hours starting with the first hour of the day beginning at sunrise and ending with the last hour of the day ending at sunrise of the next planetary day.

The period of daylight that extends from sunrise to sunset is divided into the twelve "hours" of the day. The period of darkness extending from sunset to sunrise of the next day is divided into the twelve "*hours*" of night. Combined these give the twenty-four hours of the planetary day.

As the duration of daylight and darkness varies except at the Spring and Autumn Equinoxes, on a particular planetary day the length of the hours of the day will differ from the length of the hours of the night. This is why the planetary hours are sometimes called the unequal hours. Almanacs, ephemeredes and the internet are all sources you can use to discover the sunrise and sunset times, enabling you to calculate the planetary hours.

Standard Attributions for Planetary Hours

Planetary Hours of the Day

Hour	Sunday	Monday	Tuesday	Wednesday	Thursday	Friday	Saturday
1	Sun	Moon	Mars	Mercury	Jupiter	Venus	Saturn
2	Venus	Saturn	Sun	Moon	Mars	Mercury	Jupiter
3	Mercury	Jupiter	Venus	Saturn	Sun	Moon	Mars
4	Moon	Mars	Mercury	Jupiter	Venus	Saturn	Sun
5	Saturn	Sun	Moon	Mars	Mercury	Jupiter	Venus
6	Jupiter	Venus	Saturn	Sun	Moon	Mars	Mercury
7	Mars	Mercury	Jupiter	Venus	Saturn	Sun	Moon
8	Sun	Moon	Mars	Mercury	Jupiter	Venus	Saturn
9	Venus	Saturn	Sun	Moon	Mars	Mercury	Jupiter
10	Mercury	Jupiter	Venus	Saturn	Sun	Moon	Mars
11	Moon	Mars	Mercury	Jupiter	Venus	Saturn	Sun
12	Saturn	Sun	Moon	Mars	Mercury	Jupiter	Venus

Planetary Hours of the Night

Hours	Sunday	Monday	Tuesday	Wednesday	Thursday	Friday	Saturday
1	Jupiter	Venus	Saturn	Sun	Moon	Mars	Mercury
2	Mars	Mercury	Jupiter	Venus	Saturn	Sun	Moon
3	Sun	Moon	Mars	Mercury	Jupiter	Venus	Saturn
4	Venus	Saturn	Sun	Moon	Mars	Mercury	Jupiter
5	Mercury	Jupiter	Venus	Saturn	Sun	Moon	Mars
6	Moon	Mars	Mercury	Jupiter	Venus	Saturn	Sun
7	Saturn	Sun	Moon	Mars	Mercury	Jupiter	Venus
8	Jupiter	Venus	Saturn	Sun	Moon	Mars	Mercury
9	Mars	Mercury	Jupiter	Venus	Saturn	Sun	Moon
10	Sun	Moon	Mars	Mercury	Jupiter	Venus	Saturn
11	Venus	Saturn	Sun	Moon	Mars	Mercury	Jupiter
12	Mercury	Jupiter	Venus	Saturn	Sun	Moon	Mars

Example

Let us say you wanted to work out the planetary hours for a ritual that focused on the energy of Chesed, i.e. used Jupiterian energies. Thursday is the day of Jupiter, so you decide to perform the ritual next Thursday, during the day. The process is then as follows:

Consulting an almanac you see the sun rises at 7am on that day and sets at 8.36pm. So the hours of daylight are from 07.00 – 20:36, giving 13 hours and 26 minutes.

(13 x 60) + 36 = 816 minutes of daylight. Divide by 12 = 68. So each of the 12 "hours" of daylight will be 68 minutes long.

Consulting the tables given you see the first and eighth hours of Thursday are ruled by Jupiter. So for the first hour of the day the ritual should be performed between 7.00am and 8.08am (68 minutes).

For the eighth hour more calculation is involved. Add together the "hour" length for 7 "hours" (7 x 68 = 476 minutes, or 7 hours and 56 minutes).

Then add this to the sunrise time (7:00am) + 7 hours and 56 minutes = 2:56pm). This means the eighth hour starts at 2:56pm and finishes at 4:04pm (2:56 + 68 minutes).

You then decide which of these two times will be more practical, and you have your time to perform the ritual in.

To calculate the hours of night you can simply deduct the length of a day "hour" from 120 minutes. As the amount of time left in the complete day will be the amount that makes it up to 24 hours, so the hour length will be proportionally more or less than 60 minutes depending on the length of the day hours.

50. Consecration of Talismans

When you have made your talisman you need to consecrate it. You will need the following ingredients:

— The talisman.
— An appropriately coloured piece of silk big enough to wrap it in.
— A bowl of salt
— A bowl of water
— Some incense or joss
— Almond oil

The procedure is as follows:

Having worked out the time for your ritual beforehand, and created your talisman, place it on a piece of appropriately (to the planet) coloured silk, and visualize a sphere of luminous energy (of the appropriate colour for the Sephira) about 20cm in diameter in the air over the talisman. (See the earlier Chapter *The Colour Scales*).

State the intent of the talisman, in a single concise sentence (that you have prepared beforehand).

Sprinkle the talisman with salt, as you do saying

I consecrate this talisman with the power of Earth that it may (repeat intent).

Sprinkle the talisman with water, as you do saying,

I consecrate this talisman with the power of Water that it may (repeat intent).

Pass the talisman through the incense or joss the appropriate (to the planet) number of times, as you do saying:

I consecrate this talisman with the power of Fire that it may (repeat intent).

Breathe upon the talisman the appropriate (to the planet) number of times, as you do saying:

I consecrate this talisman with the power of Air that it may (repeat intent).

As you have performed the previous four steps with the elements, for each step you should have visualised the ball becoming smaller, brighter and more intense in colour, as the energy grew stronger. Ideally it should have reduced about 4cm in diameter each time – to 16cm, then 12cm, then 8cm, then 4cm after you have breathed on the talisman.

Anoint the talisman with a drop of almond oil, saying:
I consecrate this talisman with the power of Spirit that it may (repeat intent).

See the sphere shrink further, so it is now a tiny sphere about 1cm in diameter of intense energy, almost too bright to look at.

Then put a drop of your saliva on the talisman, linking it to your energies, and see the sphere of energy descend into your talisman as you say:

I join this talisman to my life, that the (repeat intent).

Wrap the talisman in the silk and put it in a safe place.

You can of course use discs of metals or crystals for making amulets and talismans. Whilst some of these would be prohibitively expensive (such as gold), it is an option. With this in mind I would like to mention that when beads of crystals were added to Kabbalistic amulets in ancient times they were always of a red or blue stone.[105] Red was traditionally a protective colour and blue seen as a most holy colour.

---

[105] *Hebrew Amulets, T Schrire, 1966, p57-8*

PART XI

FURTHER IDEAS

51. Tree of Life Tarot Spread

Since Eliphas Levi's linking of the Tarot to the Tree of Life, this union has become an accepted part of the magickal perception of Qabalah. For this reason the Tree of Life glyph makes an excellent spread for performing tarot readings to see the energies at work in your life. Whilst it is often said that you should not read the Tarot for yourself, this spread does enable you to receive insights into what areas of your life to concentrate on.

The Rider-Waite or Thoth decks are the preferred decks for doing this spread. Apart from being the two most popular tarot decks in the world, they are also both the results of collaboration between major members of the Golden Dawn with very talented female artists – A.E. Waite with Pamela Coleman-Smith, and Aleister Crowley with Lady Frieda Harris.[106] As a result they are the decks that are most steeped in the appropriate Qabalistic symbolism, and will be of greatest benefit.

The method of performing the reading is very simple. Shuffle your tarot deck as you normally would, and lay out a Tree of Life with ten of the cards, starting at Kether and working down to Malkuth. As you lay each card say the name of the Sephira it represents.

An eleventh card may also be added at the end to represent Daath. Having laid down the cards following the path of the lightning flash, you then read up the Tree from Malkuth to Kether, using the Daath card as the outcome card, indicating possible solutions – the "*gate*" to desired outcomes.

The card in each Sephira relates to the associated areas in your life. Particular attention should be paid to obvious strengthening or weakening effects between the cards and their positioning. E.g. a 9 in Yesod, or 4 in Chesed is emphasising that Sephira and its qualities. Conversely a card like the 7 of Cups in Geburah would indicate a conflict occurring.

The number of Trumps in the reading should be noted carefully – the more Trumps, the stronger the message you are getting, as they indicate major influences. Likewise the influence of Aces and Court cards should also be noted carefully.

---

[106] *As such in this instance it could be suggested that the female artists represent the Shekinah and Binah, and the male magickians the energy of Chokmah. Together their work produced the magickal children of the Tarot decks, representing Tiphereth as oracles of Beauty.*

If a particular number occurs at least three times, e.g. three eights or four fives, this is directing your attention particularly to the energy of that Sephira as a major current influence in your life.

Whenever you perform a Tree of Life spread record the results in your magickal diary, or a book specifically for the purpose. Over time you may notice certain trends occurring in your readings, and these should also be considered to see what message you are receiving. E.g. if a particular Trump or suit seems to predominate, it is indicating this is a powerful influence in your life, giving you a pointer to which energies you can most effectively tap.

Sephira	Sphere of Influence	Reinforced Cards	Reinforced Suit
Kether	Hidden influence behind the scenes – divine force	Aces	Swords
Chokmah	Masculine influence – "Great Father"	Twos, Kings[107]	Wands
Binah	Feminine influence – "Great Mother"	Threes, Queens	Cups, Disks
Chesed	Dealings with authority, spirituality	Fours	Swords
Geburah	Energy direction or conflict depending on aspect	Fives	Wands
Tiphereth	Inner self, focus of will	Sixes, Princes	Wands
Netzach	Emotions, fertile areas	Sevens	Disks
Hod	Intellect, health	Eights	Swords
Yesod	Unconscious, dreams	Nines	Cups
Malkuth	Material life, work	Tens, Princesses	Disks
Daath	Outcome – possible solutions to indicated problems	Trumps	

[107] This would correspond to Knights in the Thoth deck.

52. Further Invocations & Meditations

A beautiful prayer from the sixteenth century by the Rabbi Joseph Tzayach (1505-73 CE) contains both Divine Names and the names of the Sephiroth, and may be used as an invocation or meditational piece.

> *Ahih Asher Ahih, Crown me.*
> *Yah, give me Wisdom.*
> *Elohim Chaim, grant me Understanding.*
> *El, with the right hand of his Love, make me Great.*
> *Elohim, from the Terror of His judgement, protect me.*
> *Yahveh, with His mercy grant me Beauty.*
> *Yahveh Tzavaot, watch me Forever.*
> *Elohim Tzavaot, great me beatitude from his Splendour.*
> *El Chai, make His covenant my Foundation.*
> *Adonai, open my lips and my mouth will speak of Your praise.*[108]

Eliphas Levi, though somewhat dated and obtuse in places, still has gems within his words that can inspire us today. Levi's Qabalistic *Invocation of Solomon* (given below) makes an excellent invocatory piece to incorporate in magickal work to help create the correct focus and mood for performing Qabalistic work.

> *Powers of the Kingdom, be beneath my left foot, and within my right hand.*
>
> *Glory and Eternity touch my shoulders, and guide me in the Paths of Victory.*
>
> *Mercy and Justice be ye the Equilibrium and Splendour of my life.*
>
> *Understanding and Wisdom give unto me the Crown.*
>
> *Spirits of Malkuth conduct me between the two columns whereon is supported the whole edifice of the Temple.*
>
> *Angels of Netzach and of Hod strengthen me upon the Cubical Stone of Yesod.*
>
> *O Gedulahel! O Geburahel! O Tiphereth!*

---

[108] *Adaptation from Meditation and The Bible – Aryeh Kaplan, 1978, p72.*

Binahel, be Thou my Love!

Ruach Chokmahel, be Thou my Light!

Be that which Thou art, and that which thou willest to be, O Ketheriel! Ashim, assist me in the Name of Shaddai.

Cherubim, be my strength in the Name of Adonai.

Beni Elohim, be ye my brethren in the Name of the Son, and by the virtues of Tzabaoth.

Elohim, fight for me in the Name of Tetragrammaton.

Malachim, protect me in the Name of Yod Heh Vav Heh.

Seraphim, purify my love in the Name of Eloah.

Chasmalim, enlighten me with the splendours of Elohi, and of Shekinah.

Aralim, act ye; Auphanim, revolve and shine.

Chaioth Ha-Qadosh, cry aloud, speak, roar, and groan; Qadosh, Qadosh, Qadosh, Shaddai, Adonai, Yod Chavah, Eheieh Asher Eheieh![109]

Hallelu-Yah! Hallelu-Yah! Hallelu-Yah! Amen.

A few words of commentary may help elucidate some of the wording of this invocation. It can be seen that the names or titles of the Sephiroth are given in the first four lines, and then repeated in the next six lines, with reference to the Black and White Pillars as well. The use of the –hel and –iel endings is in the tradition of the formation of the angelic names of the Shemhamforash (see the chapter *The Unpronounceable Name of God*). The orders of Angels are then all called upon to lend their might to the petition.

The piece by Levi below relates the numbered cards of the Minor Arcana to the Sephiroth with rhyming prose incorporating the Sephirotic names, and makes a good inspirational piece for meditation.

---

[109] *This could be translated as: "Holy, Holy, Holy, Almighty, Lord, Divine Life, I am that I am!"*

IHVH		*Four signs present the Name of every name.*
Kether	4 Aces	*Four brilliant beams adorn His Crown of flame.*
Chokmah	4 Twos	*Four rivers ever from His Wisdom flow.*
Binah	4 Threes	*Four proofs of His Intelligence we know.*
Chesed	4 Fours	*Four benefactions from his Mercy come.*
Geburah	4 Fives	*Four times four sins avenged His Strength[110] sum.*
Tiphereth	4 Sixes	*Four rays unclouded make His Beauty known.*
Netzach	4 Sevens	*Four times His Victory[111] shall in song be shown*
Hod	4 Eights	*Four times He triumphs[112] on the timeless plane.*
Yesod	4 Nines	*Foundations four His great white throne maintain.*
Malkuth	4 Tens	*One fourfold Kingdom owns His endless sway, As from his Crown there streams a fourfold ray.*

Meditation of Lights

One of the few examples we have of Kabbalistic meditation comes from Rabbi Azriel of Gerona. In the book called *The Gate of Kavanah* (*Shaar HaKavanah*) he describes a technique for concentration and meditation on the divine.

See yourself as a being of light, and all your surroundings as being made of light. In front of you in the middle of all the light see a Throne of light, and above the Throne see a glowing light.[113] Behind you see a second Throne, with a light above it emanating goodness.[114] To the right of you see a brilliant light[115] and to the left of you a radiant light.[116]

Above you are three lights. Immediately above is a light emanating glory,[117] above that is a light emanating life,[118] and above that a crown of light. This crown of light is the divine and represents the emanation of Kether from the

---

[110] *"Justice" in the original, amended here for parity with the other major sephirotic names.*
[111] *"Conquest" in the original, changed as per the previous amendment.*
[112] *Levi obviously struggled to fit "Splendour" in, as Hod has few alternative titles!*
[113] *"Nogah" or "glow".*
[114] *"Tov" or "good".*
[115] *"Bahir" or "brilliant".*
[116] *"Zohar" or "radiant".*
[117] *"Kavod" or "glory".*
[118] *"Chaim" or "life".*

Ain Soph. Unite yourself with the energy of the lights around you, and then feel the divine energy descending from above through the lights to fill you, and draw your awareness up through the lights to the infinite.

53. Qabalah in Daily Life

As well as trying out the exercises and rituals, and discovering their benefits, you may wish to apply more Qabalistic principles to your daily life. By looking at where you have problems, e.g. in the workplace, or in relationships, you can see which sphere of your life needs to be focused on. By using the symbols, colours and techniques appropriate to that Sephira, you can bring more balance into the problem areas of your life by focusing the positive energies of that Sephira.

We are by nature creatures of habit, and can be very resistant to change. One of the great beauties of Qabalah is that it provides us with a map for balanced and effective change, and by working systematically through the Sephiroth. By doing this you will bring a greater sense of balance into your life, enabling you to progress more efficiently on your path through life. Harmonising intellect and emotions, will and imagination, drive and direction, practicing Qabalah brings insight, calm and success into your life.

Bathing
Cleanliness is considered extremely important in magick, and you should bathe or shower regularly (preferably daily). Remember you can add essential oils or herbs that you feel are appropriate to your bath, and also meditate on purity and cleanliness when you are in the bath.

Diet
If you are practicing Qabalah there are certain foods you may choose to omit from your diet. These are those foodstuffs that customarily have not been eaten by Kabbalists for various reasons. Traditionally pork and seafood would never be eaten. Although there are many references in the Torah to eating meat, some people go further and point to Ezekiel 4:14[119], which indicates a vegetarian diet is preferable. Of course abstaining completely from animal products does tend to help increase psychic sensitivity, so there are benefits to such a course of action.

Bread is usually included, though traditionally unleavened, and you should check if you have wheat or gluten allergies. Practicing Qabalah does not

---

[119] *"Then said I, Ah Lord God! Behold, my soul hath not been polluted; for from my youth up, even till now, have I not eaten of that which dieth of itself, or is torn in pieces; neither came there abominable flesh into my mouth."*

mean you cannot drink alcohol, but moderation is encouraged. Using psychoactive drugs in combination with Qabalistic practice is not encouraged or recommended. Whilst some books will give you lists of drugs relating to the Sephiroth and paths, the use of these substances can result in all sorts of problems and they are not conducive to the discipline of serious magickal work.

Qabalah cards

Sometimes you don't have time to meditate, and need some inspiration or guidance quickly. A set of Qabalah cards can help with this. Get ten pieces of blank card, each about half the size of a postcard. On each card write the following information – the name of the Sephira, its meaning, number, divine name, archangel, angelic host, heaven, virtue, vice, and description.

When you need that quick answer, calm your mind, shuffle the cards and draw one. Look at the card you have chosen and see what it says to you.

Scents

The different Sephiroth are all associated with different areas of life, and each has associated scents. You may wish to burn different scents or wear oils or perfumes for their qualities based on this. You can choose scents for different occasions to help stimulate your body and mind with the appropriate energy of the Sephira you are working with.

So for day-to-day activities and earthy things like gardening choose Malkuthian scents, for dreams choose Yesodic scents, for study and intellectual stimulation Hod scents, for love and the emotions Netzach scents. For success you could use Tiphereth scents, for exercise Geburah scents, for health Chesedic scents. For understanding Binah scents, for wisdom and insight Chokmah scents, and for meditation and prayer Kether scents.

Sephirotic Days

You can follow the sequence of the planetary energies through the week and incorporate appropriate correspondences to help you learn them.
Alternatively if you have made a set of Qabalah cards, try drawing one in the morning, and then planning your day accordingly.

Wear an item of clothing of the appropriate colour for the Sephira, and if possible an item of jewellery with an appropriate crystal in. Try also wearing an oil appropriate to the Sephira, on your wrists or if you feel appropriate on the part of the body corresponding to the Sephira. Watch your behaviour during the day and try to make sure you practice the virtues and avoid the vices of the Sephira. This will help you learn Qabalah in a very practical way!

Day of the Week	Planet	Sephira
Sunday	Sun	Tiphereth
Monday	Moon	Yesod
Tuesday	Mars	Geburah
Wednesday	Mercury	Hod
Thursday	Jupiter	Chesed
Friday	Venus	Netzach
Saturday	Saturn	Binah

APPENDIXES

Appendix 1 – Hebrew & Colour Scales

Hebrew Letter	Pth	King Atziluth	Queen Briah	Emperor Yetzirah	Empress Assiah
Aleph	11	Bright pale yellow	Sky blue	Blue emerald green	Emerald, flecked gold
Beth	12	Yellow	Purple	Grey	Indigo, rayed violet
Gimel	13	Blue	Silver	Cold pale blue	Silver, rayed sky blue
Daleth	14	Emerald green	Sky blue	Early spring green	Bright rose, rayed pale green
Heh	15	Violet	Sky blue	Bluish mauve	White, tinged purple
Vav	16	Red orange	Deep indigo	Deep warm olive	Rich brown
Zain	17	Orange	Pale mauve	New yellow leather	Reddish grey inclined to mauve
Cheth	18	Amber	Maroon	Rich bright russet	Dark greenish brown
Teth	19	Yellow, greenish	Deep purple	Grey	Reddish amber
Yod	20	Green, yellowish	Slate grey	Green grey	Plum colour
Kaph	21	Violet	Blue	Rich purple	Bright blue, rayed yellow
Lamed	22	Emerald green	Blue	Deep blue-green	Pale green
Mem	23	Deep blue	Sea green	Deep olive-green	White, flecked purple
Nun	24	Green blue	Dull brown	Very dark brown	Livid indigo brown
Samekh	25	Blue	Yellow	Green	Dark vivid blue
Ayin	26	Indigo	Black	Blue black	Cold dark grey, approaching black
Peh	27	Scarlet	Red	Venetian red	Bright red, rayed azure or emerald
Tzaddi	28	Scarlet	Red	Brilliant flame	Glowing red
Qoph	29	Crimson (ultra violet)	Buff, flecked silver-white	Light translucent pinkish-brown	Stone colour
Resh	30	Orange	Gold yellow	Rich amber	Amber, rayed red
Shin	31	Glowing orange scarlet	Vermillion	Scarlet, flecked gold	Vermillion, flecked crimson and emerald
Tav	32	Indigo	Black	Blue black	Black, rayed blue

Appendix 2 - The Planetary Kameas

These are the planetary kameas as first set out in the *Key of Solomon* and used as standard ever since.

Saturn (Binah) – 3x3

4	9	2
3	5	7
8	1	6

Jupiter (Chesed) - 4x4

4	14	15	1
9	7	6	12
5	11	10	8
16	2	3	13

Mars (Geburah) - 5x5

11	24	7	20	3
4	12	25	8	16
17	5	13	21	9
10	18	1	14	22
23	6	19	2	15

Sun (Tiphereth) - 6x6

6	32	3	34	35	1
7	11	27	28	8	30
19	14	16	15	23	24
18	20	22	21	17	13
25	29	10	9	26	12
36	5	33	4	2	31

Venus (Netzach) – 7x7

22	47	16	41	10	35	4
5	23	48	17	42	11	29
30	6	24	49	18	36	12
13	31	7	25	43	19	37
38	14	32	1	26	44	20
21	39	8	33	2	27	45
46	15	40	9	34	3	28

Mercury (Hod) - 8x8

8	58	59	5	4	62	63	1
49	15	14	52	53	11	10	56
41	23	22	44	48	19	18	45
32	34	35	29	25	38	39	28
40	26	27	37	36	30	31	33
17	47	46	20	21	43	42	24
9	55	54	12	13	51	50	16
64	2	3	61	60	6	7	57

Moon (Yesod) – 9x9

37	78	29	70	21	62	13	54	5
6	38	79	30	71	22	63	14	46
47	7	39	80	31	72	23	55	15
16	48	8	40	81	32	64	24	56
57	17	49	9	41	73	33	65	25
26	58	18	50	1	42	74	34	66
67	27	59	10	51	2	43	75	35
36	68	19	60	11	52	3	44	76
77	28	69	20	61	12	53	4	45

There is not a classical kamea for Malkuth, however it is logical to assign a 10x10 square to Malkuth, to complete the sequence of kameas for use in practical magickal work. A modern attribution that is gaining more common use is given below.[120]

Earth (Malkuth) – 10x10

10	92	3	97	5	96	94	8	99	1
11	19	83	14	86	85	17	88	12	90
80	22	28	74	25	26	77	23	79	71
31	69	33	37	65	66	34	68	62	40
51	42	58	44	46	45	57	53	49	60
50	52	48	54	56	55	47	43	59	41
61	39	63	67	36	35	64	38	32	70
30	72	78	27	75	76	24	73	29	21
81	89	18	84	16	15	87	13	82	20
100	9	93	7	95	6	4	98	2	91

Talismans are made to attract the energies associated with the change you want in your life. So if you were seeking to improve your mental recall say, to pass an exam, you would draw a talisman on the kamea of Mercury. You might ask Raphael to help you, and use the divine name of Hod as the basis for the sigil you draw on the kamea. The talisman should preferably be both made and consecrated on the appropriate day of the week during the correct planetary hour.

---

[120] *From "Becoming Magick" by David Rankine, Mandrake, Oxford, 2004.*

Bibliography

Bibliography

Abelson, J. *Jewish Mysticism*. 1913, Bell, London
Achad, Frater. *QBL or The Bride's Reception*. 1972, Weiser, New York
A.H.E.H.O., Frater. *Angelic Images*. 1980, Sorceror's Apprentice Press, Leeds
Arbel, Vita Daphna. *Beholders of Divine Secrets: Mysticism and Myth in the Hekhalot and Merkavah Literature*. 2003, SUNY Press, Albany
Athanassiadi, Polymnia & Frede, Michael. *Pagan Monotheism in Late Antiquity*. 1999, Oxford University Press, Oxford
Aymar, B (ed). *Treasury of Snake Lore*. 1956, Greenberg, New York.
Bischoff, Erich. *Kabbala*. 1991, Red Wheel/Weiser, Maine
Blau, J.L. *The Christian Interpretation of the Cabala in the Renaissance*. 1944, Columbia University Press, Columbia
Bond, Bligh & Lea. *Gematria*. 1981, R.I.L.K.O., London
Bonner, John. *Qabalah: A Magical Primer*. 2002, Red Wheel/Weiser, Maine
Butler, E.M. *Ritual Magic*. 1979, Cambridge University Press, Cambridge
Butler, W.E. *Magic and the Qabalah*. 1972, Aquarian Press, London
Buxbaum, Yitzhak. *Jewish Spiritual Practices*. 1995, Aronson
Case, Paul Foster. *The Tarot: A Key to the Wisdom of the Ages*. 1995, B.O.T.A.
Charles, R.H. (trans). *The Book of Enoch*. 1917, SPCK, London
Crowley, Aleister. *777 & Other Qabalistic Writings of Aleister Crowley*. 2000, Samuel Weiser, Maine
Dan, Joseph. *Ancient Jewish Mysticism*. 1993, Israel MOD Publishing House, Tel Aviv
Davila, James R. *Descenders to the Chariot: The People behind the Hekhalot Literature*. 2001, Supplements to the Journal for the Study of Judaism, volume 70
Deutsch, Nathaniel. *The Gnostic Imagination*. 1995, E.J. Brill, Leiden
---------- *Guardians of the Gate: Angelic Vice regency in Late Antiquity*. 1999, Brill Academic Publishing, Dulles
Eliot, T.S. *Complete Poems and Plays*. 2004, Faber & Faber, London
Epstein, Perle. *Kabbalah*. 1978, Shambhala
Fanger, Claire (ed). *Conjuring Spirits: Texts and Traditions of Medieval Ritual Magic*. 1998, Sutton Publishing, Stroud
Feng, Gia-Fu & English, Jane (trans). *Tao Te Ching*. 1973, Wildwood House, London
Ficino, Marsilio. *The Letters of Marsilio Ficino* (Volume 7). 2003, Shepheard-Walwyn Ltd, London
Franck, Adolphe. *The Kabbalah*. 1967, University Books, New York
Fortune, Dion. *The Mystical Qabalah*. 2000, Revised Edition, Red Wheel/Weiser, Maine
Gikatilla, R. Joseph. *Sha'are Orah*. 1994, Harper Collins
Ginsburg, Christian D. *The Kabbalah, its Doctrines, Development and Literature*. 1970, Routledge, London
Ginzberg, Louis. *On Jewish Law and Lore*. 1970, Atheneum, New York
Goldmerstein, L. *Magical Sacrifice in the Jewish Kabbalah*. 1896, Folklore VII
Gray, William G. *The Ladder of Lights*. 1968, Helios, Teddington
Green, Arthur. *Keter: The Crown of God in Early Jewish Mysticism*. 1997, Princeton University
Green, Miranda. *The Gods of the Celts*. 1986, Sutton Publishing Limited, Stroud
Gruenwald, Ithamar. *Apocalyptic and Merkavah Mysticism*. 1980, E.J. Brill, Leiden
Highfield, A.C. *The Book of Celestial Images*. 1984, Aquarian Press, Wellingborough
Idel, Moshe. *Kabbalah: New Perspectives*. 1990, Yale University Press
---------- *Hasidism: Between Ecstasy and Magic*. 1995, SUNY, New York

----------- *Studies in Ecstatic Kabbalah*. 1988, SUNY, New York
----------- *The Early Kabbalah*. 1986, Paulist Press, New York
----------- *Golem*. 1990, SUNY, New York
Ifrah, Georges. *The Universal History of Numbers*. 1998, The Harvill Press, London
Janowitz, Naomi. *Icons of Power: Ritual Practices in Late Antiquity*. 2002, Pennsylvania State University Press, Pennsylvania
Jordan, Michael. *Encyclopedia of Gods*. 1992, Kyle Cathie Ltd, London
Kanarfogel, Ephraim. *Peering through the Lattices: Mystical, Magical, and Pietistic Dimensions in the Tosafist Period*. 2000, Wayne State University Press, Detroit
Kaplan, Aryeh. *Meditation and Kabbalah*. 1982, Red Wheel/Weiser, Maine
----------- *The Sepher Yetzirah*. 1997, Red Wheel/Weiser, Maine
----------- *The Bahir Illumination*. 1979, Red Wheel/Weiser, Maine
----------- *The Living Torah*. 1981, Moznaim
----------- *Jewish Meditation: A Practical Guide*. 1995, Schocken Books
King, Francis & Skinner, Stephen. *Techniques of High Magic*. 1997, Revised edition, Affinity Publishing, London
Lesses, Rebecca Macy. *Ritual Practices to Gain Power. Angels, Incantations, and Revelation in Early Jewish Mysticism*. 1997, Trinity Press International, Pennsylvania
Levertoff, Paul P. (trans). *The Zohar* (5 volumes). 1959, Bennett, New York
Levi, Eliphas. *The Book of Splendours*. 1975, Aquarian, London
----------- *The Mysteries of the Qabalah*. 2001, Weiser, Maine
----------- *The Magical Ritual of the Sanctum Regnum*. 1970, Crispin Press, London.
----------- *Transcendental Magic*. 1995, Tiger Books International PLC, Twickenham
Locks, Gutman G. *Gematria, The Spice of Torah*. 1985, Judaica Press
Luzzatto, Rabbi Moses. *General Principles of Kabbalah*. 1970, Research Centre of Kabbalah Press, New York
MacKenna, Stephen (trans). *The Enneads: Plotinus*. 1991, Penguin Books, London
MacLean, Adam (ed). *A Treatise on Angel Magic*. 1982, Magnum Opus, Edinburgh
Malachi, Tau. *Gnosis of the Cosmic Christ*. 2005, Llewellyn, Minnesota
Mathers, S.L. MacGregor (trans). *The Kabbalah Unveiled*. 1968, Weiser, New York
----------- *Astral Projection, Ritual Magic, and Alchemy*. 1987, Aquarian Press, Wellingborough
Mead, G.R.S. *Pistis Sophia*. 1992, R A Kessinger Publishing Co.
Meltzer, David. *The Secret Garden: An Anthology in the Kabbalah*. 1976, Seabury Press Inc, New York
Myer, Issac. *Qabbalah*. 1970, Stuart & Watkins, London
Padeh, Zwe & Menzi, D.W. *The Palace of Adam Kadmon*. 1999, Jason Aronson Inc, Jerusalem
Peterson, Joseph H. (ed). *The Lesser Key of Solomon*. 2001, Weiser Books, Maine
Ponce, Charles. *Kabbalah*. 1974, Garnstone Press, London
----------- *The Game of Wizards*. 1991, Quest Books, Illinois
Ramanujan, A.K. (trans). *Speaking of Siva*. 1973, Penguin Books, Middlesex
Rankine, David. *Crystals Healing And Folklore*. 2002, Capall Bann, Somerset
----------- *Becoming Magick*. 2004, Mandrake, Oxford
Regardie, Israel. *A Garden of Pomegranates*. 1972, Llewellyn, Minnesota
----------- *The Complete Golden Dawn System of Magic*. 1984, New Falcon
----------- *The Middle Pillar*. 2000, Llewellyn Publications, Minnesota
----------- *The Tree of Life*. 1972, Weiser, Maine
Reuchlin, Johann. *De arte Cabalistica*. 1983, Abaris Books
Savedow, Steve (trans). *Sepher Rezial Hemelach: The Book of the Angel Rezial*. 2000, Samuel Weiser, Maine

Schäfer, Peter. *Mirror of His Beauty: Feminine Images of God from the Bible to the Early Kabbalah.* 2002, Princeton University Press, Princeton
---------- *The Hidden and Manifest God.* Some Major Themes in Early Jewish Mysticism. 1992, SUNY, New York
Scheinkin, David. *Path of Kabbalah.* 1986, Continuum International Publishing Group
Scholem, Gershom. *Jewish Gnosticism Merkavah Mysticism and Talmudic Tradition.* 1965, Jewish Theological Seminary of America, New York
---------- *Major Trends in Jewish Mysticism.* 1969, Schocken, New York
---------- *On the Kabbalah and Its Symbolism.* 1965, Schocken, New York
---------- *On the Mystical Shape of the Godhead.* 1991, Schocken
---------- *Origins of the Kabbalah.* 1990, Princeton University Press, Princeton
Schrire, Theodor. *Hebrew Amulets.* 1966, Routledge & Kegan Paul, London
Shochet, Jacob Immanuel. *Mystical Concepts in Chassidism.* 1998, Kehot Publications Society, New York
Scott, Walter (ed, trans). *Hermetica.* 1997, Solos Press, London
Siegel, Richard, & Strassfeld, M. & S. *The First Jewish Catalogue.* 1973, Jewish Publication Society of America
Skinner, Stephen & Rankine, David. *The Keys to the Gateway of Magic: Summoning the Solomonic Archangels & Demonic Princes.* Sourceworks of Ceremonial Magic Volume 2. 2005, Golden Hoard Press, Singapore
Stedman, E.C. (ed). *An American Anthology, 1787–1900.* 1900, Houghton Mifflin, Boston
Swartz, Michael D. *Scholastic Magic: Ritual and Revelation in Early Jewish Mysticism.* 1996, Princeton University Press, New Jersey
---------- *Mystical Prayer in Early Jewish Mysticism: An Analysis of Ma'aseh Merkavah.* 1992, Mohr Siebeck, Tubingen
Tishby, Isaiah & Lachower, Y.F. *The Wisdom of the Zohar.* 1989, Oxford University Press, Oxford
Trachtenberg, Joshua. *Jewish Magic and Superstition.* 1939, Behrman House, New York
Verman, Mark. *The History and Varieties of Jewish Meditation.* 1996, Jacob Aronson Inc, New Jersey
Waite, A.E. *The Holy Kabbalah.* 1965, University Books, New York
Wilkinson, Richard H. *The Complete Gods and Goddesses of Ancient Egypt.* 2003, Thames & Hudson, London
Wolkstein, Diane & Kramer, Samuel Noah. *Inanna: Queen of Heaven and Earth.* 1983, Harper & Row, New York
Yates, Frances. *Giordano Bruno and the Hermetic Tradition.* 1969, Random House, New York
---------- *The Occult Philosophy in the Elizabethan Age.* 1983, Ark, London
Zalewski, P. *Kabbalah of the Golden Dawn.* 1993, Llewellyn Publications, Minnesota

Index

Index

Other Books by this Author

Keys to the Gateway of Magick
Summoning the Solomonic Archangels & Demon Princes
Stephen Skinner & David Rankine
255 pages, limited edition, hb with dustwrapper
ISBN 0954763912 ; GOLDEN HOARD PRESS 2005

Practical Angel Magic of Dr John Dee's Enochian Tables
Tabula Bonorum Angelorum Invocationes
Stephen Skinner & David Rankine
292 pages, limited edition, hb with dustwrapper
ISBN 0954763904; GOLDEN HOARD PRESS 2004

The Guises of the Morrigan
Irish Goddess of Sex & Battle: Her Myths, Powers & Mysteries
David Rankine & Sorita D'Este
212 pages, PB
ISBN 1905297009; AVALONIA 2005

Circle of Fire
Sorita D'Este & David Rankine
152 pages, PB
ISBN 1905297041; AVALONIA 2005

Becoming Magick
David Rankine
196 pages, PB
ISBN 1869928814; MANDRAKE OF OXFORD 2004

CRYSTALS : Healing & Folklore
David Rankine
400 pages, PB
ISBN 1861632002; Capall Bann 2002

About the Author

David Rankine is a writer and researcher living in London, UK. He has been practising magick since the 1970s, and has always had a passion for Qabalah and Renaissance magick. He is the author of a number of books, including "Becoming Magick", Guises of the Morrigan" and "Circle of Fire" (co-authored with Sorita D'Este) and co-wrote "The Practical Angel Magic of Dr John Dee's Enochian Tables" and "Keys to the Gateway of Magic" with well-known occult author Stephen Skinner. He has also written hundreds of articles for a wide variety of pagan, magickal and MBS magazines and journals.

David regularly lectures and runs workshops on a range of subjects in the UK and Europe, including Renaissance Magic, Qabalah, Heka (Egyptian magic) and Ceremonial Magic.

When he is not writing or researching, he can usually be found reading, listening to music or catching up with correspondence.

If you would like to find out more about his work, or have comments on this book that you would like to share, please visit his website at www.ritualmagick.co.uk or write to:

David Rankine
C/O BM Avalonia
London
WC1N 3XX
England

CPSIA information can be obtained at www.ICGtesting.com
Printed in the USA
LVOW07s1012081014

407827LV00001B/100/P